SEVENTEEN BOOK FIVE

ORIGINS

A.D. STARRLING

COPYRIGHT

DEDICATION

To the real heroes

IMMORTAL EMPIRE MAP I

Immortal Empire
Land of the Hatti
Nicaea
Sardis
Attalia
Hatusa
Tarsus
Kanesh
Dara
Ugarit
Byblos
Balack
Zakros
Paphos
West Sea
Shiloh
Hazor
Dor
Tarania
Hebru
Heraclon
Tell Farah
Tjaru
Troyu
Nahal River Delta
Tjenu
Hathor
East Desert Mountains
Nuburu
Red Sea
Expansion of the Empire
Dark Sea
Caucasia Mountains
Gilan Sea
N
Cayon
Kadavan
Haran
Toros Mountains
Hazaara
Urfa
Nemrik
Hasanu
Zagros Mountains
Tigra River
Expansion of the Empire
Silak
Qataara
Ufratu River
Nawaar
Dur Untash
Kis
Terka
Marii
Larraak
Omran
Niibru
Lagaesh
Parsah
Issin
Duruin
Girisu
Uryl
Larsaa
Finiza
Eridug
Urim
South Desert
South Sea
City
Empire's Military Outpost
Royal City

IMMORTAL EMPIRE MAP II

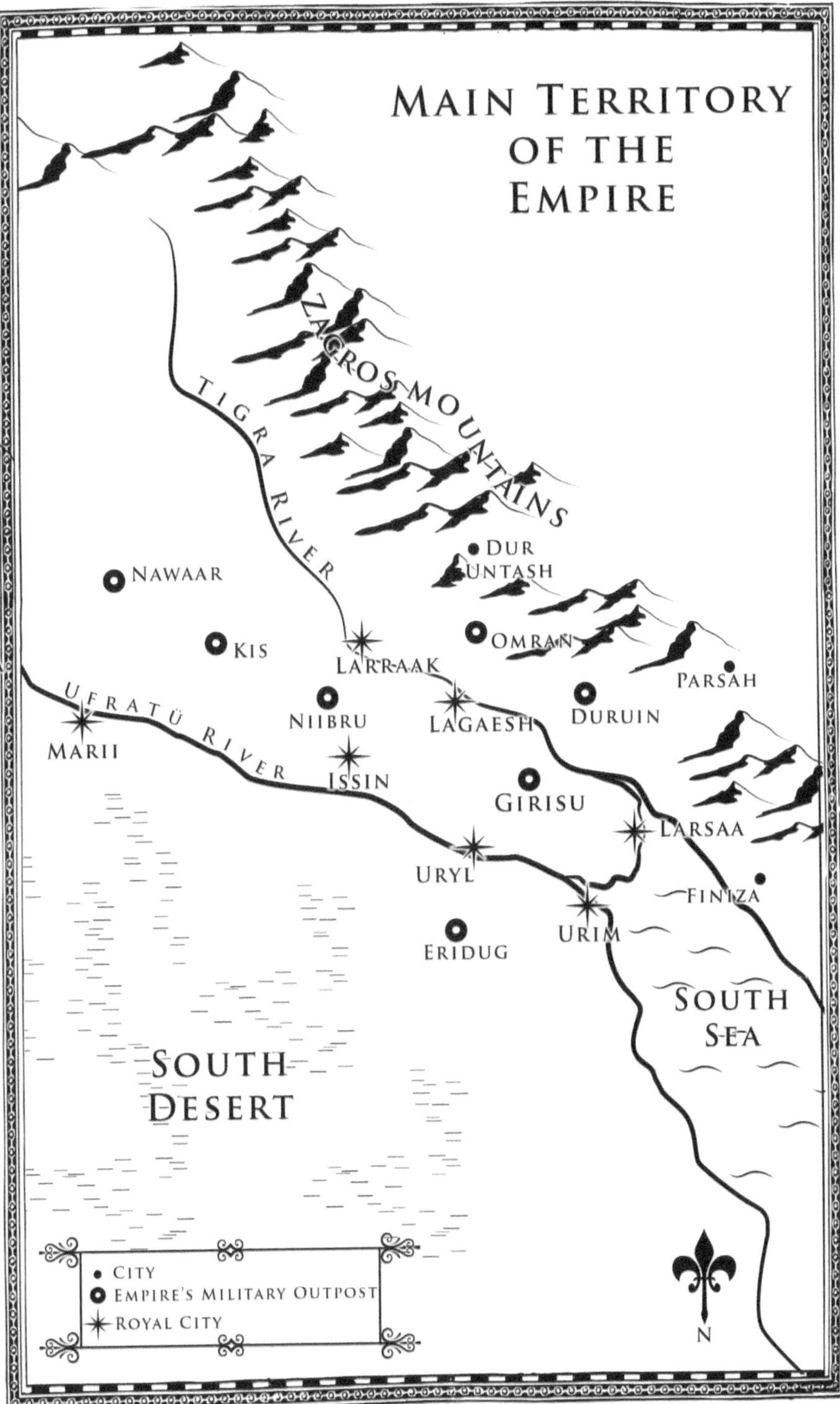

MAIN TERRITORY OF THE EMPIRE
ZAGROS MOUNTAINS
TIGRA RIVER
UFRATÜ RIVER
NAWAAR
KIS
LARRAAK
NIIBRU
ISSIN
MARII
DUR UNTASH
OMRAN
PARSAH
LAGAESH
DURUIN
GIRISU
LARSAA
URYL
FINIZA
URIM
ERIDUG
SOUTH SEA
SOUTH DESERT
CITY
EMPIRE'S MILITARY OUTPOST
ROYAL CITY
N

FAMILY TREE I

Timeline

3740-
3742 BC

ZARA
ROMERUS
JOANNA
CROVIR
BASTIAN
HELENA
SOFIA

3724 BC

HELENA
CROVIR
RACHEL
SOFIA
BASTIAN
LEAH
TOBIAS
BARUCH
HOSANNA
JARED
RAFAEL
PHEBE
YSA
NAVIA
MALACHI
BEATRIX
KRONOS

3590 BC

MILA

THE ROYAL CITIES

Uryl – Capital of the Empire
Larraak - Navia and Malachi
Marii – Jared and Beatrix
Lagaesh – Baruch and Hosanna
Issin – Mila and Kronos
Larsaa – Tobias and Ysa
Urim – Rafael and Phebe

Lunar month – one month
New Moon – first day of the month
Full Moon – fifteenth day of the month
Half Moon – one week
Quarter day – six hours
One league – approximately three miles

PROLOGUE

AND AS HE WALKED THROUGH THE KINGDOM OF HEAVEN, GOD CAME upon an Archangel looking down at the Dominion of Earth.

When He sensed the musings of the Archangel, He stopped and spoke thusly, 'I see that you are much troubled by the Fate of Mankind, oh wisest and oldest of my Angels. Speak your mind and I shall listen.'

The Archangel was quiet for some time.

'My Lord, I have seen the Future and the End of Days,' he finally said. 'I foresee a Holy War unlike any we have ever seen, between the most powerful of all your Creations. And I fear it may unleash an Era of Darkness that will consume all that was and all that will be.'

And God said, 'Do you have so little Faith in your brothers and me that you believe us unable to face such powerful foes?'

The Archangel bowed his head.

'No, my Lord,' he said. 'That you and my brothers will triumph is not in question. But the Creations you put so much love into bringing to life will perish. All of them. And that would be a great pain to bear for all who survive. Even as we speak, those who have fallen into Darkness and live in the absence of your Divine Light are filled with

hatred for your other Creations, above all Mankind, whom you made in your image. I sense their growing determination to destroy Humanity, in order to avenge themselves upon you.'

God gazed at the Archangel for a while before speaking. 'Mankind failed me once, when they succumbed to temptation. Since then, Sin has been a part of the daily life of Man. Your words lead me to think that you believe them worthy of redemption.'

The Archangel looked at his maker and saw both the challenge and the answer in his unworldly eyes. 'Yes, my Lord, I do. For they are born of you, as am I and everything in existence. We all carry your divine essence. As such, we are all worthy of redemption, even those who have fallen. That Mankind was created in your image makes them even more so. It is for this reason that I believe they should be given the chance to earn their rightful place at your side, at the End of Days. I believe their existence and their potential should not be denied.'

God smiled at the Archangel and said, 'Of all my Creations, Mankind is the weakest, both in body and in mind. Do you truly think they can stand on an equal footing with an army of Divine beings?'

The Archangel smiled back and replied, 'If you allow me, I will lend them my hand so as to make them worthy of such a station, my Lord.'

And God said, 'Then find me a man who can earn my forgiveness and who deserves your strength and wisdom.'

PART I
GENESIS

CHAPTER ONE

'In all their affliction he was afflicted, and the Angel of his presence saved them; in his love and in his pity he redeemed them; and he bare them, and carried them all the days of old.' Isaiah 63:9

3750 BC

THE MAN GAZED AT THE FIERY SUN BLAZING DOWN UPON HIM and the desert all around. At the edge of the horizon, sky and land merged, palest blue and whitest sand twisting in a rippling mirage that threatened to engulf the entire world. He wiped his brow and took another step, the staff at his side aiding his laborious trek across the shifting ground.

Seven days and six nights had passed since he left his village in search of a cure for his dying children. He had travelled east, as advised by the Elder who had spoken of a place where he could find salvation. A mountain lost in the wilderness, known to few and treacherous to reach. And inside the deepest, darkest cave within this forbidding mass of rock, a spring whose waters were said to be endowed with the power to cure all.

The Elder's words were ignored by most of the villagers, who chose only to see an old fool whose mind was lost to time and age. Even when disease befell the surrounding settlements and burning pyres darkened the sky, none believed his words. But when illness crossed his doorstep and started slowly killing his children, the man who had lived for longer than most went to the Elder to find out more. For no prayer or sacrifice could sway the sickness that had darkened the land from east to west, a plague borne on the wind that few escaped, an illness unlike anything he had seen in his extended life.

And so, four days after his sons collapsed from the fever ravaging their young bodies, and two days more after they fell into a slumber so deep none could rouse them, the man bade his wives goodbye and set off on a perilous journey from which he knew there might be no return.

This thought never deterred him, for he had faith. Faith that he would find a way, somehow. Faith that his sons would be cured. Faith that there had to be a reason for this plague and that time would tell what that reason was.

Into the desert he walked, one lone man, his father's staff at his side and a goat-skin sack across his back. Inside the sack were water-filled gourds made from sheep's bladders, dried fruit, bread, and a blanket.

The first three days passed without event, the landscape devoid of any threat bar the blazing heat and the cold nights. But as the mountains to the north faded into nothingness and he entered the true desert, the man discovered he had been lulled into a false sense of security. Soon, dunes as tall as twenty men soared in his path and vicious sandstorms whipped at his skin and clothes, slowing his progress and sapping his energy. When darkness fell and a wintry cold pricked his skin, the calls of creatures he could not see kept him awake for most of the night. Serpents and scorpions proved to be yet another, more silent threat. To pause in the shade of a rock or sit under an acacia tree meant tempting their deadly bites and stings.

As dusk descended upon his seventh day in the desert, the man discovered he was down to half a gourd of water. He had come across a shallow, dry streambed two nights previously, close to some rocks where grass and a handful of spiny shrubs grew. An hour of painstaking digging had unearthed a shallow pocket of water deep beneath the sand. The next day, he had saved his rations further by drinking from the fat leaves he had picked off the plants, which were heavy with a thick, bitter fluid that went some way toward quenching his thirst. He was also running low on food, a fact reflected in his increasingly weakened state.

When darkness fell, a full moon rose to the east and bathed the desert in an eerie light. The man stopped for a moment, startled by the sight. He had not expected the moon to be so plump and bright for another five days. Puzzled, he counted slowly on his fingers. His gaze shifted back to the white disc in the star-speckled sky. There was no doubt in his mind. Unless he had lost time in the desert he was unaware of, this was an unusual phenomenon indeed.

All thoughts of the moon were wiped away by the wave of lassitude that suddenly washed over him. He swayed where he stood. Shadows rose from the ground some fifty feet to his right. He stumbled over and discovered a clump of trees and shrubs. A scattering of dead branches and twigs lay on the ground. It was as good a place as any to stop for the night. He collected kindling and soon had a meager fire going.

IT WAS THE GROWLING THAT WOKE HIM. DEEP AND FERAL, THE sounds reverberated through his bones and roused him from the heavy slumber that had claimed him. He bolted upright, heart pounding in his chest and sweat drenching his skin despite the coolness of the night. For a moment, he thought he had dreamt the noise. It came again, low and guttural. A shiver danced down his spine, scattering the last of his fatigue. He peered into the dark and tried to see which direction the threatening sounds had come from.

A short distance behind him, something blocked out the lower section of the sky. It was a sand dune. A roar suddenly shattered the air, bringing him unsteadily to his feet.

There was little doubt in his mind that whatever was making that noise lay behind the shadowy ridge.

The fire had died down. The man threw more kindling upon it and lit the stoutest branch he could find. He hesitated, debating his choices. He could either walk out into the night, away from whatever danger lay behind him, or he could try to scare it away, whatever it proved to be.

The fact that traversing the land would be doubly perilous in the dark sealed his fate. He could also only go so far before weakness got the better of him. So the man gripped the flame torch and his walking stick and headed for the sand dune.

The ridge grew in stature the closer he got. By the time he reached the base, it rose some fifteen feet tall, curving away at the edges. He pondered his approach. Height would be an advantage against whatever he would face on the other side. He started to climb.

The sand shifted languorously beneath his sandals, wrapping around his legs almost to mid-calf in deceptively smooth sinkholes eager to halt his every step. He grunted and forged ahead, his determination growing, the torch throwing his shadow across his rapidly filling footprints. He knew he was wasting the last of his energy making undue haste, but he wanted whatever was going to happen over and done with.

He reached the summit of the dune and gasped at the sight that met his eyes.

CHAPTER TWO

THE MOON SAT DIRECTLY IN THE SKY ABOVE HIM, GHOSTLY LIGHT cast in a stark beam that lit up the incredible scene below and highlighted every ghastly detail.

To his right, a stranger stood with his back facing the west wall of the ridge. A pale, hooded cloak covered his body, masking his face in shadows. There was a simple staff in his right hand and a crow perched on his left shoulder.

Had his gaze not been drawn to the frightful beasts prowling the ground a short distance from the stranger, the man would have found the sight of the bird somewhat incongruous.

Claws stabbing sand, maws parted to reveal sharp, glinting teeth half the size of the man's hand, two large lions stood facing the stranger. The beasts were some nine feet long and almost half as tall, with luxurious, dark manes that flowed from their brows all the way down their backs. Though terrifying in appearance, they were stunningly beautiful creatures to behold.

The stranger stood still, fingers loose around his staff, his posture relaxed. The bird was similarly motionless, beady eyes focused unflinchingly on the giant creatures, feathers glossy black under the moonlight.

The man swallowed and glanced at his torch and walking stick. They seemed paltry weapons indeed against the fearsome animals below him.

One of the lions suddenly danced forward and pawed the air in front of the stranger's face, jaws open in a terrifying growl.

The man found his feet moving against his own volition. He was down the dune and into the fray in a matter of heartbeats, his path delivering him between the beasts and the stranger. And there he stood, torch held aloft in one hand, staff grasped tightly in the other, stance wide and steady despite the tremors running through his body.

For a fleeting moment, he wondered what insanity had possessed him to think he could fight off these creatures. Then he looked into the animals' snarling faces and his fear faded.

He was a man who had always done the right thing, for as long as he could recall. Though he had lived beyond the time that should have been his, on account of his exceptional ancestry, his was a simple life. On the piece of land that had been in his family for hundreds of years and that abutted the place he had called home, he grew crops and tended a mixed herd of animals. It was enough to feed his wives and his two young sons, and there were even leftovers with which to barter with the traveling merchants who came through their valley, granting them rare goods they would not otherwise find in the village.

One of the principles by which he lived was to do unto others that which he would have done unto himself. It was a life lesson indoctrinated in him by his father many years past, one that been passed down the generations of long-lived men and women in their family, a canon he was now teaching his own sons.

And this, right here, was the virtuous thing to do. Even if he died, even if it meant never finding a cure for his sons, he knew he could not live with his conscience if he did not do his utmost to save the life of another.

So he straightened, took a step toward the creatures and waved the torch, calling out, 'Away with you, beasts!'

The lions blinked, as if in disbelief. The man took another step, his resolve unshaken, and shouted the command again. The lions surged forth, deadly bodies coiling tightly for the spring. The man stood his ground, his heart drumming rapidly in his breast.

That was when the stranger spoke.

It was a sound unlike any the man had ever heard. A song reaching down into the depths of his soul, it danced down his spine and raised the hairs on his arms. It also stopped the lions in their tracks.

The beasts dropped on their haunches. Ears flicking back, they stared at a spot just beyond the man's right shoulder, where the stranger stood.

The latter spoke again, softly.

The lions lowered their heads. Then, with a timid sound, they rose and retreated silently into the darkness.

The man blinked. His knees gave way beneath him. He was still staring after the beasts when a shadow fell across him. He looked up.

The stranger stood above him, hand held out. The man took it gratefully and was surprised by the strength of the grip that pulled him to his feet. He stumbled slightly. The stranger steadied him.

'Thank you,' the man mumbled.

Close up, he could see more of the stranger's features. They were pale and beautifully refined, as if drawn by a skilled artist.

'The word you spoke, what was it?'

The stranger regarded him for a moment, a faint smile on his lips. 'I told them to leave.'

His voice was low and rich, liquid silver in the night.

The man glanced in the direction the lions had vanished. 'Maybe you did not need my help after all.'

'The outcome may have been different had you not arrived.'

The man could not help but feel the consequences would have remained in the stranger's favor. He shook off the uncanny feeling dancing on the edges of his consciousness, picked up his torch and staff, and motioned to him. 'Come, I have a place nearby where you can rest for the night.'

The stranger followed him up the dune and down the other side. When they reached the camp, the man took out a piece of bread and the water gourd from his sack, and offered them to his new companion.

'Is this the last of your supplies?'

The man shrugged. 'It is but you need not worry about that.'

The stranger shook his head and made to return the items. 'I cannot accept your generosity. You have already done more than I could ever expect.'

The man gently pushed the gourd and the bread back into the stranger's hands. 'I insist. You are my guest.' He smiled and looked around. 'Although I wish I had a better place to entertain you in.'

The stranger observed him for a moment before accepting the food and drink. The crow jumped down on his arm and pecked at the bread.

'He is a very docile creature,' the man commented, watching the bird.

'He has his moments,' said the stranger.

The crow stopped and gave him a beady stare. The man chuckled.

The stranger looked at him quizzically.

'I am sorry. It is just the exact expression Joanna has when I say something foolish.'

'Joanna?' the stranger repeated.

The man sobered. 'Yes. My second wife.' He cleared his throat. 'I have yet to introduce myself. My name is Romerus.'

The stranger dipped his chin. 'It is nice to make your acquaintance, Romerus. I am Ury'an.' He indicated the crow. 'This here is my companion Arael.'

Their names made Romerus's skin tingle. 'It is also nice to meet you.' He hesitated. 'I do not mean to pry, but why are you here? In the middle of the desert?'

'I am a traveller,' said Ury'an.

'Oh.' Romerus faltered. 'Have you a particular destination in mind?'

Ury'an shook his head and smiled faintly again. 'No. I am… looking for something.'

Romerus stared. 'What is it that you search for?'

Ury'an looked at the moon briefly. His gaze, when it landed on Romerus's face, was heated. 'I will know when I find it.'

Romerus stroked his beard. 'That is most cryptic.'

Ury'an grinned. 'What about you?' He indicated the desert around them. 'What are you doing here?'

The question brought Romerus sharply back to the stark reality of his situation. He found himself suddenly talking, words spilling out and stumbling over each other in his eagerness to share the heavy burden he had carried for so long. He spoke of the plague and his two sons by his first wife, Zara. Of his second wife, Joanna, whose spirit was as indomitable as the wind. Of the demise of the nearby villages and the Elder's promise that salvation lay somewhere to the east, in no man's land.

Ury'an listened, his handsome face impassive, eyes glinting with an indefinable emotion while Romerus spoke.

'It seems your predicament is dire indeed,' he said in the silence that followed Romerus's account. He glanced at the crow, who now perched on his shoulder, head buried under a wing. The bird's feathers trembled slightly. 'Arael agrees. We will accompany you on your travels until you find this cure you seek.'

CHAPTER THREE

Romerus blinked, uncertain he had heard him correctly. 'I—I do not know what to say.'

'Then say nothing. It is the least Arael and I can do to repay the debt we owe you.'

They settled down to rest, Romerus finding sleep hard to come by after the extraordinary events of the night. When morning came, Ury'an and Arael were still there. They looked remarkably refreshed.

They set off toward the east, a companionable silence between them. And so passed another day as they ventured deeper into the desert.

When dusk fell once more, they found a small oasis and rested on cool grass, in the shade of palm trees. There were dates to eat and Arael even caught a desert rabbit. It was the first time Romerus had seen a crow hunt. The bird did it with cool efficacy and made sure to kill the creature quickly. As the moon sailed across the sky, they talked about their lives. It was only afterward that Romerus realized he did most of the talking.

On the eve of the tenth day of his journey into the desert, a shape appeared on the skyline to the east. Romerus's heart leapt in his throat when he saw it.

'I think that is the mountain the Elder spoke of,' he said to Ury'an.

Ury'an studied the distant shadow, his face inscrutable.

Romerus barely slept that night, so filled with excitement was he at being close to finding a cure for his children. He prayed fervently that they would still be there when he returned.

It was another two days before they reached the mountain. By the time they stood in the shadow of its base, Romerus understood why the Elder had spoken of the place in such hushed tones.

It rose hundreds of feet above the desert, a towering, dark mass stabbing at the sky, forbidding and radiating an almost evil energy. The rocks crowding its sides were sharp and jagged, poised to slice through skin and impale flesh. It looked like the last place one would hope to find a miraculous spring.

He glanced at Ury'an, troubled.

'There.' Ury'an pointed. 'I see a path.'

Romerus looked where he indicated and almost sagged with relief. Ury'an's sharp eyes had seen what he could not. A narrow footpath snaked its way up the mountain some sixty feet to their right.

'Can you see it?' said Ury'an.

'The path? Yes.'

'No, farther up. It looks like there is an opening up there.'

Romerus's head snapped up. He stared and soon spotted

the blacker than black shadow Ury'an spoke of. His heartbeat accelerated. He took the lead and started up the path.

By the time they reached the mouth of the cave, Romerus's hands and shins were bloodied. Though the path helped, it did not take away from the treacherous rocks that lined it and caused him to stumble and fall.

In contrast, Ury'an seemed untouched, his breathing slow and steady compared to Romerus's pants, his clothes and skin free of tears and blood.

Romerus gave this strange fact but a passing thought as he stared into the darkness of the cave. He took a step forward and would have fallen had Ury'an not grasped his elbow.

'Steady there. You would not want to hurt yourself when you have come this far.'

Romerus swallowed and nodded shakily. He took a deep breath and ventured slowly into the gaping maw of the mountain. Ury'an followed, Arael on his shoulder.

The light dimmed and they were engulfed in gloom. The cave finally narrowed into a tiny passage they had to squeeze through. Soon, the ceiling crowded them and they found themselves crawling into even tighter spaces. Just when Romerus thought they would have to turn back, the passage started to widen.

Moments later, it ended. Romerus scrambled to his feet and stared at what lay before him.

A giant cavern some hundred feet tall and just as wide occupied what appeared to be the very center of the mountain. Arrowing down from the distant ceiling through a narrow sinkhole, a shaft of sunlight pierced the gloom and illuminated a clump of vegetation sitting in the shallow basin in the middle of the cave.

Romerus ran toward the light, his steps unsteady, his heart filled with wild hope.

It was only when he drew close that he saw the plants were brown and dead. Although the smoothness of the rock that lined the basin indicated it had once held water, there was none now. His gaze sought and found the crumbling pile of stones that should have been a spring. He sank to his knees before them, his breath catching in his throat.

Fingers trembling, Romerus reached out and touched the rocks. They were bone dry. He started moving them aside, slowly at first then with increasing desperation, fingers digging at parched dirt and stone, unheeding of the sharp edges that sliced his skin and the blood that soon colored his hands crimson.

It was only when Ury'an touched him on the shoulder that Romerus realized he was crying. He stopped then, silent sobs racking his body, his hands limp in his lap, hope all but lost.

'I am sorry,' said Ury'an.

Romerus looked up at the blur that was his companion's face. He shook his head. 'It is not your fault, my friend.'

He wiped his eyes and stared at the dead spring for a long time. Then his gaze shifted to the shaft of daylight bathing them. He rose unsteadily to his feet, turned his face to the sun, and closed his eyes.

'What are you doing?' said Ury'an after a short silence.

Had he been in a more stable state of mind, Romerus would have detected the change in his companion's voice. It had become musical once more.

'I am praying.'

'Praying?' Ury'an repeated. 'To whom do you pray and why?'

Peace slowly filled Romerus's heart as he stood enveloped by the warm light. 'To the One who gifted this world with life. And because I have Faith.'

'Faith?'

Though tears still pricked his eyes, Romerus allowed a smile to curve his lips. 'Yes. I have Faith. In the One who created my forebears. The One who has given me a longer life than most. I have done all that I can. Now, I must entrust the fate of my sons to Him.' He hesitated. 'Whatever His choice, I will accept it.'

'Is this truly what you believe?'

Romerus opened his eyes and stared into the shaft of light. He examined his mind and heart and found them filled with a simple truth. 'Yes.'

Brightness filled the cave, incandescent and hot. Romerus gasped and sheltered his eyes with a bloodied hand, wondering if the sun's path had brought it directly above them. It took but a heartbeat for him to realize that the source of the ethereal light was not the golden orb in the sky. He turned slowly. His breath froze on his lips. He fell to his knees once more.

Ury'an had shed his cloak. Instead of the clothes Romerus had become used to seeing him in, the man who had been his constant companion over the last few days had turned into a dazzling being wearing golden armor. Skin glowing where it was exposed, eyes molten silver, he was an achingly beautiful entity to behold. Only Arael remained unchanged, although Romerus could see flickers of the same unearthly radiance dancing through his black feathers. A warm breeze blew across the cavern, bringing with it the scent of spices and an oppressive pressure that drove Romerus's body closer to the ground.

'*Rise, Romerus.*'

And there it was, the voice he had heard that first night, when the lions suddenly retreated. A musical tune that echoed through his mind and body, bending his will. To disobey was unimaginable. The physical force pressing down on him abated. He found himself back on his feet.

Just as suddenly as it had appeared, the light faded and Ury'an's appearance returned to that which Romerus had grown accustomed to. Arael clucked.

'*Yes, it was,*' Ury'an told the crow.

'What?' Romerus mumbled.

'*He asked whether the dramatic display was strictly necessary,*' said Ury'an.

Romerus shook his head, dazed. 'Who—who are you?' He envisioned the dazzling light he had seen but a moment ago. 'Are you—a god?'

Ury'an smiled. '*I am not a god.*'

Romerus stared, pulse racing and blood thundering in his ears. 'You are too pleasant to be a demon.'

Ury'an shrugged. '*Demons are quite cunning creatures. But you are correct. I am no demon.*'

Arael pecked Ury'an on the shoulder.

Ury'an sighed. '*It seems my companion grows impatient with me.*'

And then he spoke. Of what he was. Of the challenge he had been given. Of the promise he had made. Of the future he wanted to mold. Of the many years he had spent scouring the face of this world, searching.

Romerus listened to it all, mind abuzz, mouth dry, body shaking from shock and awe.

'*In you, I believe I have found him,*' said Ury'an finally. '*A man worthy of His forgiveness and to whom I will lend my strength and wisdom.*'

'I—this is—' Romerus stopped, lost for words. What could he say?

'*So I will give you what you seek.*'

The hope that had died a quick death only moments past burst forth in Romerus's heart once more.

'*I will give you a cure for your sons.*'

CHAPTER FOUR

THE VILLAGE APPEARED BENEATH HIM, A CLUSTER OF CLAY AND mud-brick houses nestled in a shallow, green valley.

Romerus's pace quickened, his stick digging into the hard ground as he made his way down the winding path carved into the side of the hill. The moos of oxen and the cries of goats reached him on the evening air. He looked up, pleased to see his livestock in the pen next to his home, on the slope of the far hill.

It was only when he drew closer to the settlement that he saw the pyres of the dead, black mounds containing what were once the bodies of those who had succumbed to the sickness.

They were stacked in the shadow of a rocky overhang, next to the narrow river that coursed through the vale. Sadness filled him, for many had perished in his absence. He forged ahead, more eager now than ever to see his family.

The village was eerily quiet, doors banging open on hinges, darkness filling rooms normally lit with fires. He saw not one soul as he made his way to his home. The first tendril of fear gripped him.

It intensified when he saw his own door lying open.

He shook his head, berating himself for the treacherous thought that darted through his mind. After all he had seen, he had to keep his Faith.

He found them in the farthest room of the house.

An olive grove rose on the other side of the thick, clay walls, keeping sunlight at bay and the chamber cool. The wooden shutters were wide open and pale light streamed into the chamber.

It was enough for him to make out the four figures sleeping on a pair of straw-filled mattresses, the women's arms wrapped around the children.

Love filled Romerus's heart and tears his eyes as he beheld them. Though they looked thin and exhausted, they were here. They were still alive.

He took his sack off his back and carried it carefully to the beds.

Zara was the first to rouse, her brown eyes fuzzy with sleep. She blinked at him.

'Romerus?' she whispered. 'Is that you?'

Joanna woke. Tears filled her eyes when she saw him.

'You have returned!'

She lunged at him awkwardly and wrapped her arms around his neck. Zara joined her. The two women sobbed, their voices weak with relief.

'Did you find it?' said Zara. She pulled back and gazed at him hotly. 'Did you find the spring?'

Romerus shook his head.

Joanna cried out before clamping a hand over her lips. She glanced at the boys. They slept on, unaware of the goings on around them.

'So—so it was all in vain?' Zara said brokenly, once she could speak.

'No,' Romerus replied. 'It was not.'

He spoke then of all that he had seen in the desert, of the lions and of Ury'an. Of Arael the crow and the mountain. Of the dead spring inside the cave. Of the chance he had been given after all hope was lost.

Silence fell upon the room when he finished his tale.

His wives stared at him, their eyes reflecting their shock.

'He gave you a cure?' said Zara, hope strengthening her voice.

A troubled expression darkened Joanna's face.

'Are you sure, Romerus?'

Romerus hesitated.

'How can you say that, sister?' Zara cried. 'After all Romerus has been through—'

'I am sure,' Romerus said calmly.

Joanna was quiet for some time, her hazel gaze intent, an arrow piercing his mind. He wondered whether she could see the truth he had omitted to tell them.

'Then do it,' she said quietly.

Romerus nodded and extracted the gourds containing the cures.

There were two. One for each son.

Zara leaned forward. 'Do they have to—?'

'Yes, they have to drink it. It is the only way to get it into their body.'

And so Romerus gently lifted the head of his firstborn son, Crovir, and placed the first gourd to his parched lips. He parted the boy's mouth with his thumb and tilted the vessel. From within it, a shimmering, golden mass slid down and disappeared into Crovir's throat.

Then he lifted the head of his second born, Bastian, and repeated the process with the second gourd. The sparkling mist it held vanished inside the boy's mouth.

'It is done,' he said softly, his sons' heads resting in his lap.

A shudder ran through Crovir's body. His brother stirred beside him. Their eyes blinked open.

As he gazed down at his children through a film of tears, Romerus recalled what Ury'an had said and done in the cave.

'I WILL GIVE YOU A CURE FOR YOUR SONS. YOU WHO ARE DESCENDED *from the very first man and woman who walked this Earth. You who are pure of heart and soul. I will give you what you seek. And in this cure will be the last chance humanity receives for redemption.'*

Fear suddenly stabbed through Romerus, the enormity of Ury'an's last words so vast he could barely comprehend it.

'What do you mean?' he whispered.

'Your sons will become the first of a new race. One that will possess the potential to save Mankind.'

Romerus stared, dazed.

'My boys—*my sons.*' He shook his head. 'They are but children! How can they save humanity? And why?'

Ury'an drew closer then, his silver eyes filling with such sadness it made Romerus's heart ache.

'Because I have seen the future.' He placed his hand on Romerus's face. *'Let me give you an infinitesimal glimpse of what it holds.'*

Images flashed through Romerus's mind for a handful of heartbeats. What he saw caused him to gasp and cry and fall to his knees, a terror unlike any he had ever known drenching his body in a cold sweat.

He fell back, breaking contact.

'What was that?' he whispered, lips numb, a sick feeling threatening to empty his stomach.

'It is what awaits Mankind and all of God's other Creations at the End of Days.'

'And my sons—my sons will be able to stop *that?!*' Romerus stammered.

Ury'an fell silent. Even Arael grew still, his large eyes strangely thoughtful.

'I cannot guarantee it.'

Romerus blinked. 'What do you mean?'

'To your son Crovir, I will gift a piece of my heart. It will grant him physical and mental fortitude beyond any other man on this Earth. It will also bestow upon him relentless determination and strength of will. To your son Bastian, I will gift a piece of my soul. It will grant him singular fortitude of body and mind as well, beyond that possessed by mere mortals. It will also bestow upon him great wisdom and kindness.' Ury'an's face grew inscrutable. *'But my gifts will not take away their free will. Whatever path they choose to travel in life, it will be their choice. The decisions they and their descendants make, however, will directly affect the future of humanity.'*

In Ury'an's words, Romerus sensed a warning. Still, he watched as God's Messenger placed a hand over his chest and slowly extracted a shimmering piece of matter. This he placed inside one of the gourds in Romerus's sack. Inside a second gourd, he breathed a glistening mist that lit the air around them with a brief flash.

And so they left the cave and climbed down the mountain. When they reached the desert, Romerus turned to Ury'an. He sensed their time together was at an end.

'The gifts you have given my sons. Will they make them like you?'

Ury'an shook his head. *'No. They will maintain the appearance of Man. But they will live longer, much longer even than you, and have many children and lives.'*

Romerus's eyes widened. 'You mean—they will never die?'

Ury'an looked up at the sky. *'They will have as many lives as there are crows above us.'*

Romerus followed his gaze. Surprise darted through him when he saw the silent, circling birds that had appeared seemingly out of nowhere, bodies black against the pale blue sky. He counted seventeen of them.

'Upon the final death of your sons, their children, and all those who will descend from their bloodlines, Arael and his brethren will come for them and return their bodies to ash.'

Romerus looked at the crow. The bird stared back at him, his gaze intent but kind.

'One thing your sons must bear in mind,' Ury'an added. *'As with the first man and woman who walked this Earth, the children they bear will breed with one another to keep their bloodlines pure. But the offspring of Crovir and Bastian must never cross-breed.'*

Romerus startled. 'What do you mean?'

'The Heart and Soul must never meet. Not now. Not ever.'

Unease filtered through Romerus once more. 'Why?'

'Because a child born of pureblood descendants of Crovir and Bastian will be more powerful than any of their kin. If such a breed were created, they might prove dangerous, to both humanity and their own race.'

Romerus was silent for some time.

'Your will shall be done,' he said finally with a dip of his chin. 'I will tell my sons so.'

Ury'an stepped toward him then and lifted his hands. Romerus blinked in surprise as God's Messenger clasped his head and tilted it down to kiss his forehead.

Ury'an stepped back and watched him with a glint in his pale eyes.

Romerus raised a trembling hand to his brow. A strange

heat was spreading through his body from the spot where Ury'an's lips had touched him.

'To you, I grant some of my Divine essence. It will give you longevity beyond that of even the first man and woman, so that you may live to see your grandchildren grow.' Ury'an gave him a slight smile. 'For the hope humanity has for redemption truly lies in them.'

And then he was gone, his body dissolving into a flock of crows that soared into the air. Romerus watched, breathless, as the birds flew toward the sun. Soon, they were a vanishing black speck engulfed by the very heavens.

He stared at the sky for a long time. Then, he turned toward the desert and started to walk.

And so the Archangel returned to the Kingdom of his Lord, nearly a hundred Earth years after he had left His side.

Upon seeing him, God said, 'Have you found a man worthy of my forgiveness and your favor?'

'Yes, my Lord,' replied the Archangel.

And God looked out over the Dominion of Earth, his unworldly eyes glimmering. 'But I see darkness in the future of this man and that of his offspring. Although his heart remains pure, those of his children grow wicked. The wars and bloodshed they create will cast shadows upon the Earth for millennia to come. This, in spite of the seventeen lives you have granted them to acquire the wisdom they need to accomplish their destiny. Are you certain you have chosen well?'

The Archangel smiled and said, 'Yes, my Lord. For the challenges they will face in the times ahead will be their ultimate test. A test of the trueness of the heart and soul of humanity.'

God was quiet for some time. 'I see you have not told this man all of the truth.'

The Archangel said, 'No, my Lord. I have not.'

And God smiled. 'It seems you are willing to gamble with the Fate of Mankind after all.'

'Call it Faith, my Lord.'

The Archangel gazed upon the Dominion of Earth, his heart and soul at peace. For the warning he had given Romerus was incomplete. The bloodlines of his sons were not to mix. Not until the time was right. And what he had foreseen of the children's future indicated that many a millennia would pass until such a time was upon their descendants.

For the ones who would inherit and manifest the full potential and expression of his gifts would be born dozens of generations hence. And upon the bodies of the men and women who would be humanity's true salvation, the ones whose torturous pasts would define their futures, he would carve his marks to identify them as his true heirs.

CHAPTER FIVE

3156 BC

IT CAME ON THE WIND, THE WILD, SHRILL CALL OF A HAWK. IN the valley below, soldiers paused, weapons aloft, hands crimson with the blood of their enemies, their own bodies weeping from stabs and slashes. The sounds of war abated for a frozen moment.

Heads rose. As one, the men stared at the peak of the ridge to the east. Hearts that already raced from combat accelerated with fear and awe as they beheld the figure on a large, black horse clad in plates of armor. A murmur ran through the troops gathered on the bloodied battleground.

'The Red Queen! The Red Queen is here!'

Slowly, it grew, until it became a chant, a frenetic chorus that energized one army even as it sapped the other of its remaining strength.

The figure on the horse raised her arm in the air. The

broadsword in her hand glimmered, impossibly big in her grip, the metal catching the sun at her back and casting sparkling jets onto her gilded battle suit and chainmail tunic. On her shoulders, a cape fluttered in the wind, blood red under the golden light. On her head and limbs, polished bronze gleamed. The soldiers held their breath.

She brought her sword down and pointed it at the battlefield, heels digging sharply into the flanks of the fearsome beast beneath her. The horse neighed wildly and reared up on its hind legs before bolting down the hill toward the soldiers.

The rest of the Red Queen's army came behind her, weapons glinting, the beats of their horses' hooves making the ground tremble, their cries darkening the sky. Above them, an armor-clad hawk hovered, a silhouette against the dazzling orb. It shrieked once more before diving after its mistress.

'I DO NOT EVEN KNOW WHY WE ARE HERE.'

Mila turned away from the tent's opening toward the man who had spoken, hands stilling on the blade she was polishing. She picked a piece of ostrich meat from a bowl on the table and fed it to the hawk perched on her shoulder before giving him her full attention.

A quarter day had passed since the battle ended. They had set up their tents on a rise in the valley, a short distance from where the main troops were stationed. At the edge of the camp, the bodies of the dead burned, dark mounds sending smoke spiraling toward the sky. The stench of scorched flesh would linger in the air for a Half Moon at least. By morning, the valley would be a veritable feasting ground for vultures and other carrion birds. She knew this from past experience.

'The soldiers like to see you on the battlefield,' she said coolly.

Baruch sighed. 'The only one they want to see is you, cousin. Most of them would happily lay down their lives for the *Red Queen*.'

'He is not wrong,' murmured the man munching on an apple next to him. 'And I suspect any one of them would think they had died and gone to Heaven if you ever allowed him to grace your bed.'

Mila ignored Baruch's chuckle and narrowed her eyes at the second figure. For a moment, she entertained the thought of setting the hawk on him. The gesture, however, would be futile. Whatever injuries the bird inflicted would heal within a few days.

'Tobias, you are a prince and general in our fathers' army, as are you, Baruch.' Her tone hardened. 'I would like it if you two behaved in a manner befitting your stations.'

Tobias propped his feet up on a wooden chest and reached for a handful of olives. 'Keeping up the appearances of our rank is solely for the sake of our people and soldiers, sister. We should at least be able to be our own selves in each other's private company.'

Mila narrowed her eyes. 'After four hundred and thirty-five years, your company grows stale, brother.'

Baruch laughed loud enough to startle the soldiers guarding the tents outside.

A grin curved Tobias's lips. 'Still, though we are formidable warriors, Baruch and I both know you should be leading our men, sister. To this day, I do not know why our fathers insist on keeping you at the rank of lieutenant commander.'

Mila refrained from replying. Her gaze shifted to the opening of the tent and the pyres of the dead once more.

The uprising in Terka was just one of several rebellions that had arisen since the fourth lunar month rose on this, the five-hundredth year of the Empire. Even as she stood a few miles north of the burning city, the first and second generals of their fathers' army at her side, Mila knew some of her siblings and cousins were engaged in similar skirmishes on the boundaries of the lands that constituted the center of their domain.

It was a small price to pay for ruling a kingdom that stretched as far southwest as the Naqada population of the Nahal River, as far north as the Yamnayas of the Arals, and as far east as the Yellow River people. At last count, the Empire had dominion over nearly fifteen million human souls. And every year, even more were absorbed into their ever-growing realm as their powerful army vanquished nations farther afield.

Though Tobias and Baruch's births preceded hers by over a hundred years, Mila knew their kingdom had grown most aggressively once she joined the army as a foot soldier at age twelve. As per the custom that had applied to everyone who had come before her, their fathers had insisted that she, the last born of their children, also progress up the ranks through her own sweat and hard graft. It took Mila twenty-two months to rise to the position of captain of the troop and another five years to that of lieutenant commander, an exploit matched by none among her siblings and cousins. In that time and the years since, she had conquered more human cities than anyone else in a position of power in the army, contributing to the dramatic expansion of their realm.

Only four people now stood above her. Tobias, the first-born son of Crovir and the army's first general. Baruch, the first-born son of Bastian and its second general. And, finally, Crovir and Bastian themselves, their fathers, kings, and absolute rulers of the Empire. Below her were ranked her nine siblings and cousins, all powerful warriors in their own right, though some had assumed other roles within the Empire.

In all, fourteen governed their dominion of millions. Fourteen extraordinary beings, remarkable not only for their physical prowess and stamina in battle, but also for their ability to defeat death itself. Fourteen "Immortals". And beneath them, the grandchildren of Crovir and Bastian, also Immortals, though most were still under age. Building an empire took time and commitment, and it was only in recent years that they had been granted permission by their fathers to have their own children.

Although the Immortals were revered as gods, Mila knew their lifespans had a finite limit. As per the lore instilled in them when they were but a few years of age, she and the other children of Crovir and Bastian had been gifted seventeen lives, and physical superiority over normal men. They had also been indoctrinated with the one immutable law that governed their kind: the decree that forbade the offspring of Crovir and Bastian from ever mating with one another.

To this rule, Crovir had added another caveat. To keep the bloodlines pure, his children and those of Bastian were also prohibited from procreating with mere mortals.

A bitter smile twisted Mila's lips at that thought. Of course, the latter rule did not preclude the kings from taking human lovers themselves, something she knew her father Crovir indulged in on a regular basis.

The notion that had preoccupied her for the past Half Moon rose in her mind, sweeping aside all thoughts of her father's debauchery. Her smile faded.

'That is the fifth Terka governor we have disposed of in twice as many years,' she said quietly. 'Do you not think these uprisings are getting more frequent?'

Though she had her back turned to them, she sensed the glance Tobias and Baruch exchanged. Abu, her hawk, shifted his grip on her shoulder and nuzzled her ear.

'Come now, sister,' Tobias drawled. 'It is but a consequence of ruling so many.'

She turned to look at her brother and saw the lie in his eyes. And though Baruch studied her with a neutral expression, she could tell he also shared her sentiments.

'So, I am not the only one who thinks that,' she murmured.

A commotion drew her gaze to the west bank of their encampment. A cloud of desert sand and dust rose from the hillside. Below it, a cavalry of some twenty men approached, helmets shining under the sun. A banner fluttered in the wind at the head of the troop, a golden lion on a sea of red. The crest of the Empire.

Tobias appeared at her side. 'Ah. Your husband is here. His haste to join your side is evident, as usual.' He glanced at her. 'Not that I blame him.'

'Yes.' Baruch nodded wisely on the other side of Mila and lobbed another chunk of meat at the hawk. 'Not only is our Red Queen a fearsome sight to behold on the battlefield, she is also the most beautiful woman in our realm.'

'I am sure your wife would be thrilled to hear that,' Mila muttered.

Baruch shrugged. 'Even Hosanna admits it.'

'So does Ysa,' said Tobias. 'In fact, all our siblings and cousins agree on this matter. You are the fairest flower in our kingdom. Even Navia, with her golden hair and green eyes, is no match for you.'

Mila tried her best not to roll her eyes as she watched the man leading the troop head their way. The dust and blood smearing the coat of the white stallion beneath him grew more evident as he drew closer. She frowned. She had lost track of the number of times she had berated him for not looking after his steed.

Abu uttered a shrill cry. She raised a fist to the bird. He dropped down onto her hand, flapped his wings, and flew out of the tent.

He was not a fan of her mate.

The man on the stallion jumped down before the horse came to a full halt, barked a command at one of the soldiers outside, and marched briskly toward the tent. His bright gaze arrowed in on her face when he entered, the hunger and possessive light in his eyes blatant for all to see.

Tobias coughed diplomatically. 'How goes the rebellion in Nemrik?'

Calvary Regiment Commander Kronos, third-born son of Crovir, her older half-brother and the mate chosen for her by their father, waved a dismissive hand. 'It was a simple matter to handle, brother. The rest of the battalion is already on its way back to Nawaar. Rafael and Malachi travel ahead to the capital to join Jared and the others.'

'And what of the governor of Nemrik?' said Baruch.

Kronos looked away from her for a moment and flashed a triumphant smile at his cousin. 'He was executed in the main square yesterday, along with his family.'

Baruch raised an eyebrow in the ensuing silence. 'Was that strictly necessary? His wives and children could have been imprisoned or dispatched as slaves to the farthest reaches of our kingdom.' A frown marred his brow. 'Why slaughter them?'

Kronos blinked, genuine surprise darting across his handsome face. 'Why, he needed to be made an example of. Besides, Crovir has always been quite direct with his instructions. We are to forcefully quash any uprising and demonstrate in no uncertain terms to the human cities under our rule the cost of betrayal.' He paused, his gaze and tone turning thoughtful. 'He was very specific about what we were to do to the leaders of these rebellions and their families. He does not want any survivors who might seek revenge or stir up further revolts in the years to come. I presume you followed his orders and did the same to the governor of Terka?'

Baruch glanced at Tobias and Mila. 'The thirst for blood your father possesses knows no end, it seems. And no, we have spared the family of the governor here. They are among the cohort of prisoners currently making their way back to the capital.'

Kronos narrowed his eyes. 'You know this will displease him.'

'Then he can ask Bastian to put me over his knee and tan my hide,' said Baruch, his normally relaxed face hardening for a moment. 'They made me a general of their army for a reason. And that reason included my ability to make decisions in matters of war.'

He stormed out of the tent.

'I shall leave you two alone,' Tobias murmured before following Baruch. He dropped the tent's flap on his way out.

Kronos turned and unbuckled his sword, dropping it to the ground as he advanced toward her. Mila had to raise her head to look at him when he stopped, inches away.

'Take off your clothes.'

She balked at his commanding tone. Though he was older than her by dozens of years, she still outranked him. He must have read the expression in her eyes for he grabbed her chin and kissed her forcefully. Mila pushed him away. He tightened his grip. She shivered before surrendering to the desire growing between them.

In all the years Kronos had been her mate, he had always

pleasured her in bed, his passion for and devotion to her never dimming with the passage of time.

A sliver of guilt stabbed through Mila as he pushed her down on a sea of cushions. Despite the fact that she reciprocated his ardor and had borne him a son and a daughter, she knew her heart would forever remain closed to her husband.

CHAPTER SIX

THE CHANTS OF THE CROWD ECHOED TO THE SKIES AS THE parade proceeded through the capital's main plaza. At the head of the impressive square, two formidable, hundred-foot-tall, stone statues cast their shadows across the troops of infantry soldiers marching rigidly to the beat of drums, feet pounding the ground in perfect time to the tempo. Behind them came the archers and the cavalry, the clatter of the horses' hooves lost in the din.

From where she sat on her steed at the rear of the procession with her siblings and cousins, Mila gazed beyond the carved, life-like depictions of the kings of the Empire to the hundred steps rising toward the citadel that dominated Uryl, the capital of the kingdom. On the wide stage that fronted the towering stone ramparts, the real Crovir and Bastian sat on gilded thrones.

She glanced at the thousands lining the square. Though the humans who lived within the protective walls of Uryl cheered the soldiers, few would ever set foot inside the citadel and witness the decadent splendor of the palace of the kings.

Indeed, apart from the servants and guards who lived inside the palace, only the human leaders who swore fealty to Crovir and Bastian and were permitted to rule their own cities had stepped inside its walls. As it stood, it was only on special occasions such as this that the populace was even allowed to cross the heavily-guarded moat that separated the capital from the fortress which enclosed the citadel and housed the city's administrative quarters and a battalion of some thousand soldiers.

Movement down the line of horses distracted her from her cynical thoughts. She glanced over the row of twelve she rode in.

To her left, sitting erect on his stallion, was Kronos. On the other side of him, the rest of the row consisted of Crovir's remaining children —Tobias with his wife and half-sister Ysa, and Jared, beside his wife and half-sister Beatrix. Of the children of Crovir, only Tobias, Jared and herself were born of Crovir and *his* half-sister Helena, which elevated them in status above their half-siblings and mates, born of Crovir and his second wife Rachel.

The other half of the row to her right comprised her uncle Bastian's offspring, in the same formation. Baruch rode beside his wife and half-sister Hosanna, Rafael, Bastian's second son, by his wife and half-sister Phebe, and Navia, his youngest daughter, next to her husband and half-brother Malachi. Similarly, Baruch, Rafael and Navia were born of Sofia, their father's half-sister, and thus elevated them above their half-siblings and mates Hosanna, Phebe and Malachi, who were born of Bastian and his second wife Leah.

'Brother, will you please control your beasts? One of them just tried to slip inside my dress,' Hosanna murmured to the bearded, blue-eyed man to her right.

'Sister, that is because your skin is as pale as the almond

milk I usually feed them. They probably think it is time for their midday meal.' He stroked the snakes coiled around his neck and left arm, before catching the one that was unceremoniously tossed his way by his scowling, dark-haired half-sister.

Kronos twitched at Mila's side.

Unheeding, Hosanna leaned forward on her steed and addressed the woman on the other side of the blue-eyed man with the snakes.

'Seriously, Phebe, I am amazed you have not banned these creatures from your palace.'

'Ah, you know full well Rafael needs them for his healing arts, sister,' replied Phebe. She glanced benignly at her husband and his snakes. 'Besides, he knows not to bring them inside our bedroom.'

Rafael grimaced and patted the serpent in his lap. 'Yes. The one time that happened, you screamed the place down so loudly everyone thought I was murdering you.'

'But you learned your lesson, did you not, dearest?' said Phebe, a hard undercurrent scoring her words.

'I did,' said Rafael sheepishly.

'So long as you never forget who truly rules you,' murmured Jared from Mila's other side.

'Really?' scoffed Rafael. 'You are one to talk. I hear Beatrix made you move the course of an entire river so she could indulge her habit of moonlight bathing in the open air closer to your palace.'

'I did not ask Jared to move a river,' Beatrix protested. 'He just created a branch that could serve our home better. And how do you know of my bathing habits?'

'The whole kingdom knows of them,' Rafael stated.

Mila's attention was drawn from their bickering to activity

further along the row. She was conscious of Kronos's face growing darker by her side.

'Navia, I think Malachi just fell into slumber,' said Hosanna.

The fair-haired woman she had addressed moved in time to stop the figure next to her from sliding off his horse.

'Malachi, my love, I know you are tired but please try to stay awake,' she murmured. 'We are still in the middle of the procession.'

Malachi blinked and straightened in his saddle. 'Oh.'

He looked ahead to the citadel and swallowed a yawn.

'You need to feed him more meat, Navia,' murmured Hosanna. 'I fear his blood is thin and weak.'

Baruch grinned. 'I am not sure about that. Hey, brother, could it be that our little Navia is tiring you out in the bedroom?'

Navia blushed.

Hosanna elbowed her mate in the ribs. 'Does every word that leaves your mouth have to be so filthy, husband?'

'You know you like it that way,' said Baruch.

Hosanna's ears reddened while her husband's grin widened.

Kronos finally snapped. *'For the love of our fathers, will you all shut up and act in the manner suited to your ranks?'*

For once, Mila had to agree. Despite the fact that she was the youngest among her siblings and cousins, there were times when she felt like giving them a right ding around the ear. This was one of those times.

'It seems someone has not broken his morning fast,' Jared murmured.

'I agree. You need to learn to relax, Kronos,' said Rafael. 'Here, pet a snake.'

Phebe giggled.

Before Mila could murmur words to appease her now apoplectic husband, the troops ahead of them came to an abrupt halt and parted in a precisely rehearsed drill that she had long become accustomed to, clearing a path to the citadel.

The elaborate welcome ritual in progress was one Crovir always insisted upon whenever they came back from a significant victory. In time, their subjects had come to expect it. To Mila and the others, it was clear the ceremony was not so much a display of genuine delight at their safe return as it was a show of power.

The chanting grew louder as the twelve princes and princesses of the Empire pressed on, their formal attire and those of their steeds resplendent under the noon sun as they progressed between the rows of soldiers.

Although she was too far away to see the face of her father where he sat on his throne, Mila knew the crowd's obvious adoration displeased him. The reverence he and Bastian inspired in those they ruled was born of fear rather than admiration. It was different for their children.

Over the years, after they came into their own and became rulers of cities bestowed upon them, the brutality of their actions, as dictated by the kings, had lessened as they began to appreciate the nature of the weaker race they controlled. Bar Kronos, who still inspired distrust and fear through his uncompromising adherence to his father's style of rule, all the kings' children had come to earn the love of the people through acts of kindness, particularly Rafael, the Healer, and Navia, the Seer. Even Mila, the coldest and least approachable, had gained the respect of the populace through her sharp but fair treatment of her soldiers and subjects.

'It is almost over,' Tobias muttered as they passed the stone statues of the kings.

Baruch glanced at him, his expression sobering.

Of all her siblings and cousins, the two firstborns most

shared Mila's mounting irritation at being forced to be a part of the pompous display.

They dismounted at the base of the citadel and climbed the hundred steps to the stage where their fathers sat. At Crovir's side were his queens, Helena and Rachel. Sofia and Leah, Bastian's queens, stood next to their king. Framing the sides and rear of the platform, and lining the way to the imposing bronze doors leading into the citadel, was a retinue of some hundred servants and soldiers.

The crowd's cheers grew frenzied when the twelve princes and princesses lowered themselves onto their right knees and bowed their heads before the kings. Mila gritted her teeth, her gaze focused on the sandstone floor. Out of the corner of her eye, she read tension in Tobias and Baruch's postures. This, to them, was the worst part of the ceremony.

Bastian rose to his feet first.

'Children, welcome back,' he said in a booming voice.

He pulled each of his offspring up before dropping a kiss on their forehead and embracing them.

Crovir followed leisurely. When his arms closed around her, Mila felt little warmth in his touch. It was only when he stepped back that she registered the cold fury reflected deep in his eyes.

She looked around the stage, searching for the one person she wanted to see, conscious the act would irk Crovir further. 'Where is our grandfather?'

Bastian exchanged a glance with his brother.

'He rests in his quarters,' he said quietly. 'In the time that you have been away, his bones have grown more weary and his sight poorer. We did not think it fair to bring him here today.'

Mila twisted on her heels and stared out over the capital, her heart sinking. From this height, she could see all the way across Uryl to the outer walls encircling the city. On the distant plains beyond, on a rise in the land, rose a second, smaller citadel.

It was the home of Romerus, the father of the kings, and the person she loved the most in this world.

'I believe you may have misunderstood my instructions when I sent you to Terka,' Crovir said softly behind her.

Mila turned slowly.

Crovir glanced at Tobias and Baruch before focusing his heated stare on her once more. 'Or did you decide to disobey me, child?'

She stiffened.

'My king, must we talk of this now?' murmured one of the women standing behind him.

It was her mother, Helena. The queens had followed in their husbands' footsteps and were greeting their children. Helena hugged Mila and dropped a kiss on her cheek, her arms lingering warmly around her. Anger surged through Mila when she saw the bruise on her mother's neck.

Unlike the kings and their children, the queens were not Immortals. Helena, Crovir's first wife, and Sofia, Bastian's first wife, being the daughters of Joanna, Romerus's second wife, had inherited his longevity. Descended from a distant relative of Romerus, Rachel and Leah, the kings' second wives, were similarly gifted with long lives, but they were now long past their best years. Compared to Crovir and Bastian, men still in their prime, their spouses were weary women more fit for the role of queen mother than queen.

But it was not their lifespan or juvenescence that was at the forefront of Mila's mind. Since they lacked the accelerated healing abilities of Immortals, it took the wives as long as an ordinary human to overcome any illness or injury, a fact she had been acutely conscious of since she was a child. For Crovir regularly battered his wives, especially her mother Helena, the most vocal when it came to defying him.

Despite the passage of hundreds of years, Mila still recalled the first time she confronted her father about his barbaric behavior. Though her older siblings tried to stop her, saying the gesture would be futile, Mila could not bite her tongue the day Crovir broke her mother's arm. It was afterward that she realized why her brothers and sisters had implored her to stay quiet. Her mother's injuries doubled overnight. Whenever she dared open her mouth to challenge her father in the time that followed, the pattern repeated itself.

Only once did Mila speak to Bastian about the matter. From the troubled look that crossed his face, she realized he had been aware of the problem for some time. His reply shattered the last hope she had that he could talk sense into his brother.

'What happens between man and wife must remain a private matter,' he said quietly. 'I cannot, in good faith, interfere.'

Bastian's blind love for Crovir, and the steadfast disbelief that he could be anything but a good man, was similarly reflected in her grandfather's words when she went to plead with him.

'You must be wrong, child,' Romerus told her. 'My son could not do such things.'

So time passed and everyone turned a blind eye to the brutality of the older king. But for Mila, the memory of every single wound the wives suffered remained starkly imprinted in her mind, and each fresh one further sapped the respect she had for her father.

'Are you alright, mother?' she murmured presently.

Helena's hand fluttered to her neck. She lowered her gaze for a moment, shame and guilt flashing across her face.

'Why, this is nothing, child.' Her expression brightened and she took Mila's hands in her own. 'I must tell you of little Eleaza. She drew her first arrow the other day. Oh, it was such a wondrous sight to behold. I—'

'You can discuss such frivolous matters later, woman!' Crovir snapped.

The excitement in Helena's eyes died. She bit her lip and took a step back. Tobias and Jared stared their way.

'As I was saying,' Crovir continued, oblivious to the tension on the stage, 'I thought I made it quite clear that you were to kill that treacherous Terka snake and his family. So why did they arrive here this morning, among the prisoners you took from the city?'

'It would have been a waste of resources to kill them, my king,' Mila said in a measured tone. 'They will serve our empire better as slaves.'

Crovir leaned toward her.

'I do not care about resources, daughter,' he hissed in her ear. 'You were to make an example of them.' He drew back, his eyes growing cold. 'Do not worry though. I have corrected your blunder.'

Mila went still. 'What do you mean?'

Crovir smiled. 'I have completed the task that you could not. Even as we speak, the lions feast on the flesh and bones of the family of the Terka governor.'

She stared at her father, her blood growing as hot as the sun beating down upon them. Behind Crovir, Helena shook her head slightly, her expression pleading.

Mila swallowed her rage and dipped her chin curtly. 'Then it is done.'

CHAPTER SEVEN

She stormed past her father and marched toward the towering bronze doors of the citadel, conscious of the gaze of her husband and her siblings at her back. Servants bowed and guards lowered their heads and spears as she crossed the wide, cool passage spanning the twenty-foot-thick wall beyond the opening.

At the end of it, the palace of the kings opened up before her, a maze of opulent buildings made from the finest, sun-baked mud brick and stone from the Empire's quarries. Interlinked by a series of elaborate open-air courtyards and sumptuous gardens, the complex covered several thousand square feet. She navigated a quadrangle and entered an immense hall lined with towering granite and marble columns and gem-studded frescoes. It was one of many that graced the palace and was a stark symbol of the wasteful extravagance that Crovir insisted upon to demonstrate the Empire's wealth and power. Mila ignored the dazzling beauty of the artwork around her and focused on slowing her ragged breathing.

She doubted Crovir would inform Tobias and Baruch of

the fate of the Terka governor's family. His tormenting words were often reserved for her ears alone.

Her father's latest action only added to the poisonous thoughts that had been troubling her for some time. His cruel nature had become more evident over hundreds of years of rule, giving birth to increasingly barbaric acts, most of which were carried out many leagues from the immediate territory of the Empire, away from the eyes of Bastian and Romerus.

Mila knew she was partly at fault for his rising brutality. In as much as some of it was fueled by his unease toward her, his determination to show her his power and make her submit to his will had grown over time, until it became a scourge that blighted her days and dirtied her hands with the blood of the Empire's victims.

Though it had taken her a long time to realize it, Mila knew the reason he had never recommended her promotion to the position of general of his armies. She made him nervous. She, the last born of his children and the most powerful of the twelve princes and princesses.

She was entering a courtyard dotted with glittering water fountains and dominated by a pond swarming with fish and lotus flowers, when a cry interrupted her thoughts and drew her gaze to the gallery that ran around the open space. She slowed to a stop.

In the shade cast by fat stone pillars, a young woman clad in a sumptuous dress stood twisting a little boy's arm, her features contorted in anger as she berated him. A broken bowl lay at their feet, the contents, milk and honey, spilt across the marble floor. Behind the weeping boy, an elderly female servant prostrated herself on the floor, pleas for forgiveness tumbling from her lips. At the south end of the gallery, other servants cowered and murmured among themselves as they looked on.

They were the first to notice Mila's approach. A hush fell over the courtyard, the sudden silence broken only by the shrill voice of the woman in the lavish dress and the boy's cries. He too went mute when he saw her, his eyes growing as wide as marbles. He tried to kneel but only made it halfway to the floor, his arm still held in the vice-like grip of the shouting woman. Behind him, the old servant stared, her mouth open in a voiceless O.

It was only then that the young woman paused and looked over her shoulder. Her dark eyes narrowed to slits as she inspected Mila's official dress uniform.

'Who are you?' she spat.

From where she stopped a foot from her, Mila heard the gasps of the servants in the gallery. Even the old female servant on the floor covered her mouth with her hands, her expression a mixture of fear and shock.

Mila paid them no heed and studied the stranger before her. Though she had not seen her face before, she could guess from her attire and the gems she wore that she was Crovir's latest concubine. A sigh almost passed Mila's lips; granted, she had not been to the capital for a whole month, but she had not expected her father's former lover to last such a short time.

'Release the boy,' she said quietly.

The young woman straightened, ruby lips thinning and eyes blazing with outrage.

'I do not take orders from a soldier!' She tilted her chin defiantly. 'Do you not know that I am a princess of Tarsus?'

Mila suddenly felt tired. She truly was getting too old for this kind of irritation. As she stood there, wondering whether to ask the guards to take Crovir's concubine away or do it herself, the female servant on the floor murmured a warning.

Crovir's lover let go of the boy, took a step toward the old woman, and slapped her viciously. The latter's lip split, staining her chin with blood as she fell sideways to the ground. The boy cried out as the younger woman raised her hand once more to strike the stunned servant at her feet.

Mila's fingers closed around her wrist.

Crovir's lover twisted on her heels, mouth open on a shout that was never uttered. Her eyes widened, fear dawning in them at what she saw on Mila's face.

'*Learn your place, human!*'

Mila's roar filled the yard and echoed against the walls of the surrounding buildings. She tightened her grip on the young woman's arm until she felt flesh grind on bone, the rage that had started to abate filling her veins once more. Crovir's lover whimpered.

'In this realm, the only true princes and princesses are the children of the kings,' Mila hissed. 'As such, you will bow when you address one of them! Is that understood?'

The young woman sobbed and fell to her knees.

Mila glared at her. 'I said, is that understood?'

'Yes!' the woman wailed, her face pale.

'You will not touch another hair on this boy's head or that of his caretaker. If I ever see you lay your fingers on one of the servants or guards in this palace, if I see you threaten *anyone*, I will cut off your hand and feed it to the lions myself.'

Mila let go of the young woman's wrist and cast her aside roughly. She sprawled on the floor and stayed there, head bowed.

'I beg your forgiveness, Princess,' she whispered shakily.

Mila ignored her and turned to the boy. 'What is your name, child?'

He stared at her, goggle-eyed.

'His name is Emet, Princess,' murmured the old servant. 'He is my grandchild.'

The boy finally found his voice. 'Ye—yes, my name is Emet!'

'Your parents?' Mila asked roughly.

The boy blinked rapidly. 'My mother died giving birth to me. My father was a soldier in the army. It has been three years since he perished in battle.'

His grandmother tapped him gently on the back of the head.

'You must address the princess correctly, Emet.'

The boy paled. 'Oh. Sorry, Princess.'

Mila's anger began to fade as she studied his innocent features.

'You shall become a companion for my daughter,' she ordered impulsively. She glanced at the elderly female servant. 'And your grandmother will come with you.'

The boy gaped at her.

'Thank the princess, Emet,' his grandmother admonished with a further tap on the head.

'Yes, Princess! Thank you, Princess!' the boy blurted out, ears reddening.

'Enough,' Mila muttered. 'Gather your belongings and come to my quarters. We leave for Issin at dawn.'

She twisted on her heels and headed deeper into the palace compound, leather sandals striking the stone and marble floors briskly. At the far end of the grounds, the sound of wood striking wood greeted her as she entered her private chambers.

On a sunlit terrace outside a sumptuous day room, with the green waters of the Ufratü River flowing languorously beyond the walls of the citadel and the fortress, her nine-year-old son Kaleb and her six-year-old daughter Eleaza engaged in a play fight under the keen eyes of their attendants.

Mila stopped just inside a shadowy archway and observed them dispassionately. Unlike her siblings and cousins, motherly love was not an emotion that came naturally to her. Bearing her children had been a duty, one of a hundred others given to her by the kings of the Empire, and a responsibility she owed her husband. Compared to the thrill of battle, she found pregnancy and childbirth bothersome chores and returned to her role of lieutenant commander a day after delivering her children into the world. As such, they had spent most of their lives with the wet nurses, maids, and tutors who had raised them. Still, there was no doubt that they were happiest in her and Kronos's company.

Mila narrowed her eyes as she watched them spar. Although her husband favored their firstborn, Kaleb, it was fast becoming evident to her that their daughter would be the better fighter of the two. She made a mental note to bring her to the training grounds in Issin the next time she went there.

Eleaza noticed her first. She sidestepped a swing of her brother's sword, dropped her blade, and ran inside the room.

'Mama!' she cried, chubby arms closing around Mila's left thigh.

Mila lifted her daughter against her chest and felt the last of her anger melt away at her warm weight. 'Eleaza.'

'Is father with you?' said Kaleb, his dark eyes bright as he followed in his sister's steps.

'He will be here shortly. Now, tell me what you have been up to in our absence.'

MILA'S PLANS TO LEAVE URYL THE NEXT DAY WERE THWARTED BY Crovir later that evening.

In the privacy of the kings' dining chamber, at the end of the feast that was the culmination of the day's celebrations, her father looked to where she sat next to Kronos and directed a cold stare at her.

'I would like Mila to stay behind, please.'

She gazed steadily back at him, conscious of her siblings' and cousins' glances. Next to Crovir, apprehension filled her mother's eyes.

'Of course,' Mila murmured.

'Do you also need me to—?' Kronos started.

'No,' said Crovir, 'not on this occasion.' His gaze shifted. 'Jared, I am afraid you will also not be returning to your city tomorrow. I have a task for Mila and you.'

Beatrix shared a guarded look with Jared.

'Brother?' Bastian said with a frown.

Crovir smiled faintly.

'It is an insignificant matter, Bastian. Do not worry about it.'

Bastian hesitated before rising from the table. Soon, everyone but Crovir, Mila, and Jared had vacated the chamber.

Jared leaned back in his seat and folded his arms across his chest.

'What is this about, father? We have only just come back from the campaigns you sent us on come the last New Moon. What is so pressing that you need Mila and I to attend to it without giving us even a day in our homes?'

Crovir smiled thinly.

'It is a simple assignment. I want you to bring me the head of a pig.'

CHAPTER EIGHT

'SISTER, WE MUST STOP. THE MEN ARE TIRED, AS ARE THEIR mounts. They need to rest.'

Jared had come up beside her. Mila glanced at him before looking over her shoulder. What she saw made her frown. She leaned back in her saddle and tugged on her horse's reins. The black stallion neighed irritably and stamped his hooves as he was forced to a stop.

'There, there, Buros, calm yourself,' she murmured.

She slapped the beast gently on the neck and wheeled him around to face the troops at their back. Above them, Abu whirled and came about, wings dark against the crimson sky.

Four days had passed since they left Uryl with a battalion of three hundred men and started the journey that would take them two hundred and sixty leagues north, to where the Toros Mountains overlapped with the Zagros chain. Mila had set a grueling pace from the outset, driving the soldiers to ride from dawn to dusk toward their destination in the snowcapped peaks that now soared on the horizon. Throughout that time, the exchange she and Jared had had with Crovir on their last night in the capital resonated in her mind.

'I want you to bring me the head of a pig,' their father had stated. 'And not just any pig. I want the head of the one who rules Hazaara.'

Mila had frowned. 'Governor Nazul?'

'Yes.' Crovir's expression had darkened. 'Nazul is a traitor who plots against us. He has refused to pay his tithes since the beginning of the New Year. His greed and ambition know no bounds. I hear he is buying weapons and enlisting private soldiers to mount a rebellion against the Empire.'

Tithes were levies imposed by Crovir and Bastian on every human city under their rule. The compulsory, twice-yearly contributions were established in the very early days of the Empire and had contributed significantly to its growth and the funding of its army over hundreds of years. As the task of raising the duties grew, it eventually befell Hosanna and the horde of collectors and bookkeepers under her command. To assist them in their function, Tobias and Baruch had assigned companies of soldiers in rotation to Hosanna's administration.

'Why are you not speaking to Hosanna about this?' Jared asked.

'I have already discussed the matter with my niece,' Crovir said dismissively. 'She insists there are extenuating circumstances at play. She wishes me to forgo the tithes for the next six months.'

Mila watched her father curiously. 'And you do not believe her?'

'No, I do not.' Crovir scowled. 'I am afraid she has been taken in by the lies of that treacherous pig. Hence why I am ordering the two of you to go to Hazaara and bring me his head. No one else will dare defy me once they hear of his fate.'

Tense silence descended on the chamber.

'What if we find that Hosanna was justified in her actions?' Mila said in a level tone. 'What would you have us do?'

Crovir blinked. 'Why, I expect you to do as you are told, daughter. After all, my word is law. If I say he is a traitor, then he is one.'

Mila stared.

'As you wish then, father,' she said finally. She had glanced at Jared and seen the troubled look that flashed in his eyes. 'We shall bring you the head of the pig.'

Her brother's voice brought her back to the present moment. 'The river is nearby. We should camp there for the night.'

Jared indicated a shallow valley to the east. In the distance, she could hear the roar of the Tigra.

Mila eyed the soldiers critically before dipping her chin. Although she, Jared, and their stallions could carry on well into the night, there was no denying the truth in her brother's warning. The men they had brought with them were among the troops who had been involved in crushing the recent uprisings across the Empire. Normally, they would have had days to rest before their next campaign. Crovir had however insisted that she and Jared use them again, rather than the fresh soldiers stationed in the capital's fortress or the ones posted at their various garrisons.

For one wild moment, Mila had wondered at his rash command and speculated whether an ulterior motive lay behind it. Then she realized that he simply did not care for the wellbeing of their men. Even if they were starved, sleep-deprived and pushed beyond the limits of their endurance, he expected them to perform at their best. Failure to do so would result in their immediate execution, something she had seen time and time again when she was a child.

But more than begrudge her father his usual callous behavior and the troublesome task he had assigned her and her brother, Mila resented not being able to visit Romerus before she left Uryl.

'Do not fret, sister. Our grandfather will still be there upon our return,' Jared murmured when they were setting up tent a short while later.

'I know.' Mila hesitated. 'Did Rafael—?'

'Yes.' Jared's eyes turned cold. 'I asked him to heal the injuries of our mother before he and Phebe left for Urim.'

Mila stared out over the darkening land to the new moon rising on the eastern horizon. 'Although his unworldly abilities confound me, as do yours and those Navia possesses, we are truly blessed to have him as our kin. He has relieved much of the suffering of the queens since he came of age and his powers matured.'

'You believe the three of us to be otherworldly?' said Jared in a light tone.

Mila shrugged. 'You cannot deny that no one else in existence possesses the mystical abilities you do.'

'You say that, but I believe your skills as a warrior are also unearthly, sister.'

As she pondered her brother's words, a flash of light by the riverside drew her attention. A man sat on a rock at the water's edge. He was cleaning the arrows and spear he had used to hunt some of the hares now roasting on spits in the middle of the camp.

Mila stared. She had been aware of the stranger ever since they left Uryl. He was the only soldier who had kept up with the punishing pace she had set and he was often to be found just a dozen feet or so behind her.

'Who is that?'

Jared looked over from where he was removing his stallion's saddle and bellyband and followed her gaze.

'The archer? His name is Aäron. He is a captain of the troop. He joined my ranks some thirteen months ago.' He undid his horse's bit and noseband and slapped him gently on the rump. 'Away you go, Ibtihal.'

The chestnut-colored stallion let out a low nicker and wandered down the slope toward the river.

'He has unusual coloring.'

'You mean the fair hair and blue eyes?' Jared smiled. 'He does look a bit like our Navia, does he not? The other men tease him often enough for it. He hails from Parsah, it seems.' He paused, his expression growing thoughtful. 'He is a good man though. Pure of heart and true of bow. He kills swiftly and is kind to our prisoners.'

'Is he as skilled with his hands and his sword as he is with arrows and spears?'

Jared gazed at her curiously. 'I believe so. Our troop commander predicts he will rise quickly through the ranks.'

Mila frowned. 'What about family? Does he have a wife? Children?'

Surprise dawned on Jared's face. 'I doubt he is celibate but no, not that I know of. Why all the questions?'

'I am in need of a good archer and fighter.'

Jared cocked an eyebrow. 'Really?'

Mila sighed. 'What is that look for?'

'*You* are the best archer in the Empire. And the best sword fighter, best battle-axe wielder, best—well, you are pretty much the best at everything, sister. What do you need my man for?'

'From what you have told me, he would make a good teacher for Eleaza.'

Jared blinked. 'What of Moab, your armorer and combat instructor?'

Mila looked at him steadily. 'Have you seen Moab lately?'

'Well, no.'

'He is an old man, brother.' Mila's gaze shifted to the moon once more. 'I retired him ten years ago. His son Danae is the new armorer of our city. Unfortunately, Kronos often calls upon his services. Danae does not have time for a child.'

Jared was silent for a while. 'How time passes.' His tone turned melancholic. 'Though others envy us our long lifespans, I often think it a curse. We have watched many good people die since our birth.' He paused and gazed farther downriver, to where Buros and Ibtihal drank from the river. 'Why, even our steeds are but scions of the stallions we were gifted as children, as is your hawk.'

'Be careful, brother,' Mila muttered. 'I fear you are turning into a composer of fine words.'

Jared sighed. 'Your warrior soul is an empty husk devoid of sweetness, sister.'

Mila smiled faintly. 'If you do not mind, I shall have a word with your man. See if he is a fit for my daughter.'

Jared shrugged. 'As you wish.'

She turned and made her way through the camp, the laughter and rumble of the soldiers' conversations faltering briefly with her passage. As she headed for the river, Mila could not help but dwell on the slightly bitter twist in her brother's voice when he spoke of Navia. Though he adored Beatrix, the mate chosen for him by their father, there was no doubt in her mind that Jared's heart truly belonged to their fair cousin. And although Navia openly cherished Malachi, Mila had long suspected she held strong feelings for Jared. Still, like so many things in their Immortal lives, their love would never be acknowledged. It was forbidden and whatever yearning existed between them would forever remain a secret from their fathers.

Though she came silently at his back, Aäron noticed her approach when she was still a good twenty feet away and stilled.

He has good instincts.

She came to a stop behind him. He looked over his shoulder. Instead of jumping to his feet like so many soldiers would, he rose and turned slowly, his stance measured.

He bowed his head. 'My Queen.'

'I am not a queen.'

Though his head remained inclined, Mila thought she saw his lips twitch in a small smile.

'My apologies, Princess.'

A sliver of irritation darted through her.

'Commander will do.'

Aäron straightened and studied her calmly. He was a good foot and a half taller than her, with a hard-bodied frame.

'How may I be of assistance, Commander?'

Mila suddenly wished it were daylight, so she could see his face better. She could tell a lot by looking at a man's eyes.

Her gaze shifted to his waist. 'I see you have a sword with you.' She looked along the riverbank to a pile of boulders as tall as a man. 'Come with me.'

He followed reluctantly as she headed for the cove beyond the rocks.

There, Mila unsheathed her blade and turned to face him.

'Draw your sword.'

Aäron ignored her command and watched her silently.

'Have I offended you in some way?' he finally asked.

'No, you have not.' Mila glanced in the direction of the camp. 'Be not afraid, soldier. I only mean to test your skills. You can show them freely here, away from the eyes of others.'

Instead of asking her the reason why, Aäron pulled his sword from his leather scabbard, his expression unreadable.

'As you wish then, Commander.'

Neither moved for a moment as they measured each other up.

She attacked first, her silver gilded blade gleaming in the moonlight as she swung it toward him. Aäron sidestepped smoothly and struck from the side. She deflected his blow and twisted on her heels, bringing her sword around in a deadly arc. Metal met metal, sparks flying in the night.

Surprise darted through Mila as she watched him from the other side of the kissing blades. He had blocked the strike expertly.

He is a skilled fighter. She frowned. *Far too skilled to be a mere captain.*

She drew back and attacked again. He parried and countered, his movements swift and sure. And so they engaged for several breathless moments, each trying to set the flow of the battle, each finding their strike skillfully blocked or evaded.

A thrill ran through Mila as they moved in their artful dance of blades. *This man is talented enough to be a regiment commander.*

His sword hummed past her head, catching her unawares.

Mila narrowed her eyes. *Time to finish this.*

She blocked his next strike with her full strength. His eyes widened in the gloom as he found himself unable to move. She pushed his sword down. He resisted, jaw clenching and grip whitening on the hilt.

Mila smiled faintly. He would be no match for her physical power.

As his blade drew inexorably close to the loam beneath their feet, he did something that caused her to blink in astonishment. He released his weapon and rolled to the ground. She caught a glimpse of movement low down, jumped in the air to avoid his sweeping kick, saw him grab the hilt of his sword mid-fall, and brought her own blade down with a harsh battle cry.

Their swords clashed once more.

Aäron grinned at her where he lay in the dirt, his grip steady on his upright blade, unheeding of his weaker position.

Admiration shot through Mila.

'At ease.'

She lowered her sword and offered him her hand.

He hesitated before taking it. A tingle flashed through her palm when their skin touched. She ignored the disconcerting feeling and pulled him up.

Aäron rose and rocked to a stand inches from her. He went still then, his face cast in shadows. Mila stiffened as she registered the heat of his body. He took a step back. She inhaled shallowly, shocked that she had held her breath.

'That was a good move,' she said in a level tone. 'Have you practiced it often?'

'No. It was the first time I fought in that fashion.'

Mila raised an eyebrow. 'You adapt quickly.'

Aäron's teeth gleamed in the night.

'It seemed the logical thing to do. You are stronger and faster than I. Tactics are my only advantage in this situation.'

A slow clapping drew their gazes to the boulders looming behind them.

'That was a great show,' Jared called out from where he crouched atop a rock. Abu perched next to him, dark eyes wide with interest. Jared grinned. 'Does my archer please you, sister?'

Mila studied the silent man in front of her. 'That he does, brother.'

'Aäron, from now on, you will be under the direct

command of the Red Queen,' Jared ordered. A chuckle escaped him. 'Rejoice, for few humans ever capture her interest.'

Aäron stared between the two of them, his expression a mixture of curiosity and wariness.

'I am not sure that is necessarily a compliment,' he muttered.

Jared blinked before bursting into laughter.

CHAPTER NINE

MILA REINED IN BUROS ON THE EDGE OF A RIDGE. JARED CAME to a halt beside her, his steed stamping its hooves and snorting in excitement. A cold wind buffeted them as they gazed silently into the valley below.

'I can see why our father chose to send you,' said Mila.

Jared glanced at her before frowning at what lay before them.

It had been fifty years since he last visited Hazaara. Much had changed in that time.

The city straddled an immense crag ringed by a vertiginous drop. Behind it, razor-edged peaks rose to the skies, crowns dressed in sheets of everlasting snow and ice, flanks riddled with waterfalls. One such chute dropped close to Hazaara and was diverted into the settlement by two man-made rock channels extending across a sixty-foot-wide gorge. The resulting river snaked through the settlement along a clever system of gullies and funnels before tipping over the abyss to join the Tigra where the latter coursed at the bottom of the fathomless rift. Artificial tributaries carved off the main waterway to feed narrow terraces where the citizens grew crops disappeared in misty cataracts that coated the escarpments below in a perpetual drizzle.

The only way to reach Hazaara was over a pair of natural stone bridges that spanned the gaping void. The first now bore a hundred-foot-long breach that effectively cut the city off from the north and west; from all appearances, it looked to have been artificially created. As for the south bridge, it was secured at the city's end with massive bronze doors erected in front of the old wooden gates that usually guarded the access to the settlement. Fresh fortifications braced the metal panels and joined up to the ancient rock wall protecting the approach to the city. The wall itself now extended to surround most of Hazaara, with watergates and sluiceways for the river and its branches. From what Jared could see, the ancient ramparts had been considerably strengthened and were taller and thicker than he recalled.

There was little visible activity within the city itself. Even the fields were deserted, the once green expanses brown and dotted with dark mounds.

'Nazul has turned Hazaara into a fortress,' said Mila. 'Maybe Crovir is right and he plots against the Empire.'

'Or maybe Hosanna speaks the truth and there is more here than meets the eye,' said Jared.

Mila regarded him for a moment before dipping her chin. 'There is only one way to find out.'

Despite the passage of several days, the unease he felt following the conversation Crovir had had with them on their last night in Uryl still plagued him. As with all his siblings and cousins, he was used to the kings' bloodthirsty commands and had obeyed them almost blindly since he became the army's archery regiment commander hundreds of years past. But something fundamental had changed in recent times. The brutality of the Empire's campaigns had doubled, especially after Bastian took a back seat in their military interventions and focused his attentions on the administrative aspects of the kingdom. This left the army's major operations under Crovir's control and had opened a floodgate giving the older king free rein to exercise his own brand of ruthlessness.

Jared glanced at his youngest sister as they made their way down the steep trail along the incline. He knew he was not the only one of his siblings and cousins troubled by his father's increasingly merciless acts.

They were halfway across the south bridge when heads appeared above the parapets of the towers framing the bronze doors ahead.

'Who goes there?' someone shouted as they approached.

Surprise darted through Jared. It was a woman.

'We are representatives of the Empire, here to see Governor Nazul,' he called out. He pulled Ibtihal to a stop some thirty feet from the towering metal doors. 'Open the gates.'

The woman studied the troops crowding the bridge. 'This hardly looks like a friendly visit. Is Princess Hosanna with you? I do not see her.'

Jared exchanged a guarded glance with Mila. It appeared Hosanna had been frugal with the details when she spoke with Crovir. She evidently had a closer relationship with the people of Hazaara than she had led him to believe.

'No, my cousin is not with us today. I am Prince Jared. This is my sister, Princess Mila.'

The men atop the wall cried out, fear evident in their voices and bearing. Not so the woman. She reached down for something behind the parapet. A murmur broke out among the soldiers behind Jared when she brought up a bow and arrow. She drew it slickly and aimed it squarely at him. The men beside her hesitated before following suit.

'That the Red Queen visits us means only one thing,' said the woman steadily. 'You are here to kill us.'

'It all depends on what we find inside your city,' Mila stated coldly.

Jared masked a wince. Finesse was not one of his youngest sister's strong points.

He studied the group above them. As far as he could see, the woman and men standing defiantly atop the palisades were not private soldiers, nor were they equipped with new weapons.

'We only wish to speak with Governor Nazul,' he said. 'We have some questions for him.'

'If this is about the tithes my father owes the kings, Princess Hosanna is aware of the matter.'

Jared frowned. That the governor's daughter was defending the city walls meant something was very wrong indeed in Hazaara.

'Enough!' barked Mila. 'Open these gates so we may enter.'

The woman atop the wall hesitated. Then, in a voice that trembled slightly, she said, 'No.'

Mila raised her hand. The hawk on her shoulder flapped his wings and soared into the sky. With a noise like thunder, half the battalion raised their shields protectively behind her. At their rear, the archers sat tall on their horses, armed bows aimed at the walls of Hazaara.

'Wait!' Jared called out. 'Do not fire your arrows.'

He dismounted and approached the metal doors.

'What are you doing?' shouted Nazul's daughter. 'Stop! Do not come any—'

Her words were lost in the low rumble that rose from the thick bronze panels. The sound grew when Jared stopped before them. He flexed his fingers, laid a hand on each door, and concentrated.

The power that was his and his alone among all the Immortals surged from the middle of his chest. He savored the familiar hot energy as it snaked down his arms and shot through his hands before blasting out from his palms and fingertips.

Metal screamed and groaned. For a moment, nothing happened. Then, rivets the size of a man's thigh slowly unscrewed from the hinges holding the panels to the palisades. When the last one fell to the ground, Jared felt the full weight of the doors against his hands. He clenched his jaw, took a deep breath, and pushed.

The bronze doors slowly toppled inward, the ponderous creak accompanying their fall ending with a crash as they smashed the wooden gates behind them. The resulting boom reverberated against the sheer cliffs enclosing the valley and made his ears ring. In the shocked silence that followed, a sheet of ice and snow detached from an upper peak and tumbled harmlessly down the mountainside.

Jared straightened and lowered his hands to his sides.

There was a glint of movement from above. The arrow winging its way toward his head stopped mid-air, inches from where he stood. He ignored the gasps from the palisades, reached up, and picked the projectile from where it spun on its axis in empty space. His gaze found the woman atop the tower.

'I will say this only once,' he called out in a hard voice. 'Desist now and we enter Hazaara peacefully. Resist us further and Hazaara falls.'

Nazul's daughter stood frozen for a moment. Then, her shoulders sagged. She put down her bow and called out an order to her men. They lowered their weapons, defeat painted across their faces.

Mila appeared beside Jared, Ibtihal in tow.

'That was quite a show,' she said as he climbed atop the horse.

'A bloodless one.'

'Our father will be disappointed. No doubt he expected us to be elbow deep in gore by now.'

Jared studied Mila. Although he could not read her expression, he sensed she was testing him. He looked to the fallen gateway and the city rising beyond.

'I see no need to shed blood yet,' he said quietly.

He urged Ibtihal forward. They led the battalion into Hazaara, the din of horses' hooves deafening as the soldiers marched across the fallen bronze doors. Once inside the walls, Mila directed half the troops into defensive positions close to the entrance, much to the dismay of the men atop the ramparts.

Nazul's daughter stood waiting farther up the main thoroughfare leading into the city, her face pale. 'I am Ishvi, daughter of Governor Nazul.'

She inclined her head stiffly.

'Take us to your father,' Mila instructed.

Ishvi twisted on her heels and strode wordlessly into Hazaara.

Jared and Mila followed, some hundred men in tow. Unlike the mud-brick constructions on the desert plains and wetlands of the Empire's main domain, the buildings in the mountains were made of rock, wood, and tar. Here, roofs were tall and pitched to limit snow deposits, and ended in overhanging eaves that could cast away heavy summer rains. With space a precious commodity atop the cliff, most of the homes were narrow and built on several levels, with many hanging precariously over steep drops.

A chill ran through Jared as they climbed the narrow streets carved in the cliff face. An eerie silence shrouded Hazaara, a pall of gloom that filled the air with an oppressive weight. So far, he had seen but a few dozen living souls, most of whom retreated into the shadows of windows and doors when they saw the soldiers.

A bridge spanning the turbulent rapids of the river appeared up ahead. Beyond it rose the city's main piazza, which also served as its marketplace and arena. The governor's home stood at its head, a large, three-story building bearing metal-studded doors and an elegant roofline that had not changed in the fifty years since Jared had last been to Hazaara.

The doors opened as they crossed the square. A man with a shock of thin, white hair appeared on the stoop at the top of a flight of steps. He was short and gaunt, with hollow cheeks and over-loose clothes that attested to the fact that he had once been a bigger man. Though he had never met him before, Jared knew he was looking at Governor Nazul. His gaze dropped. He stiffened.

Nazul bore the body of a baby in his arms.

'Father?' said Ishvi in a quivering voice. She froze for a moment before dashing up the steps toward him. 'No! No, tell me it is not so!'

She took the infant off him and pressed her lips to its pale cheeks, tears streaming down her face. A low keen left her throat as she rocked to and fro. 'Hooria! My precious niece!'

Nazul turned away from his sobbing daughter, anger overshadowing the despair painted across his face.

He glared at Jared and Mila. 'I see you have come to collect the tithes Hazaara owes the Empire. Will the corpse of my grandchild do?' He pointed at the dead child in his daughter's arms, his body shaking with rage and his voice rising to a roar that echoed across the plaza. 'Will that appease the greed of that insufferable being to whom you have pledged your loyalty, that—that *demon* who takes the name of king?'

CHAPTER TEN

Tension coursed through Mila as she studied Nazul's red face and the crying woman behind him. 'What is going on here?'

The governor watched her wordlessly. He closed his eyes for a moment, took a tremulous breath, and twisted on his heels.

'Follow me,' he said roughly. He paused and looked over his shoulder. 'You will not need your soldiers, Red Queen.'

Mila narrowed her eyes. She climbed off Buros and turned to their troop commander. 'We will take ten men. The rest of you, stay here.' Her gaze found Aäron. 'You will come with us.'

He dipped his chin, his face impassive.

They headed after the figure of the governor on foot as he walked west through Hazaara. Mila observed the vacant houses they passed with increasing disquiet. That the city was in the grip of a calamity was no longer in doubt. The few people they encountered were pale and wasted, to the point where she could see their individual ribs and the cadaverous outlines of their skulls. Some responded to Nazul's tired greeting with weak nods. Others simply stared, eyes dull and faces vacant. The thing that struck her the most was the silence. She could not hear the sounds of children, nor the cries of beasts. The pens they came across held only a handful of haggard-looking livestock sitting unmoving in the dirt.

Mila frowned. *Death walks in Hazaara, of this I am sure.*

She became conscious of a stare and glanced to her left to find Aäron's eyes on her. He held her gaze for a moment before looking away.

Mila blinked. Her growing awareness of the captain perplexed her like few things could. There was more to the man than met the eye, an indisputable fact that was clear to see in the light of day. Beneath his calm demeanor and intense blue gaze, she sensed a cauldron of emotions held in check by an iron will.

Nazul exited the outskirts of the city and headed up a steep trail that cut across the fields. Mila observed the dying crops filling the terraces dotting the inclines of the cliff on either side of them. Her gaze landed on the black mounds she had seen from the ridge above the valley. She stiffened when she recognized what they were.

Nazul finally slowed. Here, the land arrowed to a promontory that projected over the abyss surrounding the crag upon which Hazaara sat astride. Two rock outcrops stabbed at the sky on the very edge of the gulf. Nazul made for the gap between them. Mila followed with Jared and the soldiers.

The mouth of a cave appeared at the end of a short gully. She slowed and watched Nazul duck and melt into the gloom beyond the low entrance. Her hand found the hilt of her sword.

The governor reappeared, his expression more weary than angry. 'You may draw your blades if you wish. You will not need them.' He slipped a piece of cloth from his belt. 'I would advise you to cover your mouth and nose though.'

Mila exchanged a cautious glance with Jared.

The ceiling rose beyond the entrance to the full height of a man. Fifteen feet into the cave, the walls narrowed to a rugged tunnel that spiraled into the very foundations of the bluff. Steps had been carved into the floor to facilitate access. Flaming torches sat in metal baskets dotting the walls and cast their shadows ahead of them as they proceeded down the stairs.

'This cave has been here since before my birth,' said Nazul. 'My brothers and I spent many a happy hour here when we were children, as did my sons and daughters. Alas, my grandchildren will not do so.' Bitterness underscored his voice. 'I had the passage enlarged when it started.'

'When what started?' said Jared impatiently. 'I wish you would speak plainly, Governor. These delay tactics may have worked with my cousin but they will not do so with—'

It was the smell that hit them first.

Jared slowed and pulled a face. 'What in the name of the Empire is that stench?'

The noise came next, a low murmur that grew to a dull roar.

Coldness filled Mila when they came to the end of the tunnel. She ignored the muffled retching from the soldiers behind her and stopped beside Nazul on the edge of a stone landing, her gaze fixed unblinkingly on what lay at the bottom of the final flight of steps.

The cavern below them measured some three hundred feet in width and was almost as long, its farthest reaches swaddled in layers of darkness broken by the odd flaming torch. The floor fell away in a series of terraces arrowing toward the north face of the cave. Water gleamed on the distant wall, a thin chute that breached the underground chamber through a rock channel before disappearing in a shallow pool.

But it was not the sight of the cavern's impressive dimensions nor the tapering rock formations hanging from its soaring ceiling that commanded her attention.

Crowding the expanse beneath them, filling almost every corner of level ground, were people.

Some lay on straw pallets, their emaciated bodies motionless beneath thin sheets. Most, however, writhed around, shivers and coughs racking their thin frames while their wretched moans filled the vast space. Here and there, pale figures tended to them, ghosts in the shadows. Mila registered the protective clothing they wore and the masks covering their faces.

'It took us a while to realize that the disease was airborne,' said Nazul quietly. 'By then, we had lost a hundred souls and twice as many lay bedridden.'

He brought his cloth to his face and headed down into the cavern. Mila removed the polishing fabric she used for her blade and held it over her nose and mouth before going after him, Jared and Aäron in her wake.

She paused and turned to the remaining soldiers. 'Stay here.'

They nodded, their expressions grateful.

'We were already struggling to pay the rising tithes over the last few years when a deadly blight ruined the past two seasons' crops,' said Nazul as they entered the foul miasma saturating the air. 'In the wake of the famine that followed, an unwelcome sickness entered our valley from the east, brought by hunters who came to trade with us. The illness is characterized by delirious feverishness and cramps that make grown men cry. It rots the lungs and gut, and robs the afflicted of their breath. Many die choking on their own blood.'

Some of the people attending to the ill looked up at his approach. A few took hasty steps back when they saw the Immortals and the soldiers, their eyes widening in alarm above their masks.

'It is alright,' Nazul called out reassuringly. 'Carry on with your ministrations.'

'I thought the tithe had been fixed for another ten years,' said Jared quietly.

Nazul stopped and eyed him coolly. 'It seems Princess Hosanna was right. The kings do not always tell their children of their dark deeds.' A muscle jumped in his jawline. 'Why do you think there have been so many uprisings of late? The people of the Empire are struggling to satisfy the selfish demands of the ones who rule them. Many can no longer feed themselves and their children. You may not have noticed, but there are hardly any pot-bellied people left in these lands, myself included.'

Mila recalled the conversation she had had with Tobias and Baruch following the conflict in Terka.

Lines creased her brow. 'Do you mean that the kings are forcing these levies through when they know people are dying of disease and hunger?'

Nazul spread his arms and indicated the cave. 'Look around you, Princess. Do you see us reveling in our wealth? Do you see our wives and children merry and plump, their cheeks rosy with health and happiness?'

There was a commotion behind them. Mila turned.

A young man barely out of boyhood had reached out from where he lay on the ground and was grasping Aäron's ankle.

'Help—help me!' he gasped, his chest shuddering with effort.

One of the caregivers looked over in consternation from where she tended to a feverish child.

She climbed awkwardly to her feet and stumbled toward them. 'I am sorry. I will—'

Aäron raised a hand and cut her off. He dropped on his haunches and took the sick man's hand in his own. A moment later, the latter took his final breath, air leaving his discolored, dry lips in a guttural rasp while his thin body relaxed in eternal rest. The captain gazed at him silently before gently closing his eyes.

He crossed the dead man's hands on his chest, covered him with the dirty sheet on the pallet, and stood up, his expression unreadable. 'What do you do with the bodies?'

Nazul eyed him steadily. 'There is another tunnel at the end of the cave. It leads to the chasm. We give the dead their last rites there.' Sorrow darkened his eyes. 'We buried and burned as many as we could at first. When the number of the dead outstripped that of the living, we decided the abyss would be a fit tomb for them. Nothing lives at the bottom of the gorge. It is a cold and dark place that never sees sunlight.'

Aäron wrapped the dead youth in the sheet and lifted him in his arms. 'Show me.'

Nazul hesitated and glanced at Mila and Jared. 'I cannot ask you to—'

'Show me,' the captain ordered, his voice hardening.

Nazul stared. 'Come with me.'

He turned and led the way further into the cavern.

'Hosanna knows of your woes?' said Jared stiffly, his gaze lingering on the sick and dying around them.

'Yes, the princess knows. She pleaded our case with King Crovir many months ago, on our behalf and on that of other cities similarly afflicted by famine.' Nazul wavered for a moment. 'Although she would curse me for saying this, she even paid our tithes out of her own pocket the past year, after the illness started. Alas, one of her collectors was loose of tongue and the matter came to the ears of King Crovir. The provisions she had secretly been sending us stopped a while ago, no doubt intercepted by soldiers of the Empire. She promised to ask Prince Rafael to come to our assistance but I gather King Crovir has kept all of you engaged suppressing the rebellions breaking out across the Empire.' Nazul's eyes grew hooded. 'Although I have not heard of other cities afflicted by this particular scourge, I fear disease will soon spread through these lands if its citizens continue to be forced beyond their endurance by hunger and war.'

A narrow passage appeared in the north face of the cave, to the left of the pool. Nazul led them through it and into a small chamber on the other side. There, they were bathed in a cool breeze that wafted through an opening in the cliff face and took away some of the pervading stench. In a silence that spoke of grief, four women carefully washed the dead and wrapped them in clean linen sheets. Two more stood on the edge of the chasm and mouthed low prayers before gently tipping the bodies into the gaping void.

One of the women on the ground looked up when she registered their presence. She watched wordlessly as Aäron laid the dead youth next to the pile of corpses to the right, then washed her hands in a bowl of water and climbed to her knees with a wince. She pulled her mask down as she approached. The lines at the corners of her eyes deepened when she stopped before Nazul.

'Your presence here can only mean one thing. Our granddaughter has gone to her eternal rest,' she said in a lifeless voice.

Nazul swallowed convulsively. 'That she has, my love.'

The old woman's gaze moved to Mila and the two men beside her. 'I see representatives of the Empire have finally come to Hazaara.' She looked back at Nazul and raised a hand to his cheek. 'Is this to be our end then, husband? Does our city fall today?'

The other women stopped what they were doing and looked up, eyes filled with fearful expectation.

Nazul took his wife's hand in his own and turned to Mila. 'That I do not know.'

Mila looked at the corpses on the ground for a long time. Then, she twisted on her heels and made her way back through the main cave, bitter thoughts and questions raging through her mind, conscious of the gazes that followed her passage and the others behind her.

It was not until she exited the gully and reached a ridge overlooking the chasm that she stopped. She inhaled the fresh, cool air and watched Abu hover in the clear blue skies above her head.

'What is it to be, Red Queen?' said Nazul in the tense silence, a trace of defiance in his voice.

Mila turned and observed the governor and his wife for a moment. She met Aäron's guarded stare and finally looked at Jared.

The grim decision she had reached was reflected in her brother's dark eyes.

'I will support you, sister,' he said in a steely voice.

Mila smiled faintly then. As the lieutenant commander of their army, she had seniority over him in their military endeavors. Whatever she decided to do next, he would have to obey. Yet, she was confident the action she was about to take would be the one he would champion were he in her position.

With a heavy heart, she raised a hand to her waist and drew her sword.

CHAPTER ELEVEN

CROVIR STOOD ON THE TERRACE OUTSIDE HIS PRIVATE CHAMBERS and stared out over the palace grounds. This high up, he could see beyond the walls of the citadel to the plains outside the capital. He brought a gold tumbler to his lips and savored the rich taste of the wine within it as he studied the horizon.

A hazy sun glowed in a pale sky, the golden rays partially obscured by the morning mist rolling off the Ufratü River. The eerie light made the air shimmer in the distance, creating ghostly shapes that danced fleetingly above the land.

A welcome breeze swept the sundeck and cooled his bare arms. Gauzy curtains fluttered behind him. He looked over his shoulder and glimpsed Delaiah, his latest concubine, sleeping naked on his bed, body exhausted and skin covered with the marks and bruises of the past night. A thin smile curved his lips. However many humans he allowed to grace his chambers, none could keep up with his carnal appetite, not even a princess of Tarsus sold by her own father for his political ambitions.

His smile faded. He had heard her lay claim to the title of

princess on several occasions now. It was a habit he would have to curb, and quickly. Although he indulged her more than his previous lovers, he would soon grow bored of her youthful body and have to dispose of her as he had done the others who came before her, either by dispatching her to one of the garrisons to serve as his soldiers' plaything, or selling her off into slavery in distant lands. She did not yet know the fate that awaited her. Indeed, not even his brother Bastian had knowledge of such dark deeds, for they were always accomplished in secrecy, under the cover of night. In the years to come, she would die, like the others, succumbing to disease or the assault she would suffer every night from the men who ravaged her body.

Crovir frowned. None but his and Bastian's children and grandchildren could lay claim to the title of prince or princess of the Empire. He stared beyond the walls of Uryl, toward the citadel of his father. A mixture of emotions assaulted him as he thought of Romerus, the one who had brought him into this world and gifted him with immortality through his mysterious actions so many moons ago.

Love, irritation, apprehension, all these he was familiar with. But increasingly, as the years went by, hate had started to seep into his heart, a hot dagger twisting inside his soul and filling him with shame.

He had lost count of the number of times he heard the tale of how, when a deadly plague shrouded the land in darkness, Romerus had ventured into the desert for twenty-one days and nights, in search of a cure to save his dying children. His mother Zara and his stepmother Joanna had never divulged the details of how exactly Romerus came by the remedies he eventually administered to his two sons, although Crovir suspected they knew the truth. And it became evident that something had happened to Romerus himself in that desert, for he continued to live far beyond the years that should rightfully have been his as a mere human, while Zara and Joanna succumbed to eternal rest.

As Crovir and Bastian grew out of boyhood, their unique abilities quickly became apparent. They were stronger, faster, and more astute than normal men. And not only did they possess accelerated healing, they could survive death itself. Crovir never truly believed the story of the seventeen lives they had inherited until he woke up in shock after his first passing, having accidentally fallen off a horse and broken his neck. In the years that followed, his iron will and determination, combined with Bastian's great tactical mind, led them to build an army that conquered villages, cities, and, eventually, entire nations. They perished on numerous occasions during those first hundred years of establishing their empire, only to rise again and again to defeat those who stood before them. Now, with the help of their children, they ruled a kingdom of more than fifteen million souls, spanning thousands of leagues.

It was in the four-hundredth year of the Empire that Bastian decided to leave the command of their army and their military campaigns in Crovir's hands, choosing instead to concentrate on managing the kingdom's increasingly complex administration. Crovir could not have been any happier at his younger brother's choice, as it allowed him complete freedom to pursue his increasingly hungry ambitions. For he wanted dominion over more lands. In the vast, unexplored territories and seas that lay beyond their realm, he sensed there were more nations to conquer and wealth to plunder.

But one person still possessed the power to make him doubt his actions. His father, Romerus. Although he knew the old man loved him and his brother unconditionally, there were times when Crovir could sense unspoken accusation and judgment in his rheumy gaze. It irked him and had given rise to the resentment that now clouded his affection for the one who had given him life and granted him his unworldly talents.

A disturbance in the palace grounds scattered his dark thoughts. Crovir looked down and caught a glimpse of a group of people striding through a garden. Leading them was a figure in a red cape.

A thrill coursed through him. It appeared Mila had accomplished the mission he had assigned her and her brother.

As he left his chambers and made his way to the throne room, Crovir reflected on his feelings for his youngest child. There was no doubt in his mind that she was the strongest warrior of all the children he and Bastian had borne. But although pride was the emotion she had initially inspired in him, unease had slowly filtered through his heart over time and given rise to the same misgivings he felt for Romerus.

Deep inside the very marrow of his dark soul, Crovir knew Mila was capable of toppling the kings and taking the Empire for herself if she so wished.

That she had any such desire was never apparent to him or the odd spy he sent to Issin. But the thought, once birthed, would not leave his mind. She was a potential threat to his aspirations. As such, he made sure to quash any sign of insubordination quickly and resolutely, like her latest action in Terka.

Crovir entered the lavishly decorated, pillared throne room through a ceremonial side door and took a seat on one of the two gilded chairs dominating the dais that presided over the grand space. He dismissed the servants who rushed up the wide marble steps lined with ten golden lion statues, signaled to the soldiers standing by the main entrance, and sat back lazily in his throne. The men opened the imposing bronze portal guarding the access to the royal hall and lowered their spears respectfully when they saw the group waiting outside.

Mila stormed across the threshold, Jared, Hosanna, Baruch, and Kronos in tow. The latter murmured urgently to his wife as they navigated the polished floor, his expression pale and pleading.

Crovir frowned.

Mila stopped before the steps below him and motioned to a soldier bearing the uniform of a captain who stood beyond the entrance.

'Let him pass,' she instructed the guards coldly.

The captain, a fair-haired man with blue eyes, headed toward them, a metal chest in his hands. He deposited it in front of the steps, bowed, and retreated behind the princes and princesses.

Mila lifted the cover of the casket. The foul smell of rotting flesh reached Crovir's nose. She removed something from inside the container and tossed it toward the dais. Red droplets sprayed the marble floor and golden lions as the object sailed through the air. It landed on the stage with a wet sound, rolled, and came to a stop against Crovir's right foot.

He stared at the gory remains. 'What is this?'

Mila cocked an eyebrow. 'Why, my king, you asked Jared and I to bring you the head of a pig.'

Fury ignited inside Crovir. He rose and stepped over the animal carcass, his body shaking with rage.

'*Your instructions were to bring me the head of the governor of Hazaara, not that of a boar!*' he roared.

His voice bounced off the domed ceiling and the granite and marble pillars. Tense silence fell inside the throne room in the dying wake of the reverberation. The attending servants and guards blanched. A figure moved at the edge of his vision. He looked around and saw Helena stop at the edge of the dais.

Mila glanced at her mother before meeting his gaze once more.

'I could not do that, my king,' she said in a level voice. 'For not only did my brother and I find no evidence of the treachery you accused Governor Nazul of, we also discovered that the mitigating circumstances Hosanna had spoken to you about were very real indeed.'

Hosanna took a step forward and glared at Crovir. 'How could you? I explained what was happening in Hazaara, about the scourge that destroyed their crops and the illness that soon followed! I told you explicitly that they cannot pay the extortionate tithes you demand, nor can most of our other cities.' She glanced at Kronos. 'I now hear the supplies I have been sending to Governor Nazul have not reached him for many a month. And as I feared, the disease has spread.'

Kronos stiffened. 'I did as I was instructed, Hosanna.' He bestowed a chilly stare upon his siblings and cousins. 'So should all of you. To disobey the commands of the kings constitutes an act of treason.'

'Then call me a traitor, brother,' snapped Jared. He frowned at Crovir. 'I am not a puppet who will dance to the will of anybody.'

'What is this I hear, my king?' said Baruch in a quiet voice. 'You have raised the levies again? When and why?' He paused. 'I know now why my wife has looked so strained these past years whenever I have enquired after her duties.'

'I am sorry, husband,' Hosanna murmured. 'I did not wish to burden you with—'

'Enough!'

Crovir glowered at the figures below him, blood pounding in his ears. That Mila was brazen enough to oppose him was one thing. For her siblings and cousins to even entertain such an idea was anathema to him.

'Have you all taken leave of your senses?' he hissed. 'What madness possesses you to defy me so? Why, I am inclined to strip you of your titles and banish you from—'

'The reason we are seeing so many revolts is down to a simple fact,' said Mila. 'Your excessive demands cannot be met. You have to lower the tithes. Not only that, you need to suspend them for the cities afflicted with famine and disease. It is the sensible thing to do. Our empire is prosperous enough to survive several years without the levies.'

Crovir blinked, shock dampening his anger for a moment. 'You have the temerity to interrupt your *King*, child? And the nerve to *dictate* to him?!'

Mila straightened and looked him squarely in the eye. She then uttered words Crovir had thought would never pass her lips.

'You have not even begun to see the limits of what I dare do, father.'

Her statement hung in the air in the deadly lull that descended on the throne room. It slowly crystallized inside Crovir's mind, a red flag of flagrant defiance that stunned and inflamed him.

'Father, please overlook this transgression,' murmured Kronos from where he hovered protectively behind Mila. 'It will not happen again.'

His plea penetrated the outrage filling Crovir's veins. 'Are you saying that you want me to disregard her blatant act of insubordination? And those of your brother and cousins?' His gaze switched between Kronos and Baruch. 'Maybe I should teach you princes a thing or two about controlling your wives.'

Helena drew a breath in sharply. Hosanna paled. Baruch took a step toward Crovir, a muscle jumping in his cheek.

Crovir ignored them, his body stilling, eyes focused on his youngest child.

'Go ahead. Draw your sword,' he said quietly.

Everyone's gaze dropped to where Mila's fingers clasped the hilt of the blade at her waist.

MILA STARED AT THE MAN WHO HAD SIRED HER, HER HEART drumming against her ribs. During their journey back to the capital, after she had slain one of the boars in the pens of Hazaara and taken its head to bring to her father, the potential ramifications of her actions had filled her thoughts.

That Jared approved of what she had done was of some comfort, as were Baruch and Hosanna's reactions when they stopped in Lagaesh to see their cousins. The two had insisted on accompanying them to Uryl and they had met with Kronos in Issin before proceeding south.

Still, Mila had returned to the capital troubled. Not because her husband was involved in Crovir's machinations, a revelation that saddened her but hardly came as a surprise; he was stubbornly loyal to the kings and never questioned their father's orders. It was what Crovir would make of her blatant disobedience that had filled her with disquiet.

Although she had been prepared to deal with the consequences of the bold deed she had just committed, the words he had spoken doused any concessions she would have been willing to make to meet the terms of his punishment. Along with the visceral wrath his callous statement invoked, a cold certainty filled her heart. She would not bow meekly before the man who dared suggest that she and her cousin be treated with the same despicable violence he exhibited toward his wives.

A hand landed on her shoulder. Kronos's fingers tightened on her skin, his quiet desperation evident.

'Mila, stop,' he said in a low voice.

'Daughter,' Helena murmured from the dais.

Her mother's voice finally broke the dangerous spell ensnaring her.

She took a deep breath and lowered her hand from the hilt of her sword, her gaze locked on the man on the dais. 'The words I speak are uttered in goodwill. What I said to you about the tithes is my sincere recommendation as the lieutenant commander of your army. I would not wish you to do anything to endanger the Empire you and my uncle fought so hard to build. You are free to take my advice or ignore it, my king. The Empire is yours, after all.' Mila paused. 'But you do not own me, or my siblings and cousins. We are not your slaves or your tools. We will not always obey you blindly.'

Kronos flinched beside her.

Mila twisted on her heels and headed for the doors, aware of the stares at her back. She passed Aäron and heard him fall into step behind her. It was not until they exited the citadel that she finally stopped, on the stage where she had greeted the kings nearly two Half Moons ago. She stood and stared beyond the fortress wall toward Uryl until the frenetic beat of her pulse finally slowed.

'Do you think me a fool, Captain?' she said after a while to the man standing silently at her side.

'No, Princess,' Aäron replied. 'You chose the right course of action in Hazaara.' He hesitated. 'Although I would personally have chosen a less flamboyant way to demonstrate resistance to the king. Bringing him the head of an actual boar and casting it at his feet was bound to enrage him.'

Mila frowned at the wry undertone of his voice. 'I was trying to prove a point.'

'You did so, Princess. Spectacularly,' drawled Aäron. 'You may not be aware, but we have many soldiers in our ranks from that city. They will be relieved to hear that you spared the governor and the citizens.'

A bitter smile twisted Mila's lips. 'Some may see my act as mutiny.'

'And for every one of them, two more will champion you.'

Mila gazed into his eyes and sensed a deeper meaning behind his words. Before she could question him further, her mother rushed through the bronze doors of the citadel and headed toward her. Aäron bowed, murmured a greeting to the queen, and moved a discreet distance away. Helena engulfed Mila in her arms.

'Oh child, I fear you have done it this time,' she said tremulously. 'I have never seen the king so angry.'

Mila hugged her mother back fiercely. 'Just answer me this. Do you believe I did the right thing by sparing the governor of Hazaara?'

Helena went still. She leaned back and stared at Mila for silent seconds. 'Yes, I do.'

'Then that is all I need to know.' Mila took a deep breath and glanced at the plains beyond the capital. 'Let us leave this suffocating place. I want to see Romerus. Will you come with me, mother?'

Helena's face brightened. 'Of course. It has been too long since I last visited him.'

Mila looked at Aäron. 'You will escort us to the citadel of the kings' father. After that, we leave for Issin.'

The captain inclined his head. 'Yes, Commander.'

CHAPTER TWELVE

Navia blocked out the sounds of the battle and clasped the head of the terrified soldier kneeling at her feet, hands bound behind his back. She focused on the latent energy inside her heart and closed her eyes, conscious of the ring of armed guards who shielded her from the bloody conflict raging around them.

Heat bloomed in the center of her being and flooded her body. She steered the unworldly power she had been born with and focused it into the mind of the man in her hold. Random images streamed across her inner vision as she probed his scattered thoughts.

Show me the fortress.

A wall of resistance rose to block her out as the soldier fought her unspoken command. Surprise flashed through Navia. It was rare that she encountered someone with the ability to deflect her mental assault.

The people of this land are indeed gifted, she thought grimly.

Still, she had yet to meet someone who could completely

match her skills. She frowned and tightened her grip on the soldier's temples. A cry escaped the man's lips as she blasted through the barriers he had erected to protect his most private memories, pain filling his skull with a red glow.

Navia paused. Though she knew it would take but moments to break his will, she had had more than her fill of suffering and death in the last three months.

She reduced the intensity of her attack. *Do you want to save your city from destruction?*

The man's consciousness froze for a moment at her question. Fear clashed with bitter hope inside his thoughts.

He sagged beneath her. *Yes.*

Navia opened her eyes and stared into his blank, defeated gaze. *Then show me how to get inside the fortress.*

The soldier hesitated, then clenched his jaw. Navia drew a sharp breath as he finally allowed her to see the thoughts he had so carefully masked. She released him and turned to one of her guards.

'Yaham, send a message to the first general. There is a hidden tunnel at the west watergate which leads inside the fortress. I will create a path for us.'

The captain nodded and vaulted onto his horse. Navia watched him disappear into the section of middle town they had conquered. She drew her sword once more and turned to face the battleground.

Three months had passed since Mila and Jared openly defied Crovir by sparing the governor of Hazaara. Following the disturbing events in the throne room in Uryl, the older king immediately set in motion a series of brutal military campaigns, much to the dismay of the army's generals and commanders. Bar Baruch, Beatrix and Kronos, all the princes and princesses were dispatched to the farthest corners of the

Empire with entire regiments, under strict instructions to crack down on any uprising they came across and claim more territories.

Tasked with expanding their East Eurasia domains, Tobias and Navia travelled through the Zagros Range and the vast plateau beyond until they reached the Toba Kakar Mountains and the territory of the Harappas, the Indus Valley nation under their rule. From the capital Mehrgar, they proceeded through a tortuous mountain pass some twenty leagues long to the cities of Nal and Balako, where they quashed minor rebellions on their way to the town of Amri, on the border of the Empire. There, they restocked on provisions and rested a full day before heading into the unknown, arid wilderness of a great desert.

On the far side of the expanse of shifting sand dunes and scorched flat plains, they discovered sweeping salt marshes and mudflats populated by onagers, flamingos, and antelopes. Finally, on the first Full Moon after they left the known frontier of the Empire, they arrived on a peninsula ringed by the Great South Sea. According to the rumors passed on to them by the ruler of Mehrgar, the land was known as Saraostas and was home to a prosperous nation skilled in growing crops, building, and the art of working with metals, clay, and precious gems.

They came upon the first cities some days later and discovered that the stories were indeed true. It took Tobias and Navia nearly two Half Moons to capture Kotada and Surkotada. After leaving factions of their army to maintain control of their newly acquired provinces, they made their way south to Laothal, the capital of Saraostas.

Situated on a protected bay that opened onto the Great South Sea, the metropolis was an impressive sight to behold. An immense, circular stone wall surrounded the city and extended part way across the cove, enclosing its flourishing port. Completing its defenses on the waterside were thick wooden ramparts that boasted a pair of massive gates which could be closed to seal off the harbor from an attack from the sea. Inside the metropolis itself, and visible from the hills to the north where Tobias and Navia had encamped their army, the advanced nature of the town structure and defenses were clear to see.

Laothal had been built around a large mound of land that featured a towering citadel protected by its own heavily fortified walls and gateways. Below this acropolis lay a middle town cleverly constructed on platforms made of mud-brick. Each one featured up to twenty residences and commercial buildings, the raised areas offering another level of protection to the city's populace. Ringed by tall ramparts with defensive towers and a wide artificial canal that could only be crossed at two bridges, one to the east and the other to the north, the middle town gave way to a crescent-shaped lower town abutting the city's main defenses.

After five days, the Empire's army finally breached the gates of the outermost wall. Once inside, Tobias and Navia rapidly conquered the lower town and concentrated their efforts on the fortifications of the middle town. They finally broke through at sunrise, on this, the tenth day of the siege. As they advanced through the city, they discovered a complex street arrangement featuring wells fed by an underground river system, public baths, drains, and large open spaces that could be closed off individually to provide another layer of security, all signs of the advanced nature of the civilization they were set to conquer.

'Princess, what would you have us do with the prisoner?'

Navia looked over her shoulder at the Laothal soldier who had just provided them with a way into the citadel where the ruler of the city had mounted its strongest defense. The man stared at the fires raging through the middle town, his agony clear to see.

Navia deflected the tormented thoughts she could sense from him and addressed the guard who had spoken. 'I made him a promise. Take him to where we are keeping the other captives. And see to it that no harm comes to him.'

Navia's grip tightened on her blood-stained sword as she studied the enemy soldiers protecting the road that led to the west of the port. Despite the grueling fight that still lay ahead, she could taste the Empire's victory on the wind. There would only be one conclusion to this battle. By sundown, the king of Saraostas would be on his knees at the end of Tobias's blade.

The vision she had had that morning promised this outcome.

'Tell our men to leave the horses here,' she told her troop commander. 'We will not need them beyond this point.'

The man's eyes widened. He glanced at the fortress on the hill. 'Did you see—?'

'Yes, I did,' Navia interrupted curtly. 'This siege ends tonight.'

A murmur of anticipation ran through the soldiers close enough to catch her words.

Navia gritted her teeth and ignored the dull pain resonating between her temples. As was the case whenever she was in the midst of a conflict, the rage and suffering of those who fell before the Empire's greater military strength, and the glee and jubilation of the Immortals' army at defeating their foes, threatened to drown her own consciousness. It was only with the strictest training that she had mastered the ability to block out the minds of entire cities and regiments. Still, it always left her with a headache.

To her, the gifts of a Seer were both a blessing and a curse.

'The battle is still not won,' she said in a grim tone. 'Do not let down your guard.'

She headed toward the enemy, her pace accelerating the closer she drew. Behind her came the Empire's soldiers, voices raised in battle cries that shattered the air.

CHAPTER THIRTEEN

Nawaar appeared on the horizon, its mud-brick ramparts dark against the setting sun. A sea of tents punctuated by the flames of cooking fires crowded the base of the tall walls. Above the encampment, the red banners of the Empire fluttered in the cool breeze coursing across the land.

Despite his weariness, Rafael dug his heels into the flanks of his stallion and urged the horse on. Next to him, Ysa followed suit, as eager as he to reach the northernmost outpost of the Empire's immediate domain.

Four months had passed since they had been sent to the Arals to expand the northernmost territories of the Empire. Of the thousand-and-five-hundred-strong army they had left Uryl with, only half remained. A third they had lost in battle. The others had been left behind to guard their newest jurisdictions in Upper Eurasia.

In the hundred wagons trailing behind their soldiers were some of the spoils of the wars they had instigated during their quest to grow the kingdom: gold, precious gems, fine pottery, wines, weapons, and slaves, all gifts for the kings of the Empire.

Ysa had not looked kindly upon any of it, especially the women and children now destined for a wretched life of servitude thousands of leagues from their birthplace; the two of them had had enough arguments about the matter on their way back from the Arals for her to make her position perfectly clear to Rafael. Still, he knew the plundered goods would go some way toward appeasing the wrath of the older king.

If it means less war and death in the future, then so be it.

A wide path stretched through the camp to the outpost's towering gates. Rafael studied the tents on either side as they galloped up the corridor, his irate thoughts concerning his uncle temporarily forgotten.

'They are here!' Ysa shouted.

He followed her excited gaze. Occupying the western portion of the camp, visible in the light of flaming torches, were several hundred tents bearing the colors of Larsaa and Urim, the cities under their direct rule.

He looked around and registered the tents of Larraak, Lagaesh and Marii, the principalities of his siblings and cousins. 'It seems the others have arrived as well.'

Ysa frowned. 'No, not everyone. I do not see the colors of Issin.'

Their troop commanders directed their soldiers to set up camp beside the other regiments while they carried on ahead. The thick bronze doors guarding Nawaar opened ponderously upon their approach and they slowed their steeds as they entered the shadows of the fortified towers flanking the entrance. Rafael dismounted outside the main barracks and handed the reins of his horse to an attendant.

'Where is the first general and the other princes and

princesses?' he asked a captain as Ysa alighted from her stallion.

'They dine in the main hall, Commander,' the soldier replied with a bow. He smiled at Ysa. 'The first general will be pleased to see you, Princess.'

'Is my husband well?' said Ysa, a trace of anxiety modulating her voice.

The captain hesitated. 'As well as can be expected, Princess. The first general and Princess Navia arrived only a quarter day before you.'

Ysa clenched her jaw. 'Thank you.'

She headed briskly into Nawaar's main fort tower, Rafael on her heels. Raucous laughter greeted them when they entered the banquet hall moments later. Seated at the long table dominating the room and picking over the remains of a meal were Tobias, Navia, Jared, Hosanna, Malachi, and Phebe.

'So I said to Navia, "Let the poor man kiss your hand at least. He has evidently fallen under your spell and will gladly grant you every city and town in Saraostas without a fight if you so command him,"' Tobias recounted with a grin.

Navia frowned. 'Very funny, cousin.'

Malachi studied the green-eyed, blonde woman seated beside him. 'My dear, do I need to worry about the number of men who appear to have been bewitched by you on your latest travels? Will a horde of them be waiting for us when we return to Larraak, eager to challenge me for your hand?'

'Not you as well, husband,' Navia grumbled, as the others chuckled. 'Like I said before, the king of Laothal was likely concussed from the blow he received to the head. Besides, I do not see Tobias offering his fingers to every pair of lips that wish to press against them.'

'That is because he knows what is good for his health,' said Ysa tartly.

Tobias's face brightened when he spotted them by the doors. He rose and crossed the chamber with a faint limp. Ysa met him halfway and responded to his passionate kiss with an ardor that drew a groan from Jared.

'Please, some of us have not seen our mates for months,' moaned Crovir's second son.

Rafael ignored him and embraced Phebe just as heatedly when she ran into his arms.

'It is good to see you, wife,' he whispered against her lips when he finally released her mouth.

Her eyes glimmered beneath him, full of desire and heated promise. 'It is good to see you too, husband.'

'I cannot believe I am saying this, but I actually really miss my filthy-mouthed spouse right now,' Hosanna said acerbically at the table.

Tobias grinned as he headed back to his seat, a flushed Ysa at his side. 'I am sure the second general is waiting for you just as keenly, cousin.'

Rafael studied the gash on the back of Tobias's calf in the light cast by the roaring flames in the hearth. 'How did you get that?'

Tobias followed his gaze and grimaced. 'My horse bolted when we came across a venomous snake earlier today.' He sighed at Rafael's expression. 'Do not worry. The snake was unharmed. I, on the other hand, looked quite the fool when I almost slipped off my saddle.'

'Here, let me heal it.'

Tobias shook his head. 'It is quite alright, cousin. It will be gone in a matter of days.'

'Do not be stubborn,' Rafael countered gruffly.

'Yes, husband,' said Ysa. 'Let him see to your wound.'

Tobias hesitated before nodding, a tired expression suddenly washing across his face.

IT WAS NOT UNTIL LATER THAT NIGHT, AFTER RAFAEL HAD USED the powers he had been gifted to mend the wounds his siblings and cousins had incurred during their recent battles, when the wine had flowed plentifully and they had had their fill of food, that they finally addressed the unspoken matters that troubled them.

'Has anyone heard from Mila?' said Jared.

He stared into his tumbler, a frown on his face.

'No,' Tobias replied. 'I sent a messenger to Hathor before we left Mehrgar. He has still not returned.'

'The folly of the king knows no end, it seems,' murmured Phebe. 'There is nothing beyond the Nahal River but the Great West Desert. Why he would send her there is incomprehensible.'

'Do you really think so, cousin?' said Jared.

A troubled expression dawned on Phebe's face. Rafael narrowed his eyes, the worrying thoughts and feelings that had plagued him during his and Ysa's four-month-long crusade surging through him once more.

'It is clear to me why our father sent Mila to the far side of the borders of our Empire,' Jared continued in a harsh tone. 'It was simply to punish her. That he paired all of us but her speaks volumes.' He looked around the table. 'He sent Hosanna and I to the cities on the West Sea, Malachi and you,' he inclined his head at Phebe, 'to Dara and Ugarit, Rafael and Ysa to the north, and Tobias and Navia to the east. Only Mila was dispatched on her own, into the most hostile of the lands that surround our kingdom. And with less than half the number of men we were assigned, no less.'

Silence fell upon the chamber.

'Had she not openly challenged our uncle, none of this would have happened,' Malachi said quietly.

Hosanna glared at him. 'Say what you will, brother, but the words Mila spoke that day in the throne room were true. To dispose of the governor of Hazaara in the callous manner the king ordered, when the circumstances I had reported to him were so dire, would have been truly barbaric.' She paused and glanced at Jared. 'It would also have unnerved the other human states and cities under our rule and led to further uprisings. I am sure both Mila and Jared thought of this fact when they chose to spare Governor Nazul.'

Malachi smiled faintly. 'I am not saying she was wrong, sister. It is just that our cousin has a way of ruffling the feathers of the older king in a manner that none of us can quite match. I think we have all noted the tension between father and daughter over the years.'

Tobias slowly drummed his fingers on the table, his eyes thoughtful.

'She scares him,' he said gruffly.

Phebe inhaled sharply. 'What?'

Rafael blinked in surprise. 'Why do you say that?'

Tobias stilled his fingers.

'Because he is my father and she is my sister,' he replied simply, his gaze locked on Rafael's face. 'I have known both of them for hundreds of years. And I have seen Mila on the battlefield on countless occasions. Baruch and I have spoken of the matter many times to the kings. There is no doubt in our minds that she should be leading our armies.'

'I concur,' Ysa murmured.

'So do I,' said Hosanna.

A bitter smile twisted Jared's lips. 'Our little Mila has grown into the most formidable warrior in our lands.'

'Would you have drawn your sword?' said Malachi after a while, a focused look on his normally placid face.

Jared gazed at him impassively in the tense lull that followed.

'Probably,' he finally replied. 'One thing I am certain of. I will not be used as a pawn in the games my father wishes to indulge in.'

'Nor will I,' said Tobias, his face hardening.

'I fear the time to choose sides may very soon be upon us,' Navia muttered.

They all looked at her, Rafael frowning at her pale face. 'Why do you say that, sister?'

Navia stared into the fire, her gaze unfocused. 'Because I see darkness in our future. A darkness that will swallow our kingdom for hundreds, if not thousands, of years to come.'

PART II
DEFIANCE

CHAPTER FOURTEEN

Mila stood on the edge of the pit, acrid fumes filling her lungs as she gazed at the burnt corpses crowding the hastily dug graveyard below.

They had spotted the smoke from half a league away, a day after passing the outpost of Kis. Urging her exhausted army toward the location of the blaze, Mila knew what she would find when they reached it. Judging from her soldiers' expressions, so did they.

This was the third village they had come upon since they entered the Empire's immediate domain, four months after leaving Uryl on a campaign to expand the kingdom's western territories. Four months during which Mila and her army of eight hundred men crossed the Nahal River and ventured into the Great West Desert, only to find the scattered remains of a long-dead civilization and the few nomadic tribes who had adopted the rocky plateaus, mountains, and seas of sand dunes as their home.

There was little to conquer in such a barren landscape, as Mila had long suspected before she left the capital. The bitterness that had been her constant companion since her father assigned her the futile mission only grew with each man she lost to the unforgiving, scorched lands they had been dispatched to. It was thanks to her survival skills and the wit of her troop commanders and captains that they did not suffer more than a dozen deaths during their campaign, even after a violent sandstorm decimated half their supplies. Only on one occasion, when nearly two Half Moons had passed without her being able to locate food or water for her soldiers, did she trade weapons with a desert tribe in exchange for sustenance.

The act shocked her commanders, who had expected her to storm the settlement and claim the goods. Mila had considered doing just that for a fleeting moment. But the faces of the people of Hazaara had risen in her mind and the words Governor Nazul had spoken had resonated in her ears as she gazed upon the peaceful commune they had stumbled upon.

Enough. I will not shed more blood for that monster than is strictly necessary.

Her relief upon finally reaching the Empire over a day ago was quickly mitigated by the devastating scenes she and her army soon came across. At first, Mila thought their kingdom was under attack, so fierce was the destruction inflicted upon the villages and so terrible the injuries sustained by the corpses she examined. But when they reached the outpost of Nawaar and found no news of an invasion, Mila's suspicions were finally confirmed.

It was the Empire's soldiers who had brutally murdered their own people, on the orders of King Crovir. When Mila questioned the battalion leader of Nawaar as to the reasons why, he evaded her gaze and murmured something about unpaid tithes.

Anger had filled her then, anger that turned to a red haze of fury when she was told Kronos had been in charge of the mass slaughters, and that the villages that had been annihilated were home to many of her men.

Mila turned from the pit and met the bitter stares of several soldiers. She opened her mouth, hesitated, and closed her lips soundlessly. There was nothing she could say to alleviate their outrage at what had happened to their families in their absence.

She gritted her teeth, marched through the silent crowd, and vaulted onto Buros. Abu descended from the skies and landed on her shoulder, his demeanor unusually restrained, as if he sensed her unease.

'What do we do now, Red Queen?' said one of her commanders in a leaden voice.

Mila glanced at the dark spirals rising from the pit before wheeling the stallion around. 'We go home.'

ELEAZA DREW HER BOW AND NARROWED HER EYES AT THE FAR side of the arena. She exhaled and released the arrow. It sailed through the air at an impossible speed and thudded dead center into the target, feathered tail vibrating to a slow stop.

'Well done, Princess.'

Eleaza grinned and looked up at the man beside her.

Aäron, the captain her mother had charged with her training, smiled back and ruffled her hair gently. Excited clapping rose behind them.

She turned to the boy who stood beaming on the steps that enclosed the arena. 'Did you see, Emet?'

'Yes! Yes, I did!' gushed the boy.

The elderly woman weaving on the steps behind him raised a stick and tapped him gently on the bottom without looking away from her loom.

'Princess,' she corrected.

'Yes I did, Princess!' said Emet.

Eleaza made a face.

'Does he have to call me that?' she asked the boy's grandmother.

It was Aäron who replied. 'If your father were to hear him do otherwise, it would result in another beating.'

Guilt filled Eleaza as she stared at the scabs on Emet's calves.

'Father was wrong to do that,' she mumbled, recalling her cries of protest at the time and how her brother Kaleb had to physically restrain her so she would not run to Emet's assistance.

'It is the duty of a daughter to follow the commands of her father, Princess,' said Aäron.

Eleaza thought about this for a moment. 'Even if it would make me unhappy to obey such orders?'

Aäron hesitated. 'Yes, even then.'

Eleaza chewed her lip. 'What if the thing he tasked me with was wrong?'

Aäron blinked. 'You are more like your mother than I thought.'

Emet's grandmother let out a low chuckle.

Eleaza smiled uncertainly at the fair-haired captain. 'Have you always done what your father commanded you to do, Aäron?'

A strange expression flashed in the blue eyes above her.

Aäron looked up and studied the training grounds with a faint smile. 'No, not quite.'

Eleaza was opening her mouth to ask another question when a disturbance at the entrance of the arena distracted her. She turned and spotted a figure flanked by soldiers in the shadows of the tunnel. A moment later, a woman stepped out into the sunlight bathing the grounds.

Elation flooded Eleaza. 'Mama!'

She dropped the bow and ran as fast as her legs could carry her to the woman crossing the arena, only to falter as she drew close. A sliver of anxiety darted through her when she registered her mother's strangely blank face.

Undaunted, she jumped and was relieved when Mila caught her mid-air. Eleaza buried her face in her neck and breathed her mother's familiar scent. To her surprise, Mila cradled the back of her head and dropped a kiss on her hair, her lips lingering on her head for a long moment.

'It is good to see you, daughter.'

Eleaza drew back and gazed worriedly into her mother's eyes. Behind the usual inscrutable expression, she sensed a storm of emotions threatening to break through.

She raised a hand to Mila's cheek. 'Are you well, Mama?'

Mila blinked. There was a noise behind them. She turned, her arms stiffening around Eleaza.

Kronos entered the arena and headed toward them.

'You should have sent a messenger,' he called out with a smile as he approached. 'I would have met you outside Niibru had I known you were coming.'

Mila slowly lowered Eleaza to the ground. 'Go to Aäron.'

Eleaza hesitated.

'Go, child,' Mila ordered in a hard voice.

Eleaza nodded shakily and rushed to where Aäron stood. The altercation began immediately. She stopped beside the captain and grabbed his hand, staring apprehensively to where her mother and father exchanged heated words in low voices.

'Do not touch me!' Mila shouted a moment later, raising an arm to block Kronos's hand as he reached for her shoulder.

Eleaza startled and felt Aäron's fingers twitch around her

own. Emet cowered behind his grandmother on the steps to their left. At the entrance of the arena, the soldiers glanced at each other, faces pale.

Tears filled Eleaza's eyes as she stared at her mother. She had never before seen the look clouding her beautiful features. It spoke of rage and disappointment and something else. Something she could not name.

'Aäron?' Eleaza whispered in a trembling voice.

The captain squeezed her hand. 'It is alright, child.'

Eleaza looked up at him then and registered the intense light in his eyes with confusion. *His* expression she could read.

It was full of hope.

CHAPTER FIFTEEN

'Again!'

Mila raised her daggers and glared at the man opposite her, air leaving her lungs in slow, steady pants. His blue eyes narrowed below his sweat-slicked hair, the fair locks dark under the late-day sun. He clenched his jaw and braced himself, his twin blades flush against his forearms and his stance firm. Mila ignored their avid audience and attacked again, her mind focused on the fight before her.

Four days had passed since her return to Issin. Four days during which she had banned Kronos from her bed and spent her every waking hour in the training grounds of the city. There was only one way to exhaust the rage that burned inside her.

After Danae, Issin's armorer, gave in following a protracted battle that lasted well after sundown three days ago, Mila challenged the best captains and troop commanders of the battalion stationed at Issin to a fight in the arena. Of all the soldiers she tested her mettle against, only Aäron still stood.

As she engaged in yet another fierce encounter with Jared's

former archer, Mila could not help but admire his tenacity. By all accounts, he should have admitted defeat that morning. Yet, here he stood, his expression as determined as it had been the day she first clashed swords with him, on their way to Hazaara.

As she parried his blows and countered deftly, a rare sense of calm suddenly filled Mila. She blinked, surprised.

Aäron hesitated. Mila glimpsed the flash of concern in his eyes, twisted out of the way of his attack, and came up behind him, one blade at his neck, the other digging into his side.

'Never show empathy for your enemy,' she said in his ear.

He froze in her embrace, his chest heaving with his breaths. 'What if the enemy deserves a second chance?'

This close, Mila felt the vibration of his words rumble through his body. She also sensed the wild drumming of his heart and the heat of his skin. It sent a shiver down her spine that had little to do with fear. She lowered her blades and took a step back, suddenly eager to put some distance between them. Despite Aäron's hooded gaze, she detected the same awareness in his posture.

Before she could question him about his cryptic words, a patter of feet to her left distracted her. Mila looked around. Eleaza and Emet were crossing the arena, faces flushed with excitement. The clamor of voices and the clash of weapons rose around them once more as the dozens of soldiers on the training grounds resumed their practice, expressions sheepish at being caught staring.

Mila sighed. It was not every day that she so readily entertained a crowd of spectators. *My standards are slipping.*

'Mama, can you show me how to do that?' said Eleaza as she drew near.

Mila smiled faintly. 'I can.'

Her gaze shifted to the boy hovering behind her daughter.

She had heard of his treatment at her husband's hands in her absence.

'What about you, Emet?'

The boy's shy expression turned to puzzlement.

'Would you like to learn how to fight?' said Mila quietly.

Emet's eyes rounded.

Eleaza giggled and clapped her hands. 'Oh! Oh, I want to teach him! I think he will make a great soldier.'

Emet gaped between the two of them, too stunned to utter a single word.

'Do you think this wise, Princess?'

Mila turned and gazed at Emet's grandmother. The older woman had come up behind the children and stood watching her warily.

'I think it is a good idea for a companion to my daughter to know how to defend himself, and her, if the need arises.'

Emet's grandmother cocked her head. 'Do you fear that he will need to do so, Princess?'

Mila read the silent challenge in the servant's eyes.

'Not while I am here. I will not let anyone lay a single finger on him while he is within my sight.' She paused. 'Not even the prince.'

Aäron stiffened beside her. She glanced at him. He was staring at something beyond her shoulder, faint lines creasing his brow. Mila twisted on her heels and steeled herself for another confrontation with Kronos.

But it was not her husband who stormed across the training grounds toward her.

KRONOS GULPED DOWN A TUMBLER FULL OF WINE AND GAZED across Issin from the terrace outside the palace's main reception hall. A quarter league to the west, the arena stood bathed in the red glow of the dying sun.

The color matched his mood. It had been too long since he held Mila in his arms. The desire and frustration he had experienced during their months of separation had grown to fever pitch in the last few days of her denying him their conjugal bed, so much so that he feared his unconsummated passion would drive him mad. He wanted to taste his mate's lips. He wanted to mark her skin. He wanted to sink into her body and lose himself in pleasure so intense it sapped at his consciousness.

Her anger at his recent actions had stunned him, even more so than her behavior in the throne room of Uryl, when she confronted their father. Although he had noticed her growing dissatisfaction with Crovir's orders over the years, Kronos never suspected she would challenge the older king so openly, and over such a trivial matter at that. As the lieutenant commander of their army, she had done much worse in the past, and had trodden over the bodies of thousands across many a blood-soaked battlefield to grow their kingdom.

He narrowed his eyes. There was also the matter of the man Mila had assigned to train Eleaza. Although he acknowledged the archer's superior fighting skills, Kronos could not help but feel that his wife had chosen Aäron for reasons that went beyond his abilities in the arena of war. There was no doubt that the human cut an impressive figure on the training grounds. And from what Kronos had gleaned from his spies in the barracks, it was also clear that he regularly refused the advances of the female attendants and servants who wished to lie with him.

A commotion at the bottom of the terrace drew his gaze. A pair of attendants rushed after two figures crossing the elegant courtyard fronting the main hall. Kronos stared. He recognized the one in the lead. She climbed the steps, crossed the deck, and stopped a few feet from where he stood, her stance rigid.

'Why?' said Phebe in a low voice.

Kronos studied her with a mixture of surprise and irritation.

'I was not aware of your impending visit.' He waved away the attendants who had followed her. 'What brings you to Issin, cousin?'

The woman behind Phebe drew back the cowl covering her head.

Kronos frowned faintly as he gazed upon the clumps of charred hair dotting her bald head and the burn marks disfiguring her face. 'Who is this?'

Phebe's face darkened. 'You dare?! You dare ask who she is after you burned down her city and killed all her people?'

Realization slowly dawned. Kronos scowled and reached for his sword.

'Stop.'

Kronos froze at the command. He blinked and looked around.

Mila stood behind him, still dressed in her battle clothes. Rafael was at her side. A short distance away, Eleaza huddled next to the captain charged with her training, fingers clasped tightly around his large hand.

The sight was a dagger in Kronos's heart.

'Is it true?' said Mila, her voice devoid of emotion.

Kronos's gaze shifted to his mate's face once more.

'Did you destroy Hazaara?' she asked softly.

Kronos straightened. 'Yes.'

His answer hung in the still air, a stark reality that caused something to shift in Mila's eyes. The emotion he thought he had glimpsed on the day she returned to Issin was now clear to see. It rocked him to the core like few things could.

'On whose orders did you go to Hazaara?' said Rafael.

Kronos registered the fury on his face distractedly.

'King Crovir, obviously.' Though his heart thudded rapidly against his ribs at his wife's expression, Kronos kept his voice firm. 'What is it to you anyway, cousin?'

'Phebe and I travelled to Hazaara at the request of Hosanna, to help with the plague that afflicts the city,' said Rafael. 'There was nothing left but ashes and burnt rock when we got there.' He glanced at the disfigured woman. 'We found one survivor. Ishvi, the daughter of Governor Nazul.'

'How could you?' snarled Phebe. 'All those men, women, and children. They were already dying, Kronos!'

'Then it was as good a way as any to make sure the plague did not spread!' he snapped.

Nazul's daughter jumped slightly.

'Is that why King Crovir ordered you to destroy the villages inside the main territory of our empire in our absence?' said Mila silkily in the tense silence. 'I was not aware they were similarly afflicted with disease.'

Kronos clenched his jaw. 'You know full well he wanted to make an example of them, to deter other villages and cities in the kingdom from forsaking their tithes.'

'Did my father know of this?' said Rafael coldly.

Kronos frowned, anger stirring inside him. 'There was no need for my uncle to be involved in the matter.'

Phebe drew a breath in sharply.

Rafael straightened and narrowed his eyes. 'I think King Bastian would not have approved.'

'I agree,' said Mila. She walked past Kronos and stopped before the silent woman who stood watching them. 'I am sorry, Ishvi. Jared and I failed in our promise to you and your father.'

Shock reverberated through Kronos. Never in all his hundreds of years of existence had he heard his mate apologize to anyone.

'It was not your fault,' mumbled Ishvi in the stunned silence. She touched her disfigured face. 'Prince Rafael wanted to heal my wounds fully but I would not let him.' Her dead gaze focused on Kronos. 'I wanted the scars to be a reminder.'

A bark of manic laughter escaped Kronos's lips. 'Come now! I do not believe what I am seeing and hearing. The princes and princesses of this kingdom bow to no man.' He scowled. 'Have you forgotten that humans exist only to serve us? Their lives and fates belong to us. Why are you—?'

Nazul's daughter moved with a speed that stupefied everyone. She snatched the dagger from Mila's waist and charged across the terrace, her mouth open in a scream of rage.

'No!' shouted Mila, fingers clutching at Ishvi's robe.

It slipped from the woman's shoulders and fluttered to the ground.

Kronos reached for his knife, blocked her attack, and stabbed her in the heart. There was a moment of frozen stillness. It was shattered by Eleaza's scream.

Nazul's daughter stared blindly at Kronos. The dagger fell from her grasp and clattered to the marble floor at her feet.

Rafael caught her as she fell. He lowered her to the ground, yanked the blade out of her chest, and threw it aside. Blood bloomed across her dress, a pulsing, crimson tide he desperately tried to quell with his hands.

They watched, motionless, as he unleashed his healing powers to save the dying woman. The flow of blood slowly abated. Sweat beaded Rafael's brow.

It was then that Nazul's daughter raised a hand and touched his face with trembling fingers.

'Let me go,' she whispered. 'I want to be with them.'

'I can save you,' Rafael said angrily.

Phebe knelt by his side, features pale with grief.

'I know,' Nazul's daughter replied. A tear slipped out of the corner of her eye and trailed down her scarred face. 'Thank you, for everything that you have done.'

Rafael inhaled raggedly before slowly lifting his hands from Ishvi's flesh. She smiled. A moment later, her face slackened and her body relaxed in death.

The lull that followed was broken by footsteps. Mila headed past them, her face locked in an icy mask that sent a jolt of fear through Kronos.

'Where are you going?' Phebe called after her.

'To stop this.'

CHAPTER SIXTEEN

MOONLIGHT BATHED THE PLAINS EAST OF THE UFRATÜ RIVER IN a pale light. On a hill up ahead, the citadel rose, dark walls flecked with the orange glow of flaming torches. Mila urged Buros on, the beat of the stallion's hooves echoing the wild drumming of her heart, her gaze focused on her destination.

She had left Issin with one thought in mind. To put an end to her father's acts of madness. There was only one person whom she trusted to stand firm at her side when she challenged him. Her grandfather, Romerus.

She glanced at the distant lights of Uryl to the right as she approached Romerus's fortress. *Tonight. I shall go there tonight, come what may.*

The soldiers in the guard towers gaped as she raced up the hill toward the towering gates. Alarmed shouts rose from the ramparts. The counterweight mechanisms that controlled the beam blocking the gateway rumbled into life as she approached. The portal opened ponderously. She slowed Buros and slipped through the widening gap.

'Our apologies, Princess,' said a captain as she pulled up outside the barracks. 'We did not receive a message about your visit.'

'I did not send one.'

Mila leapt off the stallion and headed across the courtyard toward Romerus's palace. A chariot parked to the left drew her gaze. She froze in her tracks before whirling around.

'Is the king here?' she snapped.

The captain nodded, eyes widening at her tone. 'Yes, Princess. King Crovir arrived a short while ago.'

Coldness filled Mila's veins. She steeled herself and headed inside the palace. It was not long before she came across several of her grandfather's attendants huddled in a group in one of the courtyards. The expressions on their faces slowed her steps.

'What is going on?' she said brusquely.

'Greetings, Princess,' they murmured, bowing hastily.

Mila turned to the oldest attendant.

He hesitated, his face pale. 'King Crovir ordered us to leave the chambers of his father. We fear—' he glanced at the other servants, '—we fear he may not be sound of mind right now, Princess. His mood was most strange.'

Apprehension darted through Mila. She exited the quadrangle and hurried through the palace to the garden in the center of the fortress. Her grandfather's private quarters finally appeared up ahead, a low building straddling a platform that overlooked the beautifully-sculptured grounds.

The sounds of an argument reached her ears as she passed a water fountain. Mila recognized her father's voice and silently climbed the steps to the deck that ran around the edifice. She paused in the shadows of the curtains framing one of the archways leading to an open-air reception hall. Two figures faced each other across the marble floor some dozen feet away.

'You need to rest, my son,' her grandfather said calmly. 'You are not yourself tonight. Stay and we shall talk more in the morning.'

'No!' barked Crovir. 'We shall resolve this matter right *now!*'

Mila stiffened at her father's tone. The light from the oil lamps dotting the chamber cast stark shadows across his face, lending him a cadaverous appearance.

Romerus studied Crovir with a patient expression. 'So be it. What is this matter of such urgency that you found it necessary to come and see me about it in the middle of the night?'

Crovir glared at him. 'Your disillusionment.'

Romerus blinked, shock flashing across his face.

'I can sense it,' Crovir continued. 'I have for many years, ever since the death of my mother. You regard me with contempt.'

Mila clenched her jaw. She could tell Crovir was wildly inebriated. This was clearly evident to her grandfather as well.

'I do not know what you mean,' said Romerus. 'I have supported you and your brother in all of your endeavors since you came of age.'

'Oh, yes.' Crovir sneered. 'You always do. You are the epitome of the perfect father. But that does not mean you wholeheartedly approve of our actions.'

Crovir's words sent a shard of ice through Mila's mind. Behind them, she sensed a wealth of frustration and loathing for the man who had given him life. Her unease grew tenfold.

Romerus was silent for a long time, his lined face shuttered.

'You are right,' he finally acknowledged in a steady voice. 'I cannot deny that I have deliberately chosen to remain blind to your acts over the last few hundred years. Even when Mila and her siblings spoke to me of your ill-treatment of your wives. Even when Hosanna came to tell me about the rising levies and the misfortunes befalling the cities you rule. Even when I heard of the thousands you have casually murdered in the name of growing your empire. I always refused to recognize your callous actions.'

Mila startled, stunned by this unexpected revelation.

Crovir went deadly still. '*My* empire?'

Sadness filled Romerus's eyes. 'Yes, my son. Your empire. The one you and your brother have built. I never asked for it. Neither did your mother.' He hesitated. 'But I made a promise, a long time ago, to the One who gave me the gifts that would save you and Bastian from death. I promised I would allow you free will. So I could only watch and weep and pray that you would find your way again, somehow.'

An ugly expression distorted Crovir's features. 'You think I have lost my way?'

Romerus gazed at him. 'I did not raise a monster.'

Blood thrummed in Mila's ears in the deafening lull that followed. Something flashed on Crovir's face. Something unworldly. Fear gripped her for the first time in her Immortal life. She took a step toward the threshold.

'I am sorry to hear that, Father,' said Crovir in a strangely detached voice. He crossed the floor toward Romerus. 'Here, let me end your agony.'

There was a sound then. A sound that Mila had heard countless times, on a thousand battlefields in untold lands. She froze, unable and unwilling to comprehend its significance.

A sigh left Romerus's lips. His hands rose to the red stain blooming across his robes and the blade embedded between his ribs.

Shock dawned on Crovir's face. He stepped back and let go of his dagger, his expression clearing, as if waking from a dream.

A scream built up inside Mila's throat. Tears blurred her vision. Still, the sound would not come.

Romerus stared at his bloodied fingers for a moment before lifting them to Crovir's face, a faint smile on his lips. 'I forgive you, my son.'

He kissed Crovir's brow and cheeks before slowly collapsing in his arms. Crovir gasped and lowered his father awkwardly to the ground, hands shaking uncontrollably, eyes wide with terror.

'I—Father—' he stammered, his face that of a boy once more.

Romerus turned his head and looked straight at the archway where Mila stood hidden. His smile widened.

'You came,' he breathed.

A warm breeze suddenly washed across Mila, jolting her out of her stupor and raising goosebumps on her exposed skin. There was a faint smell of spices. An intense pressure, the like of which she had never known before, gripped her head and robbed her of her breath. Deep in the bowels of her consciousness, in the place where her most basic instincts lived, she sensed a forbidding presence and knew her grandfather was addressing it.

Before she could grasp the unearthly phenomenon she was witnessing, the curtains fluttered wildly, exposing her to Crovir's view.

He blanched. 'Mila?'

She ignored her father's hoarse whisper, her gaze fixed unblinkingly on Romerus as he took his last breath. His body went slack, his unseeing eyes focused on a spot to her right, the smile still on his face as air parted his lips in a rasp.

The scream finally left Mila and with it came a flood of outrage that burned her to the core. '*No!*'

The sound jolted Crovir. His expression changed in the next moment, cold determination replacing the fear in his eyes and hardening his face.

Had her entire world not just turned upside down, Mila would have sensed the stealthy approach of another behind her. She turned at the last moment, her hand on the hilt of her sword. Something sharp entered her right flank. She stared blindly into the face of Delaiah, Crovir's lover.

The woman let go of the knife she had used to stab her, her pretty features twisted with a mixture of shock, elation, and hate.

Mila glanced at the blade buried below her ribs and realized Delaiah had seen Crovir kill Romerus and was trying to protect the king. She ignored the sickening, wet sound the knife made as she pulled it out of her body, and slashed the woman opposite her across the throat before the latter could move.

Crovir's lover made a gargling noise and raised her hands to the red flow gushing from the slash in her neck, eyes widening. Guards appeared from every direction as she slowly crumpled to the ground. They slowed when they drew near, confusion washing across their faces as they took in the woman choking in the final throes of death at their lieutenant commander's feet, and the blood-stained blade still clasped in her fingers. One of them gasped when he spotted Romerus in Crovir's arms.

'Stop her!' shouted Crovir.

He pointed at Mila.

Mila studied her father for a heartbeat. In that fleeting instant, she felt the blood ties that had held her captive to him for over four hundred years shatter as she grasped his gruesome intention. As the only living witness to the unforgivable sin he had just committed, he wanted her blood.

And he would not stop until she was dead. Even if it meant spreading the outrageous lie his command insinuated. That she was responsible for Romerus's death.

Icy resolve flowed through her body, erasing any feelings of kinship for the man who had sired her. 'Even if it is the last thing I do in this world, I will stop you.'

CHAPTER SEVENTEEN

CROVIR'S EYES WIDENED. MILA TURNED HER ATTENTION TO THE ring of guards facing her. From their expressions, they believed the unspoken accusation in her father's voice. There would be no bargaining with them. Not at this moment.

She unsheathed her broadsword and tightened her grip on the dagger in her hand, her mind and body focused single-mindedly on the irrevocable path she was about to take.

'What are you waiting for, you fools?!' Crovir screamed, rising to his feet.

The soldiers attacked. Mila danced through them, blades moving in a deadly blur. She was past them in several heartbeats and raced across the garden. More guards appeared in her path.

'Do not let her leave!' Crovir roared behind her.

Mila gritted her teeth. By the time she reached the citadel's main yard, she had disposed of thirty men. She twisted beneath the wild swings of a dozen blades and let out a sharp whistle as she slashed and stabbed at the guards blocking her.

Buros neighed wildly where he stood at the barracks. He

stamped his hooves, reared up on his hind legs, and broke into a full gallop. The soldiers charging across the grounds toward her staggered and fell as he plowed through them. Mila dropped the dagger, grabbed the stallion's saddle as he came past, and vaulted onto his back. She gripped his flanks with her thighs, snatched a stunned soldier's sword out of his hands, and wielded the long blades with unerring accuracy, cutting down the men crowding around them.

Blood swelled from her wound and drenched the lower half of her tunic.

She ignored it and cleared a path before whirling Buros around. '*Go!*'

The stallion obeyed her command and bolted for the citadel's entrance.

Mila steered him toward the left guard tower as the gates loomed up ahead. She leaned over and slashed through the thick rope holding the sandbags that controlled the portal's opening mechanism as they flew past. The counterweights thudded to the ground behind them. The thick beam barring the entrance started to rise.

Mila slowed Buros and circled the stallion around some twenty feet from the gates. Together, they faced the horde of soldiers storming toward them. Although the horse trembled beneath her, the Immortal knew it was with excitement rather than fear.

She snarled, the power that had earned her the name Red Queen rising from the very depths of her being. Buros snorted and stamped his hooves, his body resonating with the same forceful energy.

They charged through the guards, the stallion's powerful kicks and her swinging blades halving the men's number in a dozen heartbeats while the gates slowly rumbled open behind them.

Arrows suddenly streaked through the night from the direction of the ramparts and thudded into the ground around Mila. A shaft found Buros's hindquarters. He jerked and carried on stomping the men around them. She roared and moved the swords in an arc that slashed through half a dozen soldiers before turning the stallion around. She yanked the arrow out of his side and urged him toward the narrow gap that had appeared in the portal.

They slipped through the opening with a foot to spare on either side.

The whistle of a second hail of arrows came from behind as they raced down the hill. A shaft struck Mila in the back. Another found the flesh of her right shoulder. She barely flinched, her gaze centered on the landscape to the north; she needed an escape route from the soldiers who would shortly come after her on horseback and the archers whose reach she was still within.

Movement on the plains ahead made her stiffen. An arrow drifted out of the darkness and glided toward the citadel walls. A scream rose in the night. She glanced over her shoulder and saw an archer fall from the ramparts. Two more followed.

Mila stared into the gloom and made out a figure on horseback. Surprise darted through her.

'To me!' shouted Aäron.

Mila gritted her teeth and dug her heels into Buros's flanks. The sound of arrows followed from the direction of the citadel.

Aäron retaliated, shafts leaving his bow in a blur. Mila knew without looking that his projectiles would find their targets. She passed him a moment later. He turned his horse around and reached her side just as she removed the arrows from her shoulder and back.

'What happened?' he yelled.

Mila hesitated, unsure if she could trust him. The shock of all she had witnessed brought the words stumbling forth from her lips before she could stop them. 'Crovir killed Romerus. And he aims to put the blame on me.'

Aäron stared at her. Although she had expected the surprise on his face, what she had not envisaged was the sudden glint of resolution in his eyes.

The beat of horses' hooves rose behind them. They looked over their shoulders at the troop of soldiers heading in their direction.

'He will send the entire army after you,' said Aäron.

'I know.'

Aäron scowled. 'Follow me.'

Mila blinked at his commanding voice. Still, she steered Buros after him as he turned east.

The moon sailed across the star-studded sky as they raced over the land, the gap between them and the soldiers on their heels slowly growing. They had traveled six leagues when lights appeared in the distance to their right. Mila clenched her jaw. It was the outpost of Girisu.

Flares went up behind them, three flame-lit arrows that arced into the night in rapid succession. The soldiers chasing them had sent a distress signal to the garrison.

Mila knew it would be moments before half the troops at Girisu joined the men from the citadel.

'Where are we going?' she shouted to Aäron.

'The Tigra!' he replied.

Mila studied the dark plains ahead. 'There is no safe passage across the waters where we are heading! We should turn north, to Lagaesh. Baruch and Hosanna will—'

'Lagaesh is eight leagues away!' said Aäron. 'The river is closer!' His teeth flashed in a grim smile. 'And we will not be crossing it!'

Mila stared at him. Wetness on her thigh drew her gaze to the wound on her flank. She had bled a considerable amount in the time since she crossed Aäron on the plains outside Uryl.

'This is nothing,' she said at his expression.

'It sure looks like something to me, Princess,' he responded darkly.

Mila narrowed her eyes. Were it not for the fact that he had come to her rescue and they were in the midst of a chase, she would have rebuked him for his tone.

Although the river was still some distance away, they reached it in what seemed like the blink of an eye. As she had predicted, some five hundred men now followed behind them.

They pulled up on the edge of a ravine, the horses stamping their hooves and neighing at the precipitous drop before them.

Mila gazed two hundred feet down into the raging rapids of the Tigra. 'You could have picked a better spot.'

Aäron grinned. 'This is exactly where I wanted us to be, Princess. And may I say, I resent the sarcasm.' He studied the troops bearing down on them before indicating the river. 'Jump.'

Mila stared. 'What?'

'Jump,' he ordered again, his voice hardening.

The soldiers were fifty feet away and closing fast.

'Have you lost your senses?' snapped Mila. 'I can survive such a fall, but you—'

Aäron made an impatient sound and slapped Buros hard on the rump. The stallion snorted and leapt off the precipice without a moment's hesitation. Mila's heart rose in her mouth as they dropped toward the river. A wild neigh reached her above the rush of the rapids. She sensed Aäron plummeting in the air behind her.

If he does not die from this, I will kill him myself.

They hit the water hard.

MILA TORE INTO THE SMOKED FLESH WITH HER TEETH.

She paused when she felt a stare on her face. 'What?'

Aäron grinned at her from the other side of the fire and turned the barbed fish roasting in the flames. 'Nothing.'

She hesitated before chewing and swallowing.

'It is the wound,' she muttered. 'Our bodies are greedier when we are healing.'

Aäron's gaze shifted to her exposed midriff and the bandage wrapped around her waist. He looked away, his expression troubled.

A quarter day had passed since their escape from the citadel. After their jump into the Tigra, which miraculously produced nothing but bruises, Mila and Aäron let the rapids carry them and their horses south. Occasional shouts and volleys of arrows followed from the soldiers who shadowed them on the western ridge. The shafts felt harmlessly around them in the darkness, aim skewed by the currents of air above the fast-flowing waters.

It was four leagues before they exited the river, in a section of land dominated by forests and sheer bluffs, long after the sound of pursuit had died behind them. Aäron took the lead and soon headed down a narrow gully that branched off the main ravine. They headed east for another six leagues and finally stopped in the cover of a rocky overhang on the bank of the tributary, when the reddening sky heralded the arrival of dawn.

Aäron wandered off to collect tinder and wood while Mila removed the horses' saddles and bands and led them to the water.

She rested her head against her stallion's flank as he drank from the river and closed her eyes for a moment. 'You did well, Buros.'

The horse snickered and blew out a wet snort over her head. Mila smiled, grateful for his companionship. The smile faded from her lips as she recalled the events of the past night.

There had been no time to think coherently, so focused had she been on escaping the citadel and her father's clutches. That she would not have lived to see today was a strong probability, had he managed to capture her. Now that her immediate survival was no longer of paramount importance, she needed to absorb all that had happened before she could decide her next course of action.

She was distracted from her grim thoughts by the sight of Aäron appearing around a bend with an armful of dead branches and dry scrub. Although Mila insisted on helping him fish, he warded her off and handed her a clean linen bandage and a small pouch containing a strange-smelling paste instead.

'What is this?' she said suspiciously.

'It is an ointment that will help your wound.' He sighed at her scornful expression. 'Yes, I know that you are an Immortal and that that nasty cut will soon disappear, but you could still get an infection.'

She cocked an eyebrow.

'If you succumb to fever and disease, I will leave you to rot in this gully,' Aäron stated in a leaden voice.

Mila opened her mouth, hesitated, and swore under her breath. She sat by the water's edge and cleaned the cut on her flank while he went fishing farther upriver. By the time he returned, she had applied the paste and wrapped the bandage around her waist. She would only need it for another day. The laceration was already half healed.

'What about the wounds on your shoulder and back?' said Aäron.

Mila shrugged. 'They were nothing.'

He frowned. 'Still, I should take a look.'

Mila stared at him for a moment. She twisted around and slipped her tunic off her shoulders. He came up behind her. Fingers fluttered over her exposed skin and lingered on the places where the arrows had penetrated her flesh the previous night. She stiffened at his touch.

Taut silence fell between them.

'You are right. They are almost healed,' said Aäron quietly.

He moved away and set the fish to cook over the flames.

It was not until she had sated the unusual hunger that came with an Immortal's ability to self-heal that Mila sat back and gave the man on the other side of the fire her undivided attention.

'Who are you?'

He gazed at her silently, his expression growing shuttered. 'Why, I am but a humble soldier of the Empire, Prin—'

'Enough with the lies!' Mila rose and drew her sword. 'If you do not tell me the truth right now, I will kill you.'

Aäron raised an eyebrow.

He leaned back, his posture relaxed. 'Really? After everything I did for you in the past night, you wish to take my life?'

Mila straightened. 'I could have escaped without your help.'

Aäron watched her steadily. 'I do not doubt that, Princess. But you would have been in a worse state for it.'

Mila moved. Metal clashed against metal a heartbeat later.

She stared at Aäron where he stood a foot away, his blade kissing hers with equal strength. He had jumped to his feet and drawn his sword with a speed that no longer surprised her.

'You are no ordinary soldier,' she said quietly. 'This has

been clear to me for some time.' She paused, her voice hardening. 'Are you a spy?'

Aäron stepped back and lowered his sword. 'I will tell you everything if you come with me.'

Mila went still. His admission did nothing to dispel the unsettling feeling he aroused in her.

'Come with you where exactly?'

'East.' He hesitated. 'The answers you will find there may very well surprise you.'

Mila frowned. 'Why should I trust you? You could be leading me into a trap.'

Aäron sighed. 'If I wanted to kill you, I could have done so last night.'

'I would never have given you the chance,' she snapped.

Aäron put away his blade and came up to her abruptly. She startled when he grabbed her broadsword and brought the pointed end to his chest.

'You have two choices,' he said in a voice she did not recognize. 'You can either kill me now or you can follow me and have a fighting chance of defeating King Crovir.'

Surprise jolted Mila at his words.

Aäron's eyes bore into her, as blue and as clear as the sky above them. 'What will it be, Princess?'

CHAPTER EIGHTEEN

The Zagros Mountains loomed above them, snowcapped peaks painted crimson by the fading daylight. Shadows filled the valleys carved in its steep inclines.

Mila gazed at the man climbing the foothill ahead of her. His words on the riverbank that morning still echoed in her mind. Though her instincts as a warrior warned her Aäron was an unknown threat, a voice deep inside her had urged her to put her faith in him.

They left the desert east of the Tigra when the sun was still high above their heads and travelled over a vast plain dotted with marshes to the base of the Zagros, passing far from the outposts of Duruin and Omran. As the distance between them and the immediate domain of the Empire grew, so did Mila's agitated thoughts.

Following the dreadful events of the previous night, her subconscious beseeched her to turn back and seek a meeting with her mother, siblings and cousins to relate the true events that had transpired. But when their faces rose in her mind's eye, all she could see was the contempt and accusation she had witnessed in the soldiers who had attacked her at the citadel.

There was no guarantee her kin would believe her, not in the condition she would likely find them in. The rational part of her advised she would be wise to put some space between her and them for now. Once time passed and their anguish over Romerus's death abated, there might be a chance for coherent discussion.

A dull ache filled her heart as she thought of her children. She had not had time to say her goodbyes, unlike all the past times she had left their side. That Kronos would protect them from Crovir's wrath was not in doubt. Though he was loyal to their father to a fault, he loved Kaleb and Eleaza above all else. And her cousins and siblings would not stand by and allow Crovir to harm her son and daughter.

She did not dwell on what her husband's reaction would be when he heard of Romerus's murder. Deep inside, she sensed he would side with their father.

The temperature dropped as she and Aäron navigated the sheer slopes toward a narrow pass, their breath and that of their horses misting the air before their faces. Mila was glad for the wintry chill. It soothed her troubled mind.

She followed the captain as he headed through a series of tortuous gullies that took them deeper into the range. Half a league after they crossed the pass, their destination finally came in sight. Dur Untash, the city hidden in the mountains.

Mila studied the clusters of lights dotting the maze of rock and timber buildings clinging to the near vertical gradients ahead. Despite being protected by a ring of peaks, a defensive wall spanned the narrow canyon that constituted the only port of access to the settlement.

Shadows stirred on the rocky escarpments above them as they headed for the gates set in the middle of the ramparts.

Mila spotted at least a dozen archers watching them and more on the parapets ahead.

'Who goes there?' someone shouted from a guard tower.

'It is I, Aäron, son of Parsah,' Aäron called out.

There was a commotion behind the gates. Several of the archers called out greetings to Aäron. The portal finally opened and a tall, sturdy man with a scar running across his left eye strode out to meet them.

'You devil! Where have you been all this time?' he said in a voice brimming with exasperation. 'We have been waiting for word from you for over a year now. What in the name of the Heavens happened to you?' The man looked past Aäron. He skidded to a stop, his eyes widening. 'The Red Queen!' His hand rose to the sword at his waist. He glanced at Aäron with a scowl. 'What is the meaning of this?'

Shocked murmurs ran among the archers on the ridges and the men atop the walls. Metal clinked in the darkness.

'Remain still,' Aäron told Mila in a low voice. 'Our very lives depend on your silence.'

She frowned but kept quiet.

'Do not raise your weapons,' Aäron called out to the guards watching them. He looked to the man with the scar. 'The Red Queen is my guest, Darius. I need to speak to your father.' He paused. 'And we seek shelter for the night.'

The man called Darius hesitated, his hostile gaze drilling into Mila. He dropped his hand from the hilt of his blade and signaled to the archers. They lowered their bows.

'Follow me,' he said gruffly.

He turned and led the way into the city.

Aäron and Mila headed after him with an escort of half a dozen men. The gates closed behind them with a somber rumble that echoed through the narrow valley. Mila glanced over her shoulder at the forbidding portal and wondered once more if she was making a terrible mistake.

They scaled the incline and entered a labyrinth of narrow streets. Torches lined the passages they negotiated, the flames casting a mellow glow on the thatch, timber, and rock houses they passed. Few people lurked outside; it was the time of the evening meal. Random voices and the sound of laughter reached Mila's ears through open doors and windows, and she glimpsed shadowy figures gathered next to roaring fires. She thought of the other city in the mountains, the one Aäron and she had visited all those months ago.

Unlike Hazaara, Dur Untash was full of life.

Mila kept her face impassive as they approached a wide ridge dominating the valley. Breaching the rock face was a pair of caves. Darius stopped in front of the larger one and watched them dismount. She handed Buros's reins to a guard and felt a pang of loss as the stallion was led toward the other cave.

She had memorized the layout of the city while they traversed it and outlined one possible escape route. It would be a difficult but not impossible path for the stallion to navigate. The crucial issue was the number of opponents she would have to fight to get out of the valley. She could not ignore the fact that Aäron would be among them.

The thought of having to face the captain in a real life and death situation triggered the same unsettling emotion she had experienced earlier that day on the riverbank. Although she knew she would defeat him, Mila was aware she should not underestimate his skills in battle. She sensed he had not shown her all he was truly capable of, including the depths of his tactical abilities. From what she had seen of him last night, he was clearly a brilliant strategist.

They headed through the opening in the cliffside after

Darius. Mila's eyes rapidly adjusted to the gloom and she studied the unremarkable grotto around them with a frown.

Where exactly is he taking us?

She caught Aäron's faint smile beside her and felt a twinge of irritation. It was as if he could read her mind and was mocking her.

A tunnel appeared after several hundred feet. They navigated it in silence, Mila's ire growing with every step. She noted the pick marks in the walls and ceilings and traces of hoof prints on the floor. The passage had been broadened to accommodate at least two men on horseback. Before she could make sense of this puzzling observation, the gloom ahead started to fade. They exited the tunnel a moment later and entered a space nearly as big as Dur Untash itself.

Mila slowed and looked around, her heart drumming against her ribs. To the left, outside a row of barracks, animals roasted on spits atop large fires. Men ate and drank at dozens of tables lining the space around the pits. To the right, other fires burned, these more intensely in mud-brick furnaces. Smelters worked metal over them, brows dripping with sweat as they hammered away at swords, spearheads, and axes. Stacked on the floor behind them were mounds of weapons.

She ignored the stares of the men and maids they passed and studied the stables, granaries, and pens dotting the perimeter of the vast expanse. Up ahead, a natural depression in the ground served as an arena; even this late, men worked inside it, naked torsos gleaming in the light of flaming torches as they clashed swords and battle axes.

Some four hundred feet beyond the training pit rose a palace carved out of the very bones of the mountain. She glanced at the dark mouths of caves in distant walls and looked up to a vaulted roof shrouded in shadows.

The complex had been constructed inside a natural cavern,

in the center of the peak; whoever had designed it had blended the man-made spaces with the sheer, granite rock faces enclosing it. It was a masterpiece of human engineering, one that triggered another bout of apprehension within her.

Much had changed in the hundred odd years since she had last been here. For one thing, the palace and the structures around her were new. And, much like Hazaara, the city's outer defenses were more considerable than she recalled.

Mila wondered if Hosanna and her bookkeepers were aware of these developments. Besides them, there was little reason for the Empire's officials to come into these inhospitable mountains.

If she knew about this, did she deliberately keep it a secret from Crovir?

A man appeared on the steps of the majestic archway at the base of the palace, a guard on either side. Though age bowed his spine, he was still tall, and built along the same sturdy lines as Darius. It took but a moment for Mila to see the resemblance between the two. The older man watched them with an unreadable expression as they drew near.

Aäron stopped at the bottom of the stairs and greeted him with a nod. 'Governor Edras.'

The latter bowed. 'Prince Aäron.'

Shock froze Mila's feet to the ground. She stared accusingly at the captain.

He ignored her and raised a hand.

'Please, there is no need for such formalities,' he told the governor. 'Aäron will suffice.' He smiled. 'Besides, you have known me since I was a naked infant playing at your feet with Darius here.'

The governor's face softened slightly. 'Aye, that is indeed true.' His gaze shifted to Mila. 'Still, I must confess to being at a loss. We have been waiting for news ever since you departed

Parsah all those moons ago, on your mission. Yet, here you finally are, with the enemy at your side. And not just any enemy. You bring with you the most fearsome warrior in the whole empire.'

Mila stiffened and narrowed her eyes at the armed guards now ringing her.

A hard edge underscored Aäron's quiet voice. 'The Red Queen is here as my guest.'

His tone was not lost on the governor of Dur Untash or his son. Their expressions cooled.

Aäron sighed and ran a hand through his hair. 'Would you mind going with these men, Princess? I must talk with the governor and Darius. I fear your presence will only aggravate matters.'

Mila studied him silently. Although she was confident she could defeat the men around her and escape the city, her interest was piqued. It was evident that the governor of Dur Untash was building an army. And she wanted to know the reason why.

More importantly, the man who had been her constant companion since she escaped her grandfather's citadel the previous night had some serious explaining to do.

'I will do as you ask,' she said stiffly. 'But be aware that my patience is running thin, *Prince* Aäron.'

He winced. Mila felt his gaze on her back as she allowed her stone-faced escort to lead her up the steps and through the archway.

CHAPTER NINETEEN

MILA LEANED ON THE STONE PARAPET AND GAZED AT THE CAVE
some four hundred feet below. The hour was late and the fires
outside the barracks had long died down. Only the smelters'
furnaces still smoldered, oozing red light in the gloom.

'Do you need anything else, Princess?'

Mila looked at the servant hovering nervously by the bed in
the room behind her.

'No, that will be all.'

The woman bowed, gathered the tray containing the
remains of a meal, and hurried out of the room. Mila caught a
glimpse of the guards outside before the door closed.

She had been given a guest chamber in the palace. Although
it did not boast any of the luxuries she was accustomed to, it
was clean and comfortable.

*At least they had the decency to grant me a room. They could
easily have locked me in a cell.*

That, however, would not have gone down well. The
governor of Dur Untash and Aäron no doubt realized this.
Much as the events at the citadel had stunned her, she was still

the lieutenant commander of the Empire's army and would not have tolerated such treatment lightly.

Mila frowned. She was willing to keep her peace for now. How long this state of affairs lasted depended on the answers a certain captain with fair hair and blue eyes owed her.

The door of the guest chamber opened. The man in question walked in. Mila straightened and turned, elbows on the low wall separating her from the deathly drop at her back.

'Have you eaten?' said Aäron.

He crossed the floor and joined her on the narrow terrace outside the room.

Mila noted the lack of honorific with dry amusement.

'I have.' She turned and looked out over the shadowy cavern once more. 'A hidden city inside a hidden city. I am keen to hear the reasons behind this secret Dur Untash, my prince, and about this "mission" you were supposedly sent on.'

Aäron sighed and rubbed his stubbled jaw. 'You are not going to let this prince thing go, are you?'

Mila was surprised by the involuntary smile that curved her lips. 'No.'

They studied the expanse below in companionable silence.

'It is too late to hide the evidence of what you have seen in these mountains,' Aäron finally said. 'You also know that I am not who I claimed to be when I joined your brother's army a year ago.'

Mila waited expectantly.

'Your kin have built an empire like none have seen before. Had they ruled it with fairness and wisdom over the hundreds of years past, they would have earned the respect and loyalty of those they governed. No doubt there would have been some who wanted more and who would have stirred unrest among the populace. But a just sovereign would have garnered the support of those true to him and handled those situations shrewdly.' He turned to her then, his eyes glinting in the gloom. 'Alas, the ones who reign over this kingdom are anything but kind. With each year that passes, their lust for power and riches grows, and with it come wicked acts of the most vile nature, and levies that sap people of their most basic subsistence. Even as I speak, entire cities starve. And unbeknown to the ones who sit on the thrones of Uryl, the disease that struck Hazaara slowly spreads its tentacles south and west across the Empire.' His face hardened. 'In truth, King Crovir likely knows these facts. He has ears everywhere. But he does not care.'

Mila's pulse accelerated as she digested his words. There was no denying their truth. And it was not as if she had not mulled over such thoughts herself in recent times.

Aäron looked out over the cave. 'It began with a promise.'

Mila frowned. 'What do you mean?'

'One hundred and seventeen years ago, my grandfather made a promise to his father. A promise to assemble an army that would challenge the tyrants that rule us. A promise of war.'

A chill ran through her. 'War?'

'Yes. This was after King Crovir sent an emissary to Parsah, demanding a second tithe. A larger tithe than the one my great-grandfather had already submitted to the collectors of the Empire that year.' Aäron's tone grew cold. 'Our people were already suffering from the effects of a severe drought at the time and they were left with barely enough grain to feed half the city. As a result of the cruel demands of the king, hundreds of men, women and children died from hunger and many more succumbed to the sickness that inevitably followed. My great-grandfather was among those who contracted the disease that killed nearly all of those who survived the famine.' He paused, a muscle jumping in his jawline. 'It was as he lay dying that my grandfather resolved to one day end the dominion of the Immortal kings. In the time since that promise was made, the rulers of Parsah created secret alliances with other human leaders throughout the Empire, leaders who would be loyal to our cause and who would contribute troops and resources for our plans. Forty years ago, they elected my father as the first monarch of this new faction.' He stared at her. 'We aim to depose King Crovir and King Bastian.'

Mila blinked. A bark of incredulous laughter escaped her. 'Did the fall in the Tigra affect your mind? What makes you think you have a fighting chance against the soldiers of the Empire, let alone my siblings and cousins?'

'Because you will be at our side, Red Queen,' said Aäron steadily. 'And you will help me lead the human army that will defeat the Immortals.'

CARRION BIRDS CIRCLED HIGH ABOVE, WINGS SILENT AGAINST THE pale blue sky as they drifted on invisible air currents. A southerly breeze brought a stench of rotting flesh to Mila's nostrils. The carcass of an onager appeared up ahead.

'How much farther is this place?' she said after the animal's body disappeared behind them.

Aäron glanced her way. 'Not far now.'

She narrowed her eyes at him. 'You said that before.'

He grinned. 'Patience is not one of your virtues, is it?'

'Honesty does not appear to be one of yours,' she snapped.

His smile faded. 'My lies were a necessary evil. We would not be here right now had I not stretched the truth somewhat.'

'Stretching the truth is putting it lightly. If there ever were a prevarication contest, you would be the champion of it.'

Aäron burst out laughing.

Mila glared. 'I am glad my words amuse you, Prince.'

'You have no idea, Princess,' he said, eyes sparkling.

Mila felt her pulse jump despite her annoyance.

She looked away from his warm gaze and studied the sheer bluffs on either side of them. 'Still, all I can envisage at the conclusion of this path is a dead end.'

'Have faith, Princess.'

He dug his thighs into the flanks of his steed and broke into a canter. Mila urged Buros on and followed.

Nearly a day had passed since they departed Dur Untash. As dawn swept across the canyon protecting the hidden city in the Zagros Mountains, Governor Edras and Darius stood at the gates and watched them leave.

Edras's last words to Aäron rang in her ears, even now. 'Let us all hope that you were wise in your choice of companion, prince of Parsah. I do not envy you the task of convincing your father why bringing one of our enemies into the fold is a good idea.'

A hard expression had flashed across Aäron's face. 'I will deal with my father.' He dipped his chin at Darius. 'You shall receive word of our plans soon.'

It was midday by the time they left the snow-capped peaks behind and ventured onto the desert foothills bordering the plateau that extended hundreds of leagues east to the Toba Kakar Range and the Indus Valley. Arid wilderness soon gave way to a landscape of lush, green plains and forested elevations spread across a wide basin. A while later, the Zayande River came in sight and with it a handful of villages abutting the fertile fields on its banks.

Aäron followed the meandering waterway until a city appeared on the horizon. Mila tensed slightly when she recognized Parsah shimmering in the heat waves rising off the valley floor. Surprise had darted through her in the next moment.

Instead of keeping to the road that would lead them there, Aäron turned and headed for the dark massifs looming to the south.

Mila pulled Buros to a stop. 'Where are you going?'

'Home.'

She stared at the distant city, puzzled. 'I thought home was Parsah.'

'It is. And it is not.'

Mila frowned. 'Your cryptic words strain my patience, Prince.'

'I have come to expect nothing less, Princess.'

Buros snorted impatiently beneath her. She studied the man ambling toward the mountains, sighed, and dug her thighs into the stallion's flanks.

It was another four leagues before they reached the canyon in the foothills of the peaks. The land rose and the gorge narrowed the farther along it they travelled. Twilight soon filled the spaces around them, the vertiginous walls on either side at times obscuring the heavens. A short time after they passed the dead onager, the passage grew so cramped they had to navigate it in single file. It widened again into a short gully flanked by cliffs on three sides some half a league later. Up ahead, a thin crevasse shrouded in shadows split the rock face.

Mila reined Buros in and scowled. 'Like I said, a dead end.'

Aäron ignored her and guided his steed into the breach in the mountain. It was just wide enough to take them.

'Let me guess, is there a hidden Parsah beyond this?' Mila said sardonically as his figure faded in the gloom.

'Are you coming or not?' he called out.

Mila hesitated as she recalled what Aäron had told her the

past night, on the terrace of the guest chamber in the hidden Dur Untash.

'You will help me lead the human army that will defeat the Immortals.' He had paused then, his eyes darkening with an unfathomable emotion. 'It is the only way you can avenge the death of Romerus and stop your father.'

She studied the path behind her and cursed under her breath before steering Buros into the chasm after Aäron.

The light dwindled the farther they advanced through the tight, rocky corridor. True darkness finally engulfed them after a third of a league.

Mila looked up. The sky had disappeared. In its stead was a vaulted ceiling of jagged rock. She gazed from the roof of the tunnel to Aäron's dim shape up ahead, her curiosity growing.

The air grew cooler the deeper they ventured inside the bones of the mountains, the corridor twisting and branching several times. Aäron headed confidently down what seemed like random passages, his pace never faltering. A while later, the sound of running water reached Mila's ears. It was followed by a faint luminosity that broke the all-encompassing gloom in front of them. They exited a tunnel and entered a space lit by a thousand stars.

Mila slowed Buros and stared. Glowworms clung to the glistening walls of the cave around them. On the far right, a stream merged into the underground lake filling the middle of the cavern, the trickle and splash echoing to the domed ceiling. Ripples danced across the dark surface, the water reflecting the eerie radiance from the worms a hundredfold until the lake resembled the very heavens at night.

'We had best hurry up,' Aäron called out. 'It will be dusk soon.'

Mila looked from the glittering worms to where he had

paused in the mouth of another tunnel and guided the stallion after him.

They crossed more passages and caves, some dark and empty, others bearing underground streams and pools and lined with eerie, luminescent moss and glowworms.

A league after they entered the belly of the mountains, muted daylight finally appeared at the end of a tunnel. With it came the roar of falls. Aäron exited the corridor and disappeared in a faint, white mist. Mila nudged Buros after him, eager to leave the oppressive darkness of the massifs behind. Dazzling brightness assaulted her eyes when she cleared the opening. She blinked and reined the stallion in.

Her breath caught in her throat when her vision finally adjusted to the light.

CHAPTER TWENTY

A VALLEY OPENED UP AHEAD OF THEM. OVER TEN TIMES THE width of the canyon that held Dur Untash, it spread over a rolling landscape of fields carved by a river and surrounded by sheer cliffs that curved to form a distant, rocky dome nearly a league high. Rising in the middle of the vast gorge, soaring towers bathing in beams of sunlight that arrowed down from an unseen sky, was a city.

Voices reached her above the din of the falls. 'My prince, you have returned!'

Mila tore her gaze from the astonishing sight before her and stared through the fine spray rising from the chutes tumbling down the bluff on either side of them. Three men approached on horseback from the left, soldiers dressed in colors she did not recognize. A guard tower stood on a rocky outcrop beyond a gurgling brook at their backs.

They slowed as they drew near, curiosity washing across their faces as they studied her. The one in the lead suddenly scowled.

'The Red Queen!' he hissed, and drew his sword.

'What?' said one of the other soldiers, alarmed.

'That woman is the Red Queen,' spat the first man. 'I recognize her from when I was a slave in Uryl.'

Mila straightened in her saddle, conscious of the weight of the sword at her waist.

Aäron maneuvered his steed in front of her. 'Stop!'

The soldiers drew their horses to a halt a few feet away, the animals snorting nervously when they detected their riders' agitation.

The man with the drawn blade hesitated. 'Prince Aäron, we have awaited your return for a long time. For you to come back with the enemy unfettered and carefree at your side is quite a shock.'

'It is not my intention to shock or cause distress, Kayan,' said Aäron steadily. He glanced at Mila. 'Events took a surprising turn two nights ago and I was forced to leave sooner than I had expected, with the princess as my companion.' He stared unblinkingly at the hostile soldier. 'I know of your past and your history with the capital of the Empire. I am aware that you have no love lost for those who reign over it. But you are no longer a slave, Kayan. You are a captain in my army. As such, I expect you to extend a civil welcome to my guest.'

The man clenched his jaw. For a moment, Mila thought he would ignore his commander's order. She blinked droplets of water from her eyes and assessed the immediate layout of the land, confirming two possible escape routes. She did not want to face an entire city on her own, not until she got answers to some burning questions.

The captain finally swallowed the words threatening to spill past his lips and nodded curtly. 'As you wish, my prince. It would be a privilege to escort you and your...guest to the palace.' He steered his horse around and looked to the soldiers at his side. 'Stay here and man the tower.'

They nodded wordlessly, their hot gazes following Mila as she headed after Aäron and the captain.

'This is going well,' she drawled.

Aäron frowned. 'I fear the worst is yet to come.'

Kayan glanced at them over his shoulder, a mirthless smile twisting his mouth for a moment.

Mila stared at the city they were headed for and wondered what other mysteries awaited her within its bounds. A defensive wall almost as tall as the one protecting Uryl ringed the crowded metropolis, its parapets dotted with guard towers that overlooked the river at its base. A bridge spanned the waterway and connected it to a settlement of flat-roofed buildings and tents on the opposite bank.

It was not until they drew near that Mila realized what she had taken to be a lower town was a vast encampment. A low murmur of activity greeted them as they approached the ragged boundaries. Among the voices of men, Mila was surprised to hear those of women and children.

'The city is packed to the rafters,' Aäron explained as they entered the main thoroughfare crossing the outpost. 'With so many joining our ranks, we had no choice but to set them up out here.'

Mila glanced at him before examining the busy scenes around them. She spotted several armed women bearing soldier's clothing and glimpsed laughing children darting through the cramped spaces between tents. Banners fluttered atop poles across the camp. They all depicted a red eagle with open wings on a golden field.

'How long has this place been here?'

'The camp? Five years.' Aäron studied the buildings looming on the other side of the river. 'As for the city, it has stood on this site for over a hundred years. The village that preceded it was over three times as old.' He looked up and smiled faintly. 'It was one of my ancestors who discovered this valley, many moons past. She nearly fell into it when she was but ten years of age, or so the story goes.'

Mila followed his gaze and saw a crescent of sky high above her, past the birds dancing in the rays of the fading sun.

'It was around the time that the Immortal kings conquered what was then Parsah,' Aäron continued, his voice growing melancholic. 'Some of our people fled the city during the battle and took refuge in this valley. There has been a second Parsah in these mountains since then. One that now wishes to rise against the very same kings who vanquished us.'

Mila looked at him thoughtfully. She was about to ask another question when a commotion to the left distracted her.

'It is *her*! It is the wife of that snake, the one from Issin!' a man shouted.

She saw something coming at her out the corner of her eye, whipped her dagger out, and stabbed it in mid-air. It was a rotten egg.

Fetid fluid oozed from it and dribbled down her hand. She cast the brown mess aside and felt something splash against her back. A foul stench filled the air.

'Stop!' said Aäron.

He turned and circled Mila protectively, a scowl darkening his face. Kayan slowed his steed and returned to their side reluctantly.

Mila drew her broadsword and studied the angry crowd gathering around them with narrowed eyes.

'I heard they killed their own people and burned down dozens of villages in the Empire! They are monsters, all of them!' yelled a woman.

Someone cast a stone. Mila batted it aside with the blunt

side of her blade. A second egg found her tunic. She fielded another rock with her forearm just as mud struck her right thigh and Buros's hide with a wet splat. The stallion snorted and stamped his hooves.

'*I order you to stop!*' Aäron roared. He drew his sword and rose on his saddle. 'By the gods, the next person who dares throw something will taste the sharp end of my blade!'

A hush came over the assembled mass. It was broken by shocked whispers as people finally registered Aäron's presence.

The sound of hooves striking stone reached Mila. She looked past a sullen Kayan to the group of soldiers galloping toward them from the direction of the city, the eagle banner flapping at their head. They crossed the bridge and entered the camp, the crowd parting to make way as they drew near.

The dark-haired man in the lead slowed and brought his horse to a standstill a few feet from their group. A smile split his face, warming his blue eyes. Riding in front of him was a young boy with a serious expression.

'Brother, you have returned,' said the man.

Aäron's face softened. 'Megash. It is good to see you.' He looked down. 'Gilga, you have grown.'

The boy acknowledged this with a solemn nod.

The man studied the hostile horde with a puzzled air. His gaze finally found Mila.

His smile faded. 'Son of a dog.'

The boy grinned.

CHAPTER TWENTY-ONE

Bastian stared out over the plaza, his hands fisted at his sides. Below, in the shadow of the kings' statues, the citizens of the capital paid tribute to the pyre upon which Romerus burned. Bar the shuffle of feet and the occasional sob, people were mostly silent, their figures painted crimson by the spitting flames. Out on the plains to the east rose the citadel of the dead father of the kings, walls red in the light of the dying sun, as if they too shed tears of blood at the dreadful scenes they had witnessed two nights past.

The shock and horror he had felt at Romerus's murder had slowly transformed into rage in the time since the terrible news reached his ears. Even now, he could barely comprehend his brother's reluctant admission as to the identity of the person who had taken their father's life.

Footsteps sounded behind him, distracting him from his dark thoughts. Baruch, his firstborn, appeared at his side.

'Is it true?' he said in a low voice.

Bastian looked at him leadenly. 'Of what do you speak, my son?'

'Have you and my uncle issued a death sentence for Mila?'

Fury surged through Bastian. 'Do not speak the name of that monster! Why, even her own father and mother have disowned her!'

Baruch stiffened.

'Do you really believe Mila killed Romerus?' he said after a short silence.

Unease darted through Bastian. He could not deny that the improbability of Mila being Romerus's murderer had passed through his mind the day before. Of all their children, she had been the closest to him.

He had heard of the unpleasant events in Issin that precipitated her sudden visit to Romerus's citadel late on the night of the murder. Why they would have led to her taking his life in cold blood was something no one could fathom, not even her own father, who had witnessed the end of the ghastly deed. It was Crovir's obvious distress when he told them what had happened that had convinced Bastian his niece was indeed the culprit behind the dire act.

There were also the witness accounts of the soldiers who had seen the bloodied knife in Mila's hand and watched her take the life of Crovir's latest concubine.

He met his son's stare head on. 'Yes, I do.'

Baruch's expression grew shuttered, causing a further burst of disquiet inside Bastian.

'Do you wish me to be part of the man hunt to bring her in?'

Bastian studied his son's face closely, searching for something he could not put a name to. 'No.' He turned and looked out over Uryl once more. 'We have dispatched an entire garrison after her and the captain who came to her aid that night. Helena and Sofia do not wish any of you to have to dirty your hands with the execution of your own kin.' In the lull that followed, he tried to read Baruch's unspoken thoughts. 'I am aware that you are close to Mila, as are all your brothers and sisters. But she needs to pay for her sins.'

A muscle jumped in Baruch's jawline. 'The one who murdered Romerus *will* be punished, on this we are all agreed.'

Bastian frowned as the meaning behind his son's words sank in. 'You do not believe Mila is the culprit?'

Before Baruch could reply, soft footfall rose from the direction of the citadel. Navia appeared, her face pale and her eyes red-rimmed. She slowed as she drew near, her gaze swinging from him to her brother.

She wavered for a moment before focusing on Baruch. 'Brother, may I have a word?'

Baruch glanced at Bastian. The latter dipped his chin and watched his first and lastborn head back inside the citadel, his mind a storm of thoughts. Chief among them was the startling realization that Baruch, the second general of their army, was not convinced Crovir had told them the truth.

MILA EXAMINED THE CEILING ABOVE HER AND COUNTED TEN roaches roaming the uneven rock surface. She locked her hands behind her head, closed her eyes, and did her best to settle on the thin straw pallet.

Bar the distant drip of water and the odd voice carrying from the lower levels of the palace, eerie silence filled the space around her. As prisons went, this was an oddly peaceful one.

She waited a while before releasing a sigh. 'Your mother must surely be looking for you, child.'

Someone sucked in air in the gloom beyond the metal bars at her back. 'How did you know I was here?'

Despite her anger at her current circumstances, Mila allowed a dry smile to curve her lips. 'I have keen ears.'

'Oh.' A lull followed. 'So it is true, then.'

'What is?'

'What people are saying about you. That you are a monster with ungodly powers who has come here to destroy us all.'

Mila opened her eyes and stared at the ceiling for a moment before sitting up.

She swung her legs over the edge of her prison bed and looked at the dim shape lurking in the shadows beyond her cell. 'Gilga, is it?'

'It is Gilgamesh, actually,' said the boy primly. 'Prince Gilgamesh. Only those close to me are allowed to call me Gilga.'

Mila acknowledged this with a solemn stare. 'I see that you are not afraid to speak with monsters then, Prince Gilgamesh. You are a very brave human indeed.'

The boy shrugged. 'Father and Uncle Aäron say that monsters only have real power when we allow them to fill us with fear. And grandfather says we should face them head on, with all of our strength and courage.'

Crovir's face flashed across Mila's inner vision. She looked down at her hands, the irony of the boy's words not lost on her.

'Your grandfather may be the wiser of the two of us,' she murmured.

Gilgamesh dipped his chin gravely. 'He is the king, after all.'

'That he is,' said Mila with a faint smile.

A companionable silence fell between them.

'Is it true they call you the Red Queen because your hands are soaked with the blood of more than a thousand men?' said the boy after a while, his eyes gleaming in the gloom.

Mila hesitated. Before she could muster an appropriate

reply, the glow of flames broke the darkness of the dungeon. Footsteps echoed against the rock walls as someone came down the passage. The shadows retreated.

Aäron appeared, figure outlined in a golden light and face lit starkly by the torch in his hand. There was a bundle of clothes under his arm.

He glanced at her before studying the boy. 'Your mother is looking for you.'

'I know,' the boy responded levelly. 'I heard her call my name.'

'In that case, you must have perceived the cries of your sister. Her wailing has deafened half the palace and threatens to bring the very dead back to life. Never have I seen an infant with such powerful lungs. Your mother would be grateful if you could see to her. You are the only one who can appease her when she is in this state, apparently.'

A chagrined expression washed across the boy's face. 'Ah. That is indeed true. Aaliyah can scream with the best of them.'

He stood unmoving, his gaze switching from his uncle to Mila.

Aäron cocked an eyebrow. 'Well?'

The boy blinked. 'Well what?'

'Are you leaving or not?' said Aäron, a trace of exasperation underscoring his voice.

'I will, but first, I want to hear what you have to say to the Red Queen.'

Aäron ran a hand through his hair, a distracted look darting across his face. 'I am afraid it is not a matter for your ears.'

'Oh.' The boy looked disappointed. His expression cleared after a moment. 'Is this like those times father and mother shut me out of their bedchamber, when they were busy making a baby sister for me?'

Leaden silence followed his words. Mila arched an eyebrow at Aäron.

He sighed. 'Remind me to have a word with your father when I see him next. Now go, before the other half of the palace loses their hearing.'

'As you wish, then.' The boy turned and gave Mila a gracious nod. 'I bid you farewell, Princess.'

She dipped her chin. 'Prince.'

They watched him disappear up the passage.

'He will make a fine man, one day,' murmured Mila.

'That he will,' said Aäron lightly. 'And you are being surprisingly civil, considering the situation.'

She rose and approached the metal bars separating them. 'Oh, do not mistake my courteous demeanor for surrender, my prince. The only thing stopping me from ripping this door off its hinges and killing you right now is vested interest. I would very much like to know the strength of your army and your plans for defeating the Immortals.'

Aäron sighed, dropped the flaming torch inside a metal basket next to him, and leaned against the opposite wall. 'You are angry.'

Mila narrowed her eyes at him. 'Would you not be, if you were in my place? You asked me to trust you and dragged me halfway across the Empire, only for your father to put me in chains and throw me in a dungeon like a common thief.'

'I do not recall carrying you bound hand and foot for all those leagues, Princess,' Aäron drawled. 'You came with me of your own free will. As for my father, he did not *actually* put you in chains. And no one in their right mind would ever confuse you for a common thief.'

'It is the same thing,' snapped Mila.

Events from the past day played out in her mind once more, rousing her irritation to new heights.

Dusk had been falling across the secret valley when they left the hostile camp outside Parsah and made their way across the bridge. Aäron's brother Megash and a group of some twenty soldiers had ridden with them, part escort, part sentry. As word spread of her and Aäron's arrival, people had gathered on the narrow, serpentine streets that wound through the metropolis and watched the procession make its way to the fortress at the top, their murmurs and stares following them all the way to a set of imposing metal gates standing in a tall, defensive wall. Beyond those stood a shallow forecourt overshadowed by a towering palace complex that rose several hundred feet tall, its distant roofs capped by turrets lost in wispy clouds.

Mila had had little time to admire the beautiful white stone and gleaming spires before them. A man with a shock of white hair extending to his shoulders had stormed out of the palace entrance and stopped at the top of a flight of narrow steps. On his head was a golden crown and in his right hand a bident, a two-pronged spear used as a farming pitchfork to break rock and hardened earth. The implement looked old, the wooden handle bleached with age. The man seemed to be using it as a walking staff.

Anger had filled his face as he stared down at them and he pointed the bident at Mila. 'Arrest her.'

Buros snorted agitatedly when soldiers surrounded them. Mila tightened her hold on the stallion's reins and murmured a soothing command.

She observed the white-haired man, who could only be Aäron's father, beyond a ring of spears. 'Do you know who I am?'

A look of contempt had flashed across the King's face. 'Of course I do.' He frowned at the man beside her. 'What were you thinking, to bring this creature here?' His eyes narrowed, his gaze swinging between them. 'Did you perhaps fall under her spell while you were on your mission?'

Aäron's face hardened at his words. 'Father, do not do this. The princess and I request a private audience with you. There is much we need to talk about, things that have happened in the past few days that will have implications for our plans.'

Tense silence had fallen across the courtyard as everyone waited with bated breath. It was broken by Buros huffing and stamping his hooves.

Mila patted the stallion's neck, her eyes focused on the furious man above them. 'You would do well to listen to your son, king of Parsah.'

The king scowled. 'I do not take orders from my enemies.'

His gaze switched to Aäron and he studied his son for a moment.

'I will grant you that audience,' he said gruffly. 'After all, I can do no less for the general of our army.'

Surprise had flared through Mila. She glanced at Aäron's stony profile.

'But I will not allow the Red Queen into my council chamber,' the king continued. 'Not until you give me a very good reason to do so.'

Aäron hesitated before twisting on his saddle to look at Mila. His face softened. 'Will you grant me some more of your time, Princess?'

Mila had ignored the shocked murmurs rising around them and met his gaze with a neutral stare. Behind her mask of indifference, anger and disappointment clashed with the usual coolheadedness that had won her many a battle. That Aäron had deceived her to such an extent irked and troubled her in equal measure. She was usually good at reading people. Yet, even then, as she stared into his eyes, she could not fathom his true thoughts.

'There is a time for war and a time for truce,' she said coldly. 'This is the last chance I will give you, prince of Parsah. You have fooled me long enough.'

A strange look had flashed across his face for an instant. As she dismounted and allowed herself to be led inside the palace, Mila had wondered what it was. She was still wondering, a quarter day later.

'One thing I am most curious about,' she said presently, observing him through the prison bars. 'What of the Parsah outside these mountains? Who governs it and sends tithes to the capital on behalf of the city?'

Aäron smiled. 'A cousin of my father. They look remarkably alike.'

Mila digested this before narrowing her eyes. 'So, what was the outcome of your audience with the king?'

Aäron rubbed the back of his neck. 'It took some time to convince him that recent events will ultimately play out to our advantage. Megash came around much faster, as I expected.' His expression turned uncomfortable. 'My father will speak with you in the council chamber.'

Mila's frown deepened. 'I sense a precondition coming.'

Aäron hesitated. 'If you win a contest.'

'What contest?'

Aäron sighed. 'I do not know the exact details but I suspect it will be a battle with some of our best fighters.'

She stared at him incredulously. 'Really? Your father has the chance to have me as an ally and he would rather risk losing my favor and the lives of some of his men in order to satisfy a whim than grant me an audience?'

Aäron looked discomfited.

Mila sighed. 'Since you are the general of the army, I take it you or your brother would be among the chosen fighters.'

Aäron shook his head. 'He did not ask either of us, which is strange.'

'You sound bitterly disappointed.'

He smiled at her acerbic tone. 'I have no wish to cross swords with you, Princess, and neither does my brother.' He paused, his face sobering. 'Not at the moment, anyway.'

Mila registered the unspoken threat in his words. 'And if I say no to this contest?'

Aäron's expression grew shuttered. 'Then I am afraid my father will never let you leave this place.'

Mila stared. No prison would ever hold her, not while she had breath left in her body. She could fight her way out of the hidden Parsah. Deep down inside, she sensed Aäron knew this, which explained his warning. He would protect his city if she attacked.

They gazed at each other in the silence that followed, he waiting for her answer, she trying to decide on the most strategic course of action.

'When and where is this contest to take place?'

CHAPTER TWENTY-TWO

The roar of the crowd was a solid wall of noise. It bounced against the stone walls and echoed into the distant sliver of pale blue sky high above.

So much for a battle ground with some dozen spectators, Mila thought.

They came for her at dawn, as Aäron had warned they would the previous night. But instead of being taken to the training ground inside the palace complex, where he had told her the contest would most likely be held, she was led outside the fortress and into the city, to a large arena overlooking the valley.

Seating galleries rose in tiers around her, above the twenty-foot-high enclosure that made up the perimeter of the fighting ground. They were packed with so many bodies Mila wondered whether the entire population of Parsah had come to witness the match. Then she heard the chants rising beyond the arena. There were more people outside.

She stood in the middle of the pit, bare-handed but for the battle clothes she had been wearing when she left Issin on that fateful night; they had been returned to her that morning, clean and stench free. Her gaze spanned the sea of faces before settling on the figures under the heavily-guarded canopy on a terrace at the head of the arena. She studied King Gishur and his entourage calmly.

Despite the look of irritation darkening his face, Aäron flashed her an encouraging smile. Next to Megash was a beautiful woman with long, brown hair braided into a plait. From her clothes and bearing, Mila deduced her to be the second prince's wife. She observed Mila with an inscrutable expression before leaning sideways and speaking to the boy beside her. Gilgamesh listened attentively to his mother, head half-cocked. He blinked when he met Mila's gaze and gave her a small wave. Surprise darted across his mother's face. She straightened and stared at Mila thoughtfully.

Aäron's father rose to his feet and approached the edge of the terrace. The din of the crowd abated as the citizens of Parsah looked to their king.

His voice boomed across the arena. 'To all of you gathered here today, I say welcome.'

His words were met with raucous applause and a vigorous stamping of feet.

He raised a hand until silence fell once more. 'You have all heard by now of the guest Prince Aäron brought with him upon his return to the city the past day. I, more than most, was surprised by the identity of the person who traveled with him from the heart of the Empire.' King Gishur glanced at his son. 'Many of you here have wondered at the sudden disappearance of the prince over a year ago. Only a handful among us knew where he had gone.' He paused and drew himself to his full height. 'For the past eighteen months, your prince and general has lived a double life inside the stronghold of our enemy, on a secret mission to gather the crucial information and supporters we will need for the future war against the Immortal tyrants who rule us.'

Shocked murmurs broke out among the gathered masses until a low rumble rose above the pit. For the first time that morning, Mila felt her pulse jump. She observed Aäron's contrite expression with narrowed eyes.

'Your general has seen and heard much while he was among our enemies and he has created further alliances with human cities to the north and west of the Empire. The connections he has made have already proven fruitful, with the arrival of more men and women willing to join our ranks in the past months. But, above all, what he has told me of the events of the last few months and days has given me hope that we can win the upcoming war and crush the army of the Immortals.' The king's expression grew cool as he gazed at Mila. 'For this to happen, he tells me that I should put my trust in the woman you see before you. That we should *all* put our trust in her. This, the strongest warrior among the Immortals. The one we all know as the Red Queen.'

Boos and angry shouts came from the crowd. Someone cast a stone into the pit. It landed a few feet from where Mila stood. The next one arced into the sky and sailed toward her head.

She caught it in mid-air, her movement so fast it brought gasps from all around. A hush fell upon the arena. The sound of the stone being crushed was unnaturally loud in the lull that followed.

Mila sifted the remains through her clenched fist, the fragments falling to the ground in a faint white cloud, her gaze still locked on the king's face. 'Your words try my patience, King. If you mean to talk, talk. If you mean to fight, fight. Let us end this farce before I break my promise to your son and destroy this city with my bare hands.'

Jeers echoed around the arena once more. King Gishur

frowned before glancing at a soldier standing on the terrace. Mila recognized Kayan, the captain who had once been a slave of the Empire. The latter raised his sword, a grim smirk hovering on his lips.

At his signal, one of the four metal grilles spanning the walls of the enclosure rose ponderously on Mila's left, exposing the dark mouth of a tunnel. A second one opened to her right, then a third dead ahead. She stretched out the kinks in her neck and loosened her limbs as she waited for the soldiers who had been chosen to fight her to come out into the arena.

Looks like this will be a bare-knuckle fight.

A sound came then, one that she had not expected. By the startled cries above her, neither had the crowd.

Something shifted in the shadows of the tunnel in front of her. Mila stared at the large, sinuous shape moving toward the light. Then, beautiful, limber, as deadly as a pit of scorpions, a lion walked out into the arena. Its golden gaze lazily swept the crowd before settling on her with the accuracy of a well-aimed arrow. At four feet tall and ten feet long, it was a monster of a beast, all muscle, claws, and teeth, its luxurious mane dark against its tan coat.

There was movement on either side of her. Mila broke eye contact with the fearsome creature some thirty feet away long enough to clock the second and third lions ambling out of the tunnels. The grilles dropped down after the animals, locking them inside the arena with her.

A buzz of anticipation built among the spectators, overlaying the initial shock and fear that had gripped them.

An angry voice rose above the drone. 'What is the meaning of this?'

It was Aäron, eyes dark as he stood on the terrace glaring at the king.

The latter studied him with an inscrutable expression before gazing at Mila once more. 'It is a contest. A battle of strength and skill. A way for the Red Queen to prove her worth to me.'

Surprise flashed through Mila. In the king's eyes, she finally registered the meaning behind the challenge he had issued.

A trace of admiration shot through her. *He is a clever man.*

'Yes, but in a fair fight!' barked Aäron. 'You never mentioned anything about these creatures yesterday! There is nothing honorable about this!'

'Aäron is right,' said Megash stonily.

The second prince had risen to his feet. Next to him, the woman with the plait held Gilgamesh's hand and spoke to the boy in urgent tones, her fingers curled in his hair as she tried to burrow his head in her chest. Gilgamesh resisted, his eyes locked on Mila and the three lions slowly circling the arena, their roars breaking through the excited voices from the gathered masses. She read fear in his eyes and pale face.

'Since when have our enemies ever been fair to us?' King Gishur said harshly. 'As for the lions, we have all heard tales of the pit in Uryl, where such beasts regularly feast on the flesh of the humans who dare defy the kings. Let us see how an Immortal fares under similar conditions!'

Mila scanned the enclosure. Several cracks in the stone wall caught her gaze. They would do for purchase if she needed to gain elevation. She studied the dust beneath her feet, dirt to most but a powerful weapon when it came to distracting an enemy.

'I demand that you stop this now, father,' growled Aäron. 'This has gone far enough.'

As she considered the three lions, Mila thought of her brother and cousins. Jared, who would have moved the creatures with his elemental powers and not allowed them within an inch of him. Navia, who would have frozen their bodies to the ground with her mind and had them cower in fear before her. Rafael, who would have healed his wounds as fast as they appeared while he battled the creatures with his staff weapon. She had none of their unearthly abilities.

'I am afraid it is too late for that. This contest must go ahead,' King Gishur responded.

A slight smile curved Mila's lips when she recalled her conversation with Jared on their way to Hazaara all those moons ago, during which he professed that her skills in battle were just as otherworldly as their gifts. She had never denied his words. For they were true. She possessed something more forceful and deadly than her brother and cousins' mysterious powers.

The soul of a perfect warrior. One who had yet to lose a single battle.

Although, I could do with a sword or two right about now.

'Then you leave me no choice,' said Aäron.

There was a commotion on the terrace. He ignored his father's shout, grabbed something, and hurled it inside the arena.

CHAPTER TWENTY-THREE

THE BIDENT THUDDED INTO THE DIRT SOME FIFTEEN FEET IN front of her, forked prongs driven an inch into the ground by the force of the throw, wooden handle drawing every gaze in the arena as it vibrated to a slow stop.

In the next moment, Gilgamesh sprang to his feet and snatched his father's dagger from the latter's waist before casting it toward Mila. The knife clattered on the ground and skittered to a stop some twenty feet to her left, metal blade glinting in the sunlight. He let out an excited shout and ignored his mother's shocked cry as she rose and took him in her arms.

Mila locked gazes with the first lion. Judging by its body language and the way it controlled the other two's movements, she was looking at the alpha. And just as she carefully assessed it, it also appraised her, the focused light in its eyes never dimming. It was a hunter's stare, one that was meant to scare and weaken prey.

Mila stared right back, stance straight and firm. She took a shallow breath and finally tapped into her hidden core, the side she rarely showed the world, the part that made her the most formidable warrior among all the Immortals.

From her heart it surged, the power that always lived beneath the surface of her skin, her own unearthly force. It sang through her veins, filling her body with strength so fierce her limbs became as hard as the stone that surrounded her. She fisted her hands and dug her heels in the earth beneath her feet, tasting its heat and reveling in its savagery, letting it fill her mind until all that was left was a single thought. To defeat the enemy, at all costs.

She bared her teeth in a feral smile.

AÄRON'S BREATH CAUGHT IN HIS THROAT. HE KNEW WITHOUT looking that everyone in the arena sensed the change in the woman standing in the pit. She stilled, an intense look of concentration dawning on her face as she stared at the lion who had circled back to a stop in front of her. Then it came, slow waves at first that were followed by a blast of such intensity it raised the hairs on his arms and the back of his neck.

Power. An energy so pure and raw it nearly rocked him back on his heels.

His ears popped, as if all the air had been sucked out from around him. Megash and the king gasped beside him, bodies driven back a step by the physical pressure. Down in the pit, the lions' paws slid in the dirt as they were pushed backward by the same invisible storm. All around the arena, people collapsed to their knees, lungs robbed of breath and faces pale.

Around the woman in the fighting ground, the air shimmered and vibrated with the ungodly force radiating from her body, suppressing all noise and creating a buzzing, oppressive silence that seemed to fill the entire city and the valley beyond. Movement around her feet caught his eyes. Heart drumming against his ribs, Aäron stared at the specks of dirt dancing on the ground.

The Red Queen smiled fiercely.

THE ALPHA HESITATED. THEN IT BLINKED AND TOOK A STEP toward her. Mila registered the slight drop of its haunches and saw muscles coil for the spring beneath its hide. Out of the corner of her eye, she saw the other two lions mimic the alpha's stance.

In the frozen moment that followed, she and the alpha glanced at the bident on the ground between them. Then they moved, woman toward beast and beast toward woman.

One.

The lion surged on its hind legs as it passed the two-pronged spear, maw open in a vicious snarl that revealed teeth half a foot in length, deadly claws exposed to stab flesh.

Two.

Mila jumped. Her leap took her high, the lion's paws skimming the air inches below her back as she somersaulted over its head.

Three.

She landed in a smooth slide that sent her hurtling on her side toward the bident just as the second lion charged across the arena.

Four.

She reached out, fingers closing around the staff as she went past, her momentum yanking the embedded prongs out of the ground while her other hand raked the dirt. The earth trembled behind her as the lion approached.

Five.

She rolled, snapped the handle of the bident as she sprang to her feet, and saw the swooping shadow to her right.

Six.

She cast the dust she had snatched into the lion's eyes, ducked beneath a powerful strike, and stabbed it in the neck with the jagged end of the handle.

Seven.

The beast roared, blood blooming past the stick embedded in its flesh as it batted at the grime clouding its vision. It spun and rose on its hind legs, front paws coming at her head to crush her skull.

Eight.

Mila dropped beneath the creature, felt its claws ruffle her hair, and drove the forked prongs into its chest.

Nine.

Ribs snapped and flesh tore as she pulled the bident out and stabbed the beast once more, puncturing its lung and heart.

Ten.

The lion sagged with a pitiful mewl as she jerked the weapon out of its body. She turned and bolted across the arena, gaze focused on her target, the beast hitting the dirt behind her with a dull thud.

Eleven.

The alpha and third lion closed in on her from opposite ends of the pit. She ignored them, dropped to the ground, rolled, and snatched the dagger Gilgamesh had thrown to her.

Twelve.

She was on her feet in a heartbeat, legs pounding the ground, the beasts' hot breaths warming the back of her calves. Cries rose from the crowd as she accelerated toward the stone enclosure.

Thirteen.

She leapt up against the wall, air leaving her lips in a harsh exhale, her speed bringing her halfway up in the blink of an eye. The lions bellowed and pulled up hard below her as she scaled the stone palisade.

Fourteen.

Hind legs skidding in the dirt, dust clouds rising around their bodies, they leapt and swiped at her with powerful paws. She veered left, out of their reach, and let the pull of the earth bring her down in a wide arc around the beasts.

Fifteen.

She pushed off the wall just before she started to fall and twisted through the air, landing hard on the ground twenty feet behind them. They whirled around and came at her, bloodlust filling their golden eyes and rage distorting their faces.

Sixteen.

Mila ran toward them, the dagger in her left hand, the pronged weapon in her right.

Seventeen.

She slipped between their bodies, raked the third lion across the face with the two-pronged spear, and slashed the alpha across the left flank with the blade, movements lightning fast, always a hairbreadth short of their teeth and claws.

Eighteen.

She raced through them and let her momentum carry her to the wall once more, never slowing as they turned and gave chase. The stone cracked beneath the power of her step when she pushed up against it. She lifted off and somersaulted in the air.

Nineteen.

The bewildered beasts went into a wild skid and rounded to face her when she touched down in a flawless landing behind them once more, feet sliding backward in the dirt.

Twenty.

The alpha roared and charged. Mila narrowed her eyes and dashed toward the beast.

Twenty-one.

She dropped to the ground just before it reached her, the bident and dagger carving deep trails in its belly as she slipped under its body and out the other side.

Twenty-two.

A loud bellow sounded at her back as she jumped to her feet and headed for the lion with the wounded face.

Twenty-three.

The animal blinked away the blood dripping into its eyes and reared up on its hind legs as she approached. Mila turned the dagger blade down against her forearm and blocked its first strike with the flat side of the metal.

Twenty-four.

She swooped beneath the second strike, pierced the pulsing life line in its neck with the bident, lunged low, and slashed the dagger across the second life line in its groin.

Twenty-five.

The beast stilled before dropping heavily on all fours. Blood gushed from its wounds. It staggered sideways and fell to the ground in an expanding crimson circle, rib cage heaving with shuddering breaths.

Twenty-six.

Mila turned and faced the alpha as it barreled toward her. Muscles coiled in the animal's powerful limbs, scarlet drops trailing from the wounds she had inflicted and staining the dirt in its passage, its golden gaze as heated as the sun.

Twenty-seven.

She stood her ground, grip tightening on the weapons in her hands, heels digging into the dirt.

Twenty-eight.

The crowd gasped as the lion sprung into the air with a bellow. Mila bent her knees and leapt, teeth bared, a snarl leaving her lips. Time slowed as they moved inexorably toward each other, the shadow of the beast engulfing her and blotting out the sky as she raised her weapons.

Twenty-nine.

The lion's paw struck her in the chest, robbing her of her breath. She thought she heard Aäron shout her name as she hit the ground hard. Then the beast was upon her, all claws and teeth and rage.

Thirty.

AÄRON'S FINGERS WHITENED ON THE PARAPET OF THE TERRACE, heart thrumming against his ribs, his gaze fixed unblinkingly on the bloodied pit and the giant, golden body of the alpha writhing in the dirt. It raised dust clouds as it moved, paws batting and jaws snapping at the invisible enemy beneath it. All around the arena, the crowd was on its feet, eyes wide with shock and bated expectation, breath frozen on parted lips.

Below them, the lion's movements suddenly slowed. Its head drooped. A moment later, it sagged to the ground, a red tide oozing from beneath its limp body. Then, it shifted slightly.

For an instant, Aäron thought the beast was about to stand again. Then he saw the figure pushing its way out from beneath it.

She rose to her feet, the dead beast at her back, blood dripping from the weapons in her hands and melting into the expanding pool around her feet. As she stood glaring at them from pale eyes, limbs locked in battle stance, clothes, skin, and hair stained crimson with the blood of the creatures she had so skillfully slain in thirty beats, body still vibrating with a powerful energy that resonated around the battle ground, Aäron finally understood.

In all the time he had known her, Mila had never shown him her true strength. Even when they had parried on the banks of the Tigra so many moons ago on their way to Hazaara, and more recently still on the training grounds of Issin, she had always held back. He felt strangely hurt by that fact, yet was utterly grateful at the same time. He was no match for her.

No one was.

He could see this reality dawn on the faces of everyone in the arena. If she so wished, the woman in the pit could walk out of the city right now and leave this valley. And all that would be left in her wake would be the bodies of the dead and utter destruction.

'The Red Queen,' Gilgamesh breathed in the stunned silence.

King Gishur smiled, his expression strangely triumphant.

Aäron ignored them and stared at the woman in the pit, something twisting inside his chest. Something that had nothing to do with fear and caused his heart to race even faster.

CHAPTER TWENTY-FOUR

Mila finished splashing water on her face and neck, and looked up to see King Gishur in the doorway of the chamber. They were still inside the arena.

She ignored the four soldiers who stood watching her guardedly from around the room and cocked an eyebrow at the king. 'That was quite a gamble.'

He smiled, crossed the floor toward her, and took a seat on a stone bench. He signaled to the soldiers. They hesitated before exiting the chamber.

'You saw through that, did you?'

'I would make a paltry lieutenant commander if I had not,' Mila said acerbically. 'Besides, you are several hundred years too young to fool me.'

She turned to the water barrel and cleaned the blood from her arms as best she could.

'But it worked. Although the commanders and captains of our army trust the judgment of my son and would eventually have come around to his way of thinking, my people needed to see you fight. So did the spies among them who will no doubt communicate the events of the day to the governors who have pledged their alliance to us.'

Faint, yet still audible through the thick stone walls that separated them from the open space of the arena, energetic chanting sounded from the crowd. They were shouting her name. Or, rather, they were shouting for the Red Queen.

King Gishur sighed. 'Do not give me that look. You and I both know that authority inevitably gives rise to envy and deceit. You and your kin must have seen plenty of that over the years of your existence. We need to be seen to be making decisions that our allies and our people understand.'

Mila studied him wordlessly as she scrubbed her hands clean.

The king's face hardened. 'As long as we all work together to achieve our common goal, that is all that matters. We can fight among ourselves afterward.' He frowned. 'The power of "The Red Queen" is now an undisputed image branded in the mind of every man, woman, and child out there. The people believe in your strength. When the time comes, they will fight by your side. Mark my words, tales of this contest will be retold for generations to come.'

Mila paused and narrowed her eyes. 'Whatever your motives, I do not appreciate being put on show.'

The king hesitated before rising to his feet.

He bowed. 'For that, I apologize.'

Mila masked her surprise behind a cool stare.

'Apology accepted,' she muttered.

The king broke eye contact and strolled around the chamber, fingers rising distractedly to touch the chainmail tunics and armor hanging on the walls. In that moment, Mila saw hints of Aäron in the older man. Amusement shot through her.

'I saw you once,' King Gishur finally said. 'At the battle of Kadavan. You hesitated before you felled the governor.'

Mila blinked. *Like the son, the father never ceases to amaze me.*

'It was the first time I suspected there was hope.' He met her eyes, his filled with the same light she had glimpsed in Aäron's gaze in the days they had spent together, a light that stirred unease inside her heart. 'Hope that the children of the Immortal kings who ruled us so cruelly were perhaps not as merciless as their fathers. Hope that one day, some of you would rise against them. That is why I sent my son to Uryl. But still, I did not trust you.'

Mila kept her face carefully blank. 'And you do now?'

'You could have resisted when I had you arrested. You could have escaped from the dungeon I had you locked in and fought your way out of this city. You could have killed all of us. But you did none of those things.'

'What makes you think I do not have ulterior motives? That I am not, right at this very moment, assessing the defenses of your palace and city? That I will not return with an army to defeat you?' Mila's hands fisted at her sides, an uncommon bout of frustration darting through her, her tone turning harsh. 'You would be wise not to trust your enemy so easily, human king, let alone an Immortal like me. Like your grandson said, we are monsters who would slaughter you as soon as look at you.'

A sad smile curved King Gishur's lips as he watched her. 'Crovir killed Romerus, his own father, his flesh and blood, and, from what Aäron has told me, the man you loved most in the world. He has framed you for the murder and made you a fugitive of the very Empire you presided over with your siblings and cousins for hundreds of years. He has driven you to abandon your family and children, and has no doubt spread lies about your ill intentions to further widen the rift between you and your kin.' He paused. 'You and I both know that he will have no choice but to issue a sentence for your arrest and execution before the next Full Moon.'

It took all of her will to clamp down on the rage and sorrow that surged through her veins at his words. She took a shuddering breath and composed her features into a cold mask once more.

'There is one last thing. One more reason why I choose to put my trust in you, Immortal child,' King Gishur added softly.

Mila lifted her chin challengingly. 'And what is that?'

'My son believes in you.'

AÄRON HESITATED BEFORE RAPPING HIS KNUCKLES GENTLY ON the door. The hour was late and silence filled the corridors of the palace. He wiped his moist palms on his tunic as he waited in the half-gloom, a burst of unusual nervousness causing his stomach muscles to clench.

'Come in,' someone called out from the other side.

Aäron opened the door and crossed the threshold, only to come face to face with the last woman he expected to see.

He scowled. '*Nisuna!* What are you doing here?'

His sister-in-law, wife of his brother Megash and mother of Gilgamesh, arched an elegant eyebrow from where she perched on the edge of the bed dominating the guest chamber.

'Why, good night to you too, brother,' she said in a saccharine voice.

Aäron's gaze skimmed the billowing curtains on the balcony, the fire in the hearth, and the oil lamps casting a warm glow on the pale stone walls, before landing on the open doorway of the bathing quarters to the far left.

'Is she in there?'

'Indeed she is, brother,' said Nisuna with a knowing grin. 'The Red Queen felt in need of another bath after that ungodly fight, so I asked my attendants to see to her.' She paused, her expression turning innocent. 'What are you doing here, brother?'

'I need to talk to her,' said Aäron, unable to mask the defensive note that crept into his voice.

'Oh my.' Nisuna's grin turned sly. 'Even though you spent all that time together at the feast we held in her honor tonight?'

'May I remind you that Megash and the king were also involved in those conversations?' said Aäron coolly.

Before Nisuna could utter a riposte, a clamor rose from the direction of the bathing quarters.

'Princess! Red Qu—! *My dear*, you cannot very well go out like that! Let us tend to you, I beg of you. Princess Nisuna will be most upset if she sees you in this state!'

A middle-aged woman walked backward out of the passage and into the main bedchamber, a large bath cloth in her hands and a pleading expression on her face. She was followed by three other maids, all looking similarly flushed and distressed.

'No, thank you, you have done enough.' Mila's cold voice echoed against the marble floor and walls of the corridor as she drew near. 'I have no wish to be pampered and sprayed with rose water from head to toe like a bride on her wedding night. All I asked for was hot water and bathing salts. And the princess is a woman. It is not as if she has never before set eyes on the female form.'

The Red Queen stormed out into the room naked, dark hair wet and skin slick with gleaming droplets, as beautiful as sin and smelling like the heavens. Aäron's breath froze on his lips.

Mila stopped when she saw him and Nisuna. She placed

her hands on her hips and glared at them. The servants gasped as they registered Aäron's presence.

Nisuna gaped, grabbed Aäron by the arm, and wheeled him around with her until they both faced the door.

'Princess, you have a guest!' she squeaked.

'I can see that,' came the icy remark from behind them.

Out the corner of his eye, Aäron saw Nisuna look over her shoulder.

Redness stained her cheeks when she turned forward once more. 'Hmm, would you mind getting dressed?'

'Why? Is my nakedness bothering you?'

Despite the rapid drumming of his heart, Aäron could not help the chuckle that escaped his throat. He could just imagine the Red Queen's pose. She had likely crossed her arms and would be staring at them with a sullen expression. Nisuna glanced at him, startled.

'Does my question amuse you, Prince?' said Mila.

Aäron hesitated. He took a shallow breath and turned to face her, his gaze focused above her neckline.

'You possess the ability to distract anyone with a pulse, Princess, be it man or woman. You have an extremely alluring figure and face.'

She arched an eyebrow. 'Only alluring?'

He looked down then, his gaze deliberately raking every naked inch of her from head to toe. From her pale eyes to her high cheekbones, from her full lips to her slim neck, from the swell of her breasts to her narrow waist, from the flare of her hips to her long, lithe, tanned limbs, she was the most perfect thing he had ever seen in his life. With his body reacting in ways that could only mean trouble, it took all of his effort to maintain a dispassionate expression.

'You are pretty easy on the eye,' he admitted calmly.

Mila's lips twitched. She walked over to the elderly maid,

took the bath cloth from her limp grasp, and wrapped it around her body, tucking the end in the valley between her breasts.

'There, does this soothe your fragile sensibilities?'

Aäron heard Nisuna and the maids exhale.

'Apparently so,' he murmured.

They stared at each other across the room, neither blinking nor lowering their gazes.

'Come, let us leave the prince and princess,' Nisuna said breezily, breaking the charged silence. 'They have much to talk about, I am sure.'

She herded her attendants out of the chamber and paused on the threshold. For the first time since he entered the room, Aäron saw genuine concern flash across her face. Despite their banter, he considered her his sister and knew she cared for him as fiercely as she did her own son. He dipped his chin imperceptibly. Nisuna responded with a small smile, her unease still evident.

The sound of the door closing behind her was deafening.

CHAPTER TWENTY-FIVE

MILA OBSERVED THE MAN STANDING ACROSS THE ROOM FROM her, skin hot from where his gaze had lingered on her body, heart drumming erratically against her breastbone.

Following the contest in the arena and King Gishur's confession in the armory, she had been welcomed as a guest in the palace and had spent the day learning the details of how the extensive human army now under the control of the ruler of Parsah had come to be. It was a fascinating tale to hear and one that unknowingly earned the king and his predecessors her grudging respect. For them to have achieved all of this under the eyes of the Empire spoke of shrewdness and fortitude worthy of the Immortals themselves.

But what fascinated her the most, and unsettled her in equal measure, was the shocking realization that, in all that time, no human spy had ever sold out this information to the Empire. She knew well the greed and treachery that dwelled in the heart of man. After all, she had used it to her advantage over the years, as had her kin. Her observations could only lead her to one irrefutable conclusion. The coming war, if indeed there was one, was very much going to be about humanity against the Immortals. Deep down inside, she was not sure how she felt about that.

It was as they parted at the end of the feast held in her honor that King Gishur had finally asked the question likely on the mind of every commander and captain seated in the banquet hall with them. 'What is your answer, Red Queen?'

Mila had paused, conscious of the stares from around the room. 'I have still to reach a decision.'

Murmurs and frowns had broken out across the chamber.

The king had watched her steadily, his expression enigmatic. 'Do you know when that is likely to happen?'

Mila's gaze found Aäron. He studied her just as inscrutably as his father.

'I have been the lieutenant commander of the army of the Empire for over four hundred years.' Silence fell as her voice echoed against the marble pillars and high ceiling of the banquet hall. 'The habits and duties of such a long life cannot be overturned in a single night.'

'So you have made your choice?' someone had called out from the floor.

Mila had scanned the sea of faces with a frown. 'I am an Immortal. Although the sins of my father can never be excused, I am not so willing to go against the rest of my kin or help you do so.' She paused and stared at King Gishur. 'All I ask is that you grant me more time. Are you willing to do that, King?'

An expectant silence had fallen over the banquet hall as everyone waited for the King's answer.

'Yes.'

She turned and exited the chamber, aware that the king's patience and that of his allies would only stretch so far. As evening melted into night, the nervous tension thrumming through her veins since the morning had grown until it filled her entire being.

More often than not, Kronos would come to her after the climax of a battle and they would mate with violent passion until they burned out the heated energy that followed a victorious campaign.

Yet, this fire in her body and mind was different. Mila felt as if she were standing on the brink of an abyss that filled the horizon from edge to edge, staring into a darkness so profound she could see no end to it, and no path to navigate it.

In the marrow of her soul, she had always suspected she might one day reach this point. More than Romerus's murder, more than her father's brutal acts over the years and his cruel determination to bend her to his will, she had always felt unease. Unease about the mysterious powers that were granted to Romerus's two sons so many years ago. Unease about what it meant to be an Immortal.

Although she had been loyal to the kings' wishes all of her life and helped them build their empire, it was as she stood staring out over the dark valley from the palace of the hidden Parsah that she finally acknowledged her doubts about the wisdom of their actions. For she could not help but feel that they, the ones who had inherited these unworldly gifts, the Immortals, were meant for more. More than absolute power over humans. More than dominion over the lands of this world.

But what that purpose was continued to elude her, as did the answer to the difficult choice she now faced. Days after the events that had precipitated her flight from the heart of the Empire, she was still mired in the shadows of her whirling thoughts.

She had decided a bath would be a good chance to clear her mind. Instead, she now found herself face to face with her second conundrum, one that continued to confound her just as much as the question the king had asked her earlier.

'Why are you here?'

Aäron blinked at her harsh tone. His gaze grew shuttered, but not before she saw a flash of the same emotion she had seen the day before, when King Gishur had had her arrested upon their arrival on the palace grounds. Guilt stabbed through her as she finally recognized it for what it was. Hurt.

'I want to talk.'

Mila found her gaze dropping to his lips as he spoke. 'We have done plenty of talking for one night, do you not think?'

She walked over to the bed, grabbed one of the bath cloths the maids had left, and started drying her hair briskly in front of the fire.

She heard his slow steps and straightened. Though the flames before her warmed her exposed skin, his presence when he stopped behind her scorched her even more.

A familiar heat seeped through her, one that sent a shiver down her spine. 'What do you want, Prince?'

Shock darted through her at the sound of her own voice, causing her to stiffen. It had been low, throaty, a tone she did not recognize.

She frowned, allowing surprise to turn to irritation. 'Are you here to fool me once more with your lies? To deceive and manipulate me into doing what you want me to do?'

Taut silence filled the space between them.

'It was never my intention to deceive you.'

Mila twisted on her heels, hand rising toward his face, her temper finally snapping under the storm of emotions that had been raging through her since the morning. No, longer still. Since she witnessed Romerus's murder.

Aäron's hand snaked out and grabbed her wrist before she could make contact.

'Stop,' he said, his voice hard.

Mila's breath stuttered. More than the strength in his grip, the feel of his fingers against her skin stunned her. It was the first time he had properly held her. She felt branded, forever marked by his touch, as if she would never be able to wash away the sensation of this connection.

She reacted the only way she knew how, her other hand rising to meet his face. He stopped her once more, his movement lightning fast, his fingers closing roughly on her wrist, setting her skin ablaze once more.

The motion brought them closer, their bodies almost touching as they stood facing each other.

Mila was afraid. Afraid to raise her head and meet his gaze. Afraid of what she would see. Yet, she tilted her chin. And felt air leave her lungs in a harsh gasp.

His eyes had turned the color of the storm-swept sea, pupils wide and dark, the desire burning inside them so fierce it almost blinded her. 'God, you are beautiful.'

Her pulse jumped, weakness flooding her limbs for the first time in her Immortal life, her body betraying her utterly as it fell under the spell of the man who held her. His pupils dilated further when he registered the change under his fingertips. He lowered his head.

'No,' Mila whispered when his lips were but a breath away from hers. 'Stop. We cannot.'

Aäron hesitated. He straightened and slowly released her arms.

Bitterness underscored his voice when he spoke. 'Kronos?'

Mila whirled around, fingers shaking as she gripped the cloth covering her thighs and gazed blindly into the flames.

His tone turned leaden, devoid of the passion that had burned in it but a moment past. 'Do you love him still?'

Mila swallowed. 'He is the father of my children.'

Above the buzz of blood singing in her ears, she heard his breath catch in his throat.

'But do you love him?' A sliver of hope colored his voice. 'Does he possess your heart, Princess?'

Mila's eyes widened, his questions piercing her as thoroughly as a blade.

Though she wanted to lie, to dismiss his question, she could not help the words that spilled past her trembling lips. 'No, he does not.'

Aäron moved then, his hand landing gently on her shoulder.

Mila shuddered as he turned her around.

'Can I?' His tone turned husky. 'Can I possess your heart, my queen?'

It took all her will to look up into his eyes and finally acknowledge what she had denied for so long. She wanted this man. She wanted him, just as badly as he so clearly wanted her. But more than passion, more than the intense physical longing surging through her veins, Mila felt a hunger like none she had ever known before. A hunger that could not be explained. The hunger to possess him. To bewitch and enthrall him just as he had bewitched and enthralled her. To bind him to her and make him hers in every sacred and sinful sense of the word.

She rose on the tips of her toes and answered him the only way she could, with her lips. He froze for a moment, his eyes widening above her. Then he responded with a fervor that seared her senses and stole her breath, his eyelids fluttering closed, his tongue meeting hers in a savage dance that made her legs tremble and caused her to collapse against him.

He caught her and lifted her in his arms, corded muscles bunching beneath her as he strode to the bed, his mouth still ravaging hers. She gasped when he dropped her on the mattress and tore the bath cloth from her body, exposing her to his heated gaze.

She rose up on her elbows and watched him just as hotly as he stripped, his armor and chainmail tunic thudding heavily to the floor, the only other sound in the room but for the crackling flames and their labored breathing. Impatient for his touch, she climbed to her knees and grabbed his head, a sultry moan leaving her lips as she lowered his mouth forcefully to hers again. He finished undressing and joined her on the bed, his arms closing around her as he pushed her down and covered her with his powerful frame, a low sound tearing from him when naked skin finally met naked skin, his breath melding into hers until she did not know where hers began and his ended.

As the night wore on, as Aäron's lips, fingers and tongue scorched and branded every bare inch of her, wrenching cries of pleasure from her throat, as she returned his ardor with equal passion and made him tremble and groan above and beneath her, Mila lost herself to the man who had forced his way into her life and shattered the impenetrable fortress around her heart. This was nothing like the desire she once felt for Kronos. It did not even compare.

It was not until daylight touched the land and the warm rays of the sun filtered through the curtains and kissed their skin that they finally collapsed in a tangled mess of sweaty limbs and damp sheets. As Mila lay atop him, her body weak and her mind numb, the most sated she had ever felt in her long life, Aäron stroked a lock of hair from her cheek, lifted his lips to her ear, and whispered the words that she dared not utter.

PART III
WAR

CHAPTER TWENTY-SIX

Mila laid her hands flat on the table and narrowed her eyes at the man at the head of the room. 'If we do this, we do it my way.'

It was midday and the palace's council chamber was packed. Spread across the surface of the oak table dominating the floor was a large map of the Empire.

King Gishur observed her steadily from where he sat. 'I am listening.'

'First, let me make one thing clear.' Her voice grew cool. 'I have but one aim in mind. To stop Crovir. At all costs. I will destroy anyone and anything that stands in my way.'

Megash frowned. 'Does that include the other Immortals?'

Mila hesitated, conscious of Aäron's gaze on her face. Though he stood four feet to her right, he might as well have been touching her, so strong was the connection she now felt to him. She straightened, her stance causing a faint smile to curve his lips, and spoke the words she had already said to him that morning, while they lay in each other's arms.

'I need time. To set up a meeting with my kin. To talk to them about all that has happened.'

One of the commanders snorted. 'Are you trying to trick us?'

Another glared at her as a drone of discontented murmurs rose around them.

He turned to the king. 'She no doubt seeks to return to the Empire and bring the war to us! Do you not see that she aims to betray us?'

King Gishur gave the men a cool stare before meeting Mila's gaze once more. 'I see no such thing. If the Red Queen had wished to cross us, we would all be dead by now.'

'I agree,' said Aäron. He looked around the room. 'I have lived among our enemy for a long time and I can tell you this with confidence. Not all the Immortals are our foe. I have witnessed their acts of kindness and their willingness to forgive.' He stared at Mila. 'Indeed, I am willing to bet that some will choose to stand by our side in the war to come.'

Warmth flooded Mila's chest as she gazed at him. The fact that he believed her filled her with fresh conviction; the decision she had come to that morning was the correct one, and the path she had chosen to follow would lead her and her kin through the darkness ahead and out the other side.

A change came over the room as the commanders and captains glanced at each other. In that moment, Mila glimpsed how highly they held Aäron in their esteem and how great a king the man she had begun to know could one day be.

'What do you propose we do, Red Queen?' said Megash.

THEY LEFT THE CITY AT DAWN THREE DAYS LATER, A TROOP OVER a hundred men in strength at their side.

Instead of the tortuous path Aäron had used to bring her to the hidden Parsah, they took another secret route out of the valley and through the mountains, one that brought them onto the plains bordering the Zayande River.

From there, they split, the larger contingent heading for the Zagros Mountains while messengers disguised as the Empire's soldiers started on the long journeys that would take them to the leaders of the human alliance spread throughout the kingdom, to the cities of the West Sea and the Nahal River, to the Indus Valley to the east, and all the way north, to the Toros Mountains and the Land of the Hatti, then up to the Caucasia Mountains and the Arals.

As she rode at the head of the company with Aäron at her side, Mila felt filled with purpose for the first time in over a hundred years. Now, more than ever, she was confident she had made the right choice by electing to stand at the side of King Gishur and the human army. All that remained to be seen was whether the plans they had made in the council chamber would come to fruition.

'I still think they look strange!' said Aäron as their horses pounded the foothills of the ice-capped mountains ahead.

'What do?'

'Your new weapons!'

Mila glanced at the fresh blades kissing the skin of her outer thighs. They felt cool now compared to their original state last evening, when she finished forging their shapes.

The idea for them had come to her the morning when she stood in the arena, soaked in the blood of the beasts King Gishur had challenged her with. As the crowd unfroze and started to chant her name, Mila had looked from the dead lions to the crimson bident and dagger in her hands. A flash of intuition had bolted through her and she had seen the design of an entirely different kind of pronged weapon in her mind.

'You want to use a furnace?' King Gishur had asked at the end of the first day she spent in the council chamber.

'Yes.' Mila had ignored his arched eyebrow and puzzled expression. 'And I want to take a closer look at your bident.'

A mournful look had come over the king. 'Ah, yes. The bident.' He sighed. 'That had been in our family for generations, ever since our ancestors tilled the land where the first Parsah was born.'

An uncommon pang of remorse had stabbed through Mila. 'Will you lend it to me?'

The king had hesitated before dipping his chin. 'Why not? I am curious to see what you will make of it.'

And so they had watched as she worked at a smelter's furnace outside the palace armory for the next two days. Most of the time, it was Gilgamesh who had kept her company, his curious eyes observing her every move as she molded, dipped, and hammered at the red, glowing metal. The king and Megash had come by on the odd occasion, after they had finished putting together the finer details of the plans they had made in the mornings.

On the second day, Nisuna visited with her daughter. Soon after they arrived, the baby started bawling. After tolerating several excruciatingly painful moments of the child's shrieks, Mila put down the hammer and tongs she was using, strode across to where Nisuna was trying to comfort her, and took her from her shocked mother's arms.

She stared at the wriggling, warm bundle she held at arm's length. 'Stop that infernal noise.'

The baby's face screwed up further, her wails reaching a pitch that threatened to shatter the very heavens.

Mila winced, then scowled. 'This is your second and final warning.'

The baby paused and hiccuped. Her face slowly cleared.

She gazed solemnly at Mila from limpid blue eyes. Then, she giggled.

Mila blinked, nonplussed. She became aware of a muffled snort to her left and looked around to see Nisuna with her hand over her mouth, stifling her laughter, tears streaming down her face. Next to her, Gilgamesh stood gaping, eyes filled with wonderment and adoration, clearly impressed that someone other than he had tamed his sister.

'Your daughter has no sense of danger,' Mila muttered to Nisuna.

She plunked the baby back in her mother's arms and had turned to walk away when something gripped her. She looked down and saw the baby's chubby hand clutching her tunic. As she stared into the infant's smiling eyes, Mila thought of her own children. Sorrow surged through her. She had not spent much time with them when they were of this age.

In a daze, Mila raised a hand and stroked the baby's soft cheek with a gentle finger. The infant cooed and blew a bubble.

Footsteps rose up ahead, distracting her. She looked up and saw Aäron drawing near. She had not seen a lot of him after their mornings in the council chamber. As the general of the extended army, he had had much to do.

The tired expression on his face melted away when he saw her, only to be replaced by one that twisted through her heart and stole her breath. Though it lasted the briefest of moments, Mila registered the intense longing that flared in his eyes when he looked at her and the baby.

An ache started deep inside her, one that she knew he would assuage that evening, as he had the past two, repeating the frighteningly intense passion of their first night. Though she knew every inch of his body, every scar, every spot that brought him pleasure, she craved more still, as did he. They had barely slept these last days, too drunk and lost in each other to care for rest.

Out of the corner of her eye, Mila saw Nisuna stare between the two of them.

Aäron slowed to a stop at their side, face composed once more. 'Are they almost ready? We leave tomorrow.'

Mila swallowed and nodded. 'Yes, they will be done soon.'

It was a while later that she finally laid down the implements she had been using. As dusk fell across the city and the valley beyond, Mila raised the two weapons she had forged, testing their weight in her hands. The fading light caught the edges of the short, twin, three-pronged spears. Longer than a dagger and shorter than a sword, they were slender and fitted her grip perfectly.

She spun them in her hands, the blades moving lightning fast as she experimented with their hold, at times resting one against her forearm while she thrust out with the other.

A slow clapping sounded behind her. She turned to see Megash join Gilgamesh and Aäron, Nisuna having taken her daughter away to feed her.

'Those look deadly,' said Megash with a grin. 'What are they though?'

Mila had stared from him to the weapons in her hands. 'The notion came to me three days ago, in the arena, when your brother threw the bident to me and your son your dagger. They are a combination of the two.'

Megash arched an eyebrow. 'So, another type of bident?'

'A trident,' said Aäron.

They turned to him. He shrugged. 'Well, it is a three-pronged spear.'

Mila had mulled over the new name. 'Trident. Yes, I like that. Trident daggers.'

She cast the weapons high up in the air. They spun, glinting as they were kissed by the last rays of the sun, before falling toward the ground, blades humming.

Gilgamesh gasped when Mila caught them, the short handles settling into her palms as if they belonged. She flashed a grin at him. He grinned back.

'Was that envy I heard in your voice, Prince?' Mila said presently as they rode into the Zagros Mountains, her lips curving in an amused smile.

Aäron's eyes widened at her teasing tone, his steed dropping slightly behind Buros for a moment.

'No, it was not,' he said with a grunt. 'I would likely stab myself in the gut if I were to use one of those.'

Mila laughed, the sound carrying across the vale as clear as a bell. Some of the soldiers stared, open-mouthed. Aäron's face softened.

They reached Dur Untash at sundown and conferred with Governor Edras and Darius in the hidden palace inside the mountain long into the evening. Though they retired to separate bedchambers, Aäron came to hers as he had done the past nights. As they lay in each other's arms, hearts racing, their labored breathing filling the flame-lit room, Mila lifted her head and ran her fingers gently down his face, lingering on his eyes and cheeks and lips.

'What is it?' he murmured, his breath warming her skin.

Mila hesitated, feeling strangely vulnerable. She swallowed before lowering her face to his chest.

As she listened to the strong beat of his heart, she whispered her confession. 'I have never known this before. This…peace.'

Aäron was quiet for the longest time.

'You do not know how deliriously happy that makes me,' he finally said, his voice husky.

He pulled her up until she lay full length on his body and cradled her head in his hands for a long, deep kiss.

'Can you tell, my queen?' he breathed against her lips, his eyes glinting below her.

Mila placed her hands on his chest and felt his heartbeat pick up.

She wriggled her hips and grinned when he groaned and cursed. 'Well, the lower part of you is.'

He twisted, flipping her onto her back, pressing her into the bed with the weight of his body. Then he brought his mouth to her ear and whispered every sinful thing he wanted to do to her, before proceeding to do them, teasing her mercilessly with his lips and tongue as she arched helplessly beneath him, his hands pinning her wrists above her head, his breath scorching her skin as she sought the cradle of his hips with her own. When he finally melded his body with hers, wrenching a sob from her throat, their sensuous dance cast sinuous shadows across the walls of the room long into the night.

Mila thought she would never tire of this. This perfect bliss. This heavenly joy she had never before experienced.

Dawn came too soon and they parted ways briefly before meeting again outside the palace, where the extended troop waited for them, now some two-hundred strong, with soldiers stationed in Dur Untash joining their ranks for their upcoming mission.

'May the Sun and the Moon guide your path and see you safely to your destination,' said Darius as he watched them leave. Like the men around them, his face was filled with a burning light, galvanized by the prospect of finally seeing all their years of planning come to fruition. 'I shall see you both in sixteen days, at the meeting point.'

Mila dipped her chin before wheeling Buros around, Aäron at her side.

CHAPTER TWENTY-SEVEN

The call came from the east, once, then twice, a nighthawk's shrill cry swiftly lost in the cool breeze coursing across the waters of the lake.

A thrill shot through Mila.

She glanced at the soldier next to her. 'Remember. If we have to engage them, we should aim to wound, not to kill.'

Kayan hesitated, then nodded. As they travelled north across the plateau east of the Zagros, the captain had started to thaw toward her. Though she still sensed his inherent mistrust, his respect for Aäron, the one who had freed him from slavery and who was now his general, overshadowed whatever ill feelings he held against her.

That realization only served to support Mila's growing certainty that the man she had so recently become intimate with would play a crucial role in the war to come.

They moved silently up the hard-packed earth, toward the fortress crowning the hill of the largest island on Lake Kadavan, faces and limbs covered with mud to mask their skin, weapons shrouded with cloth lest the moon and stars revealed the glint of metal.

'Kadavan?'

King Gishur's startled expression had been mirrored by those of the men in the council chamber eight days past, on the morning she first told them her plans.

'That city is long dead.' A frown had furrowed his brow. 'After the destruction you and your kin rained upon it, the only things fit to survive in its ruins are snakes and scorpions.'

Mila leaned over the table. 'The city may be dead.' Her finger moved across the map. 'But the lake next to it is not.'

As puzzled murmurs resonated around the room, understanding had dawned in Aäron's eyes.

A hint of admiration laced his voice. 'So the rumors are untrue?'

'What rumors?' said a captain.

'That the souls of the dead walk in Kadavan.' Aäron glanced around the chamber. 'There have been scattered reports over the years, after the city fell at the hands of the Empire, stories of a place of ill omen. Travelers speak of strange lights in the sky and ghostly shrieks that would unnerve the bravest of men.'

Mila straightened as she became the object of dozens of penetrating stares.

'What is on Lake Kadavan, Princess?' Megash had asked.

A grin curved her lips. 'The biggest secret of the Empire. And it is not just on the lake, but beneath it as well. A prison holding some thousand men, among them governors of cities we have conquered and the fighters still loyal to them.'

Gasps had sounded around her.

King Gishur rose from his seat, his face pale beneath his crown. 'What—how?!'

Mila shrugged. 'We are good at keeping things hidden.'

She felt Aäron's eyes on her and turned to meet his gaze.

An excited smile hovered on his lips, mirroring the hot glint in the blue depths. 'Something tells me the Empire has not spared those men out of good will.'

Mila dipped her chin, an equally charged thrill running through her. 'You are correct. However callous my father is, he is not one to waste valuable resources.' She tapped the drawing of the lake on the map. 'Inside the fortress is one of the Empire's largest arsenals. Scores of armor and weapons, all forged by those very same prisoners.' She saw realization wash across the faces of the men watching her. 'If we take Kadavan, not only can we gain a significant addition to our forces in the form of the inmates and the governors who still hold sway over them, we also secure more arms for our men.'

'Son of a dog,' Megash had muttered in the stunned silence.

It had taken them four days to travel to the ruined city of Kadavan from Dur Untash, both Mila and Aäron setting a brisk pace that the soldiers eagerly followed. As their mounts ate up the leagues separating them from their destination, Mila was reminded of the time she rode to Hazaara with Jared and Aäron, at the behest of Crovir. Except on this occasion, hope and fire filled her heart as opposed to unease and rage.

They had passed the dead city and reached the mountains circling the lake shortly after nightfall. After taking a short rest and securing the horses in a gully, they had made their way stealthily to the shore. It had taken but moments to capture the small group of soldiers manning the guard towers dotted around the lake and a pier which held a dozen boats and barges. Instead of taking the vessels, they had used driftwood and felled logs stacked in the shallows next to the dock, timber destined for the fires of the fortress, to help carry them across the water.

Once on the main island, they had separated, Mila taking

half the men to the south while Aäron went east with the rest of the soldiers. They would be attacking on two fronts.

At the sound of the fake nighthawk's call, the cue that Aäron was in position, Mila and her troop scaled the slope of the hill until they reached the base of the forty-foot wall enclosing the fortress. From there, they spread along the palisade to the strategic positions she had predetermined, away from the light cast by the fires atop the ramparts.

Then, they waited.

At midnight, a shuffle of steps sounded high above as a soldier climbed a guard tower. Outlined against the dark sky, he leaned across the guard rail on the rooftop and waved a flaming torch. Mila looked over her shoulder. From the shoreline to the south came a corresponding light tracing a golden arc in the gloom. Then, lights came from the east and west. Though she could not see it, she knew there would be one from the northern shore as well.

As per her instructions, the soldiers she and Aäron had left behind to watch over the guard towers they had secured on the edge of the lake were responding to the main fortress's signal, one issued four times a day to check there was no sign of any imminent danger to the prison.

At the evidence of the all clear, the call of a horn sounded from above and echoed across the fort. The soldiers inside were about to proceed to a change of guards.

Mila undid the cloak covering her weapons and grappling hook and cast it aside. The men next to her did the same, the message passing along the line. They had but moments to scale the wall before the next guards reached the towers.

She spun the hook above her head, slow at first, then accelerating rapidly, the rope twisting in her hand. The metal hummed as it left her grasp and sailed through the air, the claws sinking into the stone parapet above a heartbeat later.

The faint clunk was mirrored by others as her men secured their ropes to the wall. By then, she was halfway up the palisade.

By the time the first of them reached the rampart, she had already knocked out four guards. They moved swiftly in the shadows, silencing the soldiers they encountered by covering their noses and mouths with cloths soaked with the juice of the joy plant, a powerful sedative obtained from seeds harvested in the valley of the hidden Parsah, where they were being grown for medicinal purposes in anticipation of the upcoming war.

The alarm was raised when they were halfway across the fortress's main grounds, a gargled scream released from a soldier who had managed to fight off one of her men. Although Mila had not expected their subterfuge to last long, she was pleased it had endured long enough for them to take the armory by the main gates.

She left her sword and trident daggers untouched and narrowed her eyes at the wave of soldiers pouring out from the barracks around them.

'Stand your ground,' she ordered in a hard voice. 'This will be over soon.'

Kayan and the others glanced at each other before nodding grimly, hands frozen on the handles of their blades.

Recognition flashed on the faces of several of the Empire's soldiers as they drew near. They faltered, feet skidding in the dirt, the ones behind them colliding into their backs and sending some sprawling to the ground.

Cries of '*The Red Queen!*' echoed around her.

Then she saw him, the soldier wearing the uniform of troop commander, the warden of the prison. He was a giant, some six and a half feet tall, all muscle and sinew, face and limbs covered in scars. He stormed past his men and stopped a short distance away, his broadsword looking fragile in his large hand. A sneer distorted his features as he studied her.

'I see the traitor and killer of kings has come to us!' he shouted to the crowd before glaring at her once more.

Angry calls and shouts rose in the night.

Mila frowned. 'Romerus was not a king.'

The clamor stilled at her words. A hush fell over the grounds.

'He was my grandfather and one of the people I cherished most in this world. I did not—' she paused, her breath locking in her throat for a moment, '—could *never* slay him.' Her voice resonated against the walls around them, hard and steady. 'King Crovir killed him.'

Uproar shattered the lull. Cries of *'Traitor!'* and *'Liar!'* filled the air. Out the corner of her eye, Mila saw Kayan's knuckles whiten on his sword.

'I never thought I would see the day the Red Queen would resort to such cheap tactics.' A bitter smile twisted the troop commander's lips. He glanced at his soldiers. 'See how the mighty fall, men! The kings will compensate us richly when we deliver her to the capi—'

Mila's foot collided violently with his jaw, the power of her flying kick knocking three of his teeth out and snapping his head sideways. He grunted and staggered back several steps while she dropped lightly to the ground before him.

By the time he turned and started to raise his sword, a livid roar emerging from his throat, she had jumped, grabbed his shoulders, and rammed her right knee in his gut, robbing him of his breath. She twisted and swooped at the waist as she landed in the dirt, bringing her left leg around and up to deliver two lightning-fast kicks to his chest.

A wheeze left the giant's lips. His eyes widened comically as he stumbled and doubled over.

'Perfect,' murmured Mila.

She grabbed his chin and punched him in the face. The troop commander went down hard, his sword clattering to the ground, eyes rolling back in his head and blood pouring from his broken nose.

Shocked silence fell across the crowd. Mila straightened and studied the soldiers. Fury slowly replaced surprise on many of their faces.

'I do not want to fight you.' She drew her broadsword and daggers and dropped them at her feet. Dozens of pairs of eyes strayed briefly to the weapons.

'*Are you mad?*' hissed Kayan behind her.

Mila ignored him, her gaze focused on the hostile figures around them.

Now that she had taken out their immediate superior, she knew she had the soldiers' undivided attention. 'All I ask is that you listen to what I have to say.'

Doubt flashed across the faces of most of the men.

'And if we do not?' someone shouted challengingly.

'There are six hundred of us,' another called out. 'You number what, a fifth of that?'

Nervous laughter broke out among the soldiers. A discordant noise rose above it. It was the sound of hinges squeaking.

She smiled.

CHAPTER TWENTY-EIGHT

Aäron surfaced slowly, the handle of his dagger gripped securely in his mouth, sword strapped to his thigh with a leather band so it would not rattle. Water dripped down his face and body as he emerged, the faint splashes lost in the noise from the smelters' hearths some fifteen feet away. He climbed out of the underwater channel, his men rising silently behind him.

The furnaces beneath Kadavan never slept, the flames burning all day and night while the prisoners worked grueling shifts to produce arms for the Empire. It was this light that had guided them as they navigated the cold darkness of the submerged tunnel linking the lake to the forges deep beneath the island.

Skin drying rapidly in the hellish heat of the cavern, he crept up to a guard who stood watching the prisoners toiling over the fires, clamped his hand over the man's mouth, and dealt him a sharp blow to the base of the neck with the end of the dagger's handle.

The soldier slumped in his arms. In the shadows to his

left and right, other guards fell, knocked unconscious or drugged with pads imbued with the soporific sap of the joy plant he and his men carried in waterskin pouches at their waists.

A prisoner saw him when he was disposing of his fourth guard and froze for a moment, hammer stilling above glowing metal, eyes widening as he glanced around and registered the other intruders in the gloom. Aäron placed a finger against his lips, gaze flashing to the guards who were still oblivious to their presence. The prisoner, a middle-aged man with a face scarred by pockmarks, dipped his chin slightly and continued beating the sword he was molding.

They had incapacitated a third of the soldiers guarding the forges when one managed to escape the grip of Aäron's men and uttered a harsh cry. A scuffle broke out in the middle of the cavern, drawing the gaze of prisoners and guards alike. Aäron moved swiftly toward the struggling figures, eyes flickering to the soldiers closest the exit, a locked grille at the north end of the cavern.

Shouts broke out when the guards finally detected the enemies in their midst, the noise mercifully muffled by the furnaces and the clash of tools against metal. One drew his blade and moved toward the doorway, a keyring rattling in his grasp.

Aäron snatched his bow from his back and fired two arrows swiftly. The shafts whizzed through the air and pierced the soldier's hands. He screamed, the keys and sword dropping at his feet.

A prisoner tripped a guard who rushed to help the injured man and felled him with a blow to the back of the head. Another pierced a soldier in the thigh with a red-hot blade, the man's shriek echoing against the rock walls as his flesh sizzled around the glowing metal.

'Do not kill them!' shouted Aäron as more prisoners turned on the guards.

'What?!' The man with the pockmarks came up beside him, a hammer in each hand. He spat in the dirt, a scowl darkening his grimy face. 'I do not know who you are, son, but if you expect us to take pity on these swine, you have—'

'Our plan depends on keeping these soldiers alive!'

Aäron crossed the floor and grabbed a prisoner's arm just as the latter swung a mallet at a guard struggling with one of his men.

He snatched the weapon out of the stunned inmate's hand and cast it in the gloom. 'We will take this prison. And we will do it without killing a single soldier, is that understood?'

The prisoner with the pockmarks glared at Aäron while the soldiers from Dur Untash and Parsah took care of the remaining guards.

'Who in the name of the seven hells are you?'

Aäron returned his hard stare. 'Someone you do not want to cross.'

The man opposite stilled and studied him with a calculating expression. Aäron met his gaze unflinchingly, conscious of the prisoners' watchful eyes and the tension in the air.

It would take little for them to turn on us. And it seems this man holds some sort of sway over them.

'My name is Aäron of Parsah,' he said to the crowd circling them. 'My men and I are here to free you. But we need your help.'

The man with the scarred face hesitated. 'I am Tanis of Cayon.'

Surprise darted through Aäron.

He masked it behind a slight frown. '*The* Governor Tanis?'

'Aye,' the man grumbled, dipping his chin.

Aäron arched an eyebrow. 'I thought you long dead.'

Tanis grinned. 'You thought wrong, Aäron of Parsah.'

'Do you know where the other governors are?'

Tanis blinked, smile fading. 'How do you know about them?' His gaze swept over Aäron and his men. 'And how in the blazes did you discover the underwater channel?'

Aäron shrugged. 'I have my source. Now, here is what I want you to do.'

Incredulity dawned on the faces of the prisoners as they listened to his plan.

'Have you been drinking the juice of the joy plant?' snapped Tanis when he finished talking.

Aäron smiled faintly. 'No.'

Creases furrowed Tanis's already-lined brow. 'And you say there are more of you on the surface, led by this source of yours?'

Aäron kept his face carefully blank. *If they knew who it was, they would kill us in the blink of an eye.*

'Yes,' he replied. 'They move at midnight.'

Tanis rubbed his chin. 'Midnight is not far off. There will be a change of guards before fresh prisoners take over the shift.'

'We know.' Aäron stifled a burst of impatience. 'Will you help us?'

Tanis's gaze moved to the prisoners. 'What say you, men?'

Murmurs rose around them.

'We have nothing to lose,' someone called out.

'Better to go in a blaze of glory than fester in this stinking pit as their prisoners,' growled another.

'Speak for yourself,' scoffed someone. 'We smell like roses compared to you, Salem.'

Raucous laughter rose from the crowd.

A fierce smile curved Tanis's lips. 'Lead the way, Aäron of Parsah.'

With Tanis confirming Mila's outline of the layout and location of guard rooms and armories inside the complex, it did not take them long to put the next soldiers they came across out of action and release the other governors from their cells. Once they freed some hundred inmates and armed them, taking out the rest of the opposition was shockingly straightforward. By the time they worked their way up through the labyrinthine prison and reached the surface, midnight had come and gone.

It was as he came to one of the exits that led to the fortress grounds that Aäron heard Mila's voice.

'All I ask is that you listen to what I have to say.'

'And if we do not?' someone called out in a hostile voice.

'There are six hundred of us,' said another man. 'You number what, a fifth of that?'

Laughter came next, high-strung and mocking.

Aäron unlocked the opening, pushed the grille up, and climbed out. 'I am afraid your tally is not quite right.'

The metal bars clanged onto the dirt by his feet. Other grates swung up around him, the prisoners and his men pouring out of the prison.

Mila stood in a yellow pool of brightness some twenty feet away, posture relaxed and a small smile on her lips.

Aäron stepped into the light and grinned at the Empire's soldiers. 'Make that a thousand.'

CHAPTER TWENTY-NINE

'THAT WAS A STROKE OF MADNESS.'

'It was the princess's idea,' said Aäron.

They were in the dining hall of the main fortress barrack. It was the only room big enough to accommodate all of them. Across the table, captains of the Empire and former prisoners glared at each other.

With the troop commander still unconscious and under guard in another part of the building, Mila had gathered his subordinates for the meeting. The rest of the soldiers had been secured in the prison beneath the island.

A wry grimace had crossed her lips as she watched the Empire's men being herded away. The prison's design and security measures had been Tobias and Baruch's creation. They were not going to be pleased when they discovered she had taken their precious fortress so easily, and with not a single life lost among the men who guarded it to boot, although there had been inevitable injuries.

This was the one condition Mila had insisted upon when she spoke of her idea in the council chamber of Parsah. That the Empire's soldiers not be killed during their attempt to capture the prison. She had seen too much death as it was in her Immortal life, without adding to it the slaughter of those who once stood by her.

Besides, they deserve to be given the chance to choose sides in the coming war.

The man who had spoken grunted and frowned at her across the room as he stroked the stump of the missing little finger on his left hand.

'I have heard of this supposed...alliance. Most of us who governed cities inside the Empire have.' He paused. 'Like everyone else, I thought it a fanciful rumor. Now you say there is an army willing to fight the Immortals who rule us and that a human king controls it?'

A bark of laughter sounded two seats to his right. 'Come now, Yakaad! Has it been so long since you governed Urfa that you would fall for such lies?' This man had a rough voice and a face scored by scars and pockmarks. 'I too heard those tall tales when I ruled Cayon. I always believed them to be part of an elaborate trap set by King Crovir to test our loyalty to him.' He sneered, his dark eyes glowing hotly at Mila where she stood next to Aäron at the head of the table. 'He is twisted enough to try something like that. Mark my words, this too is a trick. Only this time, it is his snake of a daughter who seeks to deceive us, just as she did when she took my city by stealth, after she poisoned my men in the middle of the night. And she seems to have fooled this so called prince.'

Aäron stiffened next to her.

'Calm down, Tanis,' murmured the figure beside the scowling governor. He was tall and thin, with long white hair he had managed to keep clean despite being in Kadavan for fifteen years. 'Red Queen, although I too have gleaned word of this alliance from some of the prisoners who have come to

Kadavan in recent years, it is impossible to believe the story you and the—' he glanced at Aäron, '—*general* of this alleged army have just recounted. It is too far-fetched.'

Mila narrowed her eyes. 'Which part? The one where Crovir killed Romerus or the one where we just freed you from a life of slavery?'

Aäron laid a hand on her arm.

She took a shallow breath and clamped down on the frustration surging through her. 'Prince Aäron and I did not think it would be easy to convince you of the truthfulness of our words. Indeed, he warned me it could take days to bring you around. But we do not have days.' She paused and clenched her jaw. 'The captains currently sitting in this room will confirm that Crovir has accused me of the murder of my grandfather and has issued a warrant for my arrest and execution.'

Several of the soldiers hesitated before nodding reluctantly, faces pale as they watched her.

Mila turned to the man with the pockmarks. 'Governor Tanis, I cannot undo the past, nor can I take back my actions in Cayon.' Her gaze shifted to the silent man next to him. 'Governor Ibrahim, you may choose to believe that we fabricated this entire story, but it still does not change one important fact.' She straightened, her face settling in grim lines as she studied the figures in the room. 'There *is* a war coming and it is one that will swallow the lands of this kingdom. You can either choose to stand with us or you can side with the kings who sit on the thrones of Uryl.'

'Say we believe you,' growled Tanis. 'Say we trust you and we win this—this *war*! What then? What happens once you depose your father and uncle?' A bitter scowl distorted his features. 'Will we have other Immortals take the throne instead? Will *you* become the queen of the Empire?!'

Mila stilled. This was the question she had feared the most, the one thing she had struggled to answer for herself since discovering Aäron's true identity and agreeing to help King Gishur.

She took a deep breath, conscious of the warmth of the man beside her, comforted by his very presence. 'There will be no Empire.'

A hush fell across the room at her words. Several men gaped.

Tanis blinked, blood slowly draining from his face. 'What?'

'If we win this war, the Empire will fall. And you will all gain your freedom.' Mila's voice hardened. 'Every man, woman, and child in the kingdom shall be delivered from the dominion of the Immortals. On this, you have my oath.'

'That looks like a good place to stop for the night,' said Aäron.

Mila studied the formation he indicated. It jutted out of the desert, a craggy collection of dark rocks cradling the otherwise barren landscape. The fronds of a palm tree were visible against the reddening sky. She nodded and followed him toward the hillock.

Three days had passed since they departed Kadavan and headed south.

'My prince, I feel it is unwise for the two of you to go there. At least take some of the men from Parsah with you,' Kayan had urged back at the fortress when he had heard their plan, trepidation in his eyes.

All around them, soldiers and former prisoners worked side by side, making preparations and arming themselves for the journey ahead, united in their common goal and invigorated by the promise Mila had made the night before. Supervising them were the captains and fallen governors. Even the troop commander had reluctantly joined their ranks, after he awoke and heard all that had passed.

How long this new found fervor lasts remains to be seen, Mila thought as she watched the bustle. *Some may still choose to defect and stand with the kings in Uryl.*

'It is quite alright.' Aäron smiled and patted Kayan's shoulder. 'Besides, what have I to fear when the Red Queen rides with me?'

They had left the fortress with enough supplies to last them until the next Half Moon and soon crossed the tapering tail of the Zagros Range. Once they reached the plains beyond and crossed the northern border of the Empire's domain, they moved more stealthily, on the lookout for soldiers from the garrison at Niibru still out searching for them, according to the captains in Kadavan.

They set up camp in the shade of the palm tree and soon settled in each other's arms. As stars flashed above them and their horses grazed on desert scrub, they shared stories from their lives, as they had done the past two nights.

Mila smiled as she listened to Aäron's tales from his childhood, of perilous dares and adventures with his younger brother that had regularly earned them their father's wrath and turned their mother's hair grey long before she passed prematurely from illness when he was ten. Like the previous evenings, sadness and a sliver of envy stabbed through her at the obvious warmth and affection in his words. It was a childhood as far removed from her own as the Moon was from the Sun.

All too soon, the desire that lived just below the surface of their skin swelled once more and they mated under the shimmering heavens, movements all consuming, their hunger unabated despite the many times they had melded their bodies together.

When Aäron's breathing slowed and he fell asleep in the cradle of her arms, his head against her breast, Mila gently stroked his hair and finally whispered the words he had spoken to her that first morning they had lain with one another, the sky above glimmering through a thin film of tears.

For she understood. However much she wanted to be with him and he with her, to merge into one for all of eternity, they would remain separate entities, until death parted them. It was because of this that they chose to join their bodies repeatedly, to complete each other, however ephemerally short a time their physical union lasted, using their earthly forms to convey the heartfelt wishes their souls could not express in words. For in him she had found the other half of her, as he had in her, a missing piece unbeknown to them until they kissed and touched for the first time, a precious part they could no longer do without. A connection she had never felt with Kronos.

A noise woke her some time later. She blinked and raised her head, gaze sweeping the landscape and the horses standing in the lee of the rocks on her right. Her breath misted before her face in the chilly air, the remains of their fire a faint glow smoldering in the gloom. To the east, the lightening horizon heralded the arrival of dawn.

The sound came again. Mila sat up slowly, her heart drumming rapidly against her breast.

Aäron woke, startled, and looked at her. 'What is it?'

A short distance away, Buros snorted, bridle jingling as he shook his head and cocked his ears. The stallion recognized the noise as well.

Mila rose and started pulling her clothes on. Aäron followed suit and grabbed his blade.

'Where?' he said quietly.

'To the south.'

He glanced at her, a muscle jumping in his cheek. 'How many and how far?'

Mila lowered herself on her haunches and laid her hand against the ground.

'Two horses,' she murmured after a moment. 'About half a league away.' She paused. 'He will get here first.'

Aäron frowned as she rose and stared into the fading night. 'Who will?'

Mila lifted her head and hand, searching for the familiar shape among the dwindling stars. He came in a flurry of wings and a shrill cry, the sound joyous and admonishing at the same time, claws digging into her skin.

'Abu,' she breathed.

The hawk blinked at her sullenly before giving her wrist a few angry pecks. Then he stilled as she gently stroked him, her fingers running down his body from his brow all the way to his tail. A low rumble erupted from his chest and he closed his eyes, butting his head lovingly against her touch.

Mila smiled. 'I missed you too.'

Then she heard it, a voice in her head, one filled with as much anger as she had expected. *Found you!*

CHAPTER THIRTY

'You retarded imbecile!' roared Jared.

Mila blinked.

'Calm down,' pleaded Navia.

'Why did you run?' he shouted at Mila. He turned and grabbed Aäron by the neckline of his tunic, his handsome features dark with anger. 'And you! Why did you not bring her back?'

'It is good to see you too, Commander,' murmured Aäron. 'And I think you presume a lot of me if you think I have the capacity to control the actions of your sister.'

Mila sighed. 'Let him go. We were on our way to Larraak, to see Navia.'

Jared scowled, chest heaving with his breaths, before slowly releasing Aäron. 'Good Gods, do you know how long and how far we have searched for you?'

Mila flinched at the raw pain on her brother's face.

'Our mother is out of her mind with worry and our cousins and siblings have been scouring all the corners of the kingdom for—'

'Mother—' Mila interrupted. She paused and took a shallow breath, '—so, mother does not think I killed Romerus?'

Navia and Jared shared a troubled glance.

'None of us do,' said Jared. 'Deep down inside, I think even Kronos does not.'

Guilt flashed through Mila at her husband's name. She sensed Aäron's gaze on her.

'How is he?' she said haltingly. 'And the children? Eleaza and Kaleb? Are they well?'

'As well as can be, considering Crovir has convinced the entire Empire that their mother is a murderer and a traitor,' said Jared with a bitter grimace. 'And Kronos has taken to drinking heavily.'

'So they are still in Issin?' Mila said insistently.

Navia nodded.

Relief flooded Mila. She had feared Crovir would have taken them to Uryl. She was silent for a while.

'How come—why did you not believe Crovir when he accused me of murdering Romerus?' she said finally. 'The soldiers at the citadel did.'

'Because I know you, sister,' said Jared between gritted teeth. 'We all do. And we know of your devotion to Romerus. Once the shock of the news of his demise passed, we realized there was no way in this world you would ever have laid a finger on him, however much he provoked you.' He looked at Navia. 'Besides, there was something else that sealed our conviction.'

Mila's gaze shifted to her cousin.

'I could not read his mind,' Navia murmured. 'When I tried to probe the consciousness of the king to confirm the facts of his statement, I saw only darkness and emptiness.'

'You have always found it hard to truly read and control

Immortal minds, cousin,' said Mila. 'Especially those of Crovir and Bastian, the first among us.'

'That was why it was crucial we find you,' said Jared. 'To confirm what we all fear. Our darkest suspicions.'

Navia moved then and knelt before Mila where she sat on a rock. 'Can I, cousin?'

Mila hesitated before nodding. She bit her lip as the Seer lifted her hands to her temples. Cool fingers brushed her consciousness a heartbeat later. She glanced at Aäron. He smiled at her encouragingly, causing Jared to stare between the two of them with a frown.

She fought down her natural instinct to resist the strange force probing her mind, took a deep breath, and let go.

Lines furrowed Navia's brow as she closed her eyes and concentrated. Then she gasped, the blood draining from her face. In the frozen moment that followed, a low sob escaped her lips and tears seeped from beneath her eyelashes.

Jared stepped toward her, fingers reaching out before he stopped and clenched his fist, his hand falling to his side.

Navia finally released her and opened her eyes. Mila swallowed as she registered the agony in their green depths. In that moment, she lived it all over again. The vile words Crovir had spoken to Romerus. The dagger in his hand. The abominable act that had followed. The blood. The agony of seeing her grandfather pass from this world.

And that strange presence, the one she had forgotten about in her desperate flight from the citadel and all that came after. The sensation that someone else had been there, had witnessed it all. Had waited, as if expecting Romerus's death.

Navia cried quietly, shoulders shaking, eyes fixed unseeingly on her hands where they lay in her lap.

'So it is true,' she whispered brokenly.

'Navia?'

She looked at Jared. 'It was Crovir who killed Romerus.'

Mila's brother drew a breath in sharply, his face pale. Then he twisted on his heels and glared at the rising sun, eyelashes glistening with wetness, knuckles whitening against his thighs.

Navia finally stilled her tears. She took a shuddering breath before gazing uneasily between Mila and Aäron.

Mila met her eyes unflinchingly, knowing that when she had probed her mind, she had no doubt seen all that came after Romerus's death.

'There is more,' said her cousin in a low voice.

Jared wiped a hand across his face and turned to her with a frown.

'What do you mean?'

ELEAZA GAZED OUT OF THE WINDOW OF HER BEDCHAMBER. Although the morning sky above Issin was a pale blue, she could see thunderclouds gathering above the distant mountains to the east. She shivered, a strange feeling sending icy fingers dancing along her skin.

'Princess, look, look what grandmother made for you!'

She turned and studied Emet blankly as he came skipping across the floor. His steps faltered and the cheerful expression on his face faded. Then he rallied forth and flashed her a dazzling smile before dropping a scarf on the bench where she sat.

Eleaza stared at the beautifully woven material.

'Grandmother says the days are getting cold and you will be in need of this,' gushed Emet.

She touched the thick cloth for a moment before lifting it and wrapping it around her shoulders, wishing it were her mother's arms instead. Tears filled her eyes and her breath hitched in her throat.

Emet watched her anxiously and slowly lowered himself to the floor at her feet. 'Are you sad, Princess?'

Eleaza nodded jerkily, not trusting herself to speak. Emet fell silent and traced random patterns on the marble floor with a finger.

'I too was sad, when father died,' he mumbled after a while. 'I never knew mother, so I could not mourn her.' He gazed at her once more, his face clearing. 'But I had grandmother. Then I met the Red Queen and you and Kaleb.' He smiled. 'You are not alone, Princess. You have your father and your brother, your uncles and aunts, all your cousins, and me and grandmother. We will be with you until the Red Queen returns.'

Eleaza stared at him, her heart breaking all over again. This boy, this human whose life would be a flash in the night compared to her own Immortal one, had known more loss and misery in his existence than she had ever experienced. Remorse surged through her. Though she hated the horrible things she had heard the servants whisper about why her mother had vanished and missed her presence terribly, she could not afford to be weak, not when he could demonstrate such strength after all the hardship he had borne.

She wiped her eyes, sniffed, and rose from the bench. 'Let us go, Emet.'

He jumped to his feet and stared at her, curious. 'Where?' A grimace twisted his lips for a moment. 'I mean, where, Princess?'

Eleaza giggled and felt her heart lighten for the first time in days. 'To the training ground. Let us get Kaleb and go practice our archery.'

He nodded vigorously, eyes shining with excitement.

It was as they navigated the corridor near the main hall that they heard the voices.

'You are a disgrace!' someone shouted. 'Look at you! Are you so enamored of your wife that you turn into a wreck the moment she is no longer at your side?'

Eleaza startled when she recognized her grandfather's voice. She slowed and moved quietly toward one of the marble pillars framing an archway into the chamber, a hesitant Emet at her side.

'Princess?' he whispered.

She lifted a finger to her lips to silence him and peered around the column. Her eyes widened.

'Now, bring them here,' barked King Crovir.

Slouching on the floor against one of the gilded chairs at the head of the room was her father. His hair and clothes were unkempt and a beard shadowed his face. He had been this way for days now, ever since her mother disappeared.

'Bring who here?' said Kronos in a slurred voice.

He knocked back the tumbler in his hand, red liquid spilling past his lips and dribbling down his chin as he gulped and swallowed. He wiped his mouth with the back of his hand and gazed sullenly at the king.

King Crovir scowled. 'Your children, you fool!'

Eleaza's heart leapt in her throat. She had always felt somewhat nervous around her grandfather. Today, more than ever, his presence filled her with dread.

Kronos narrowed his eyes, his expression clearing for a moment. 'Why do you want to see the children?'

King Crovir's face grew shuttered. 'They are to come with me to Uryl.'

Kronos blinked. Understanding slowly crystallized in his eyes.

Face sobering, he grabbed the chair and rose unsteadily to his feet.

'Why do you wish to take them to Uryl?' His voice hardened. 'Is it because of Mila?'

King Crovir observed him for a silent moment, as if gauging his next move. 'Yes. They will serve as a…security of sorts, should she return.'

Fear seared Eleaza. She covered her mouth with her hands and stifled the whimper that emerged from her throat. Even though she did not fully comprehend the meaning behind her grandfather's words, his expression and tone filled her with terror. Emet grabbed her dress, fingers whitening in the material.

'Eleaza?' said someone behind them.

She jumped slightly and looked over her shoulder.

Kaleb approached from the end of the corridor, a puzzled expression on his face. 'What are you doing?'

Too late, she waved her hands to hush him. Footsteps stormed across the marble floor from the direction of the hall.

King Crovir rounded the pillar. 'There you are.' He towered over her and glanced at her brother. 'Good, I have found both of you. Come with me.'

Kaleb's gaze switched between Eleaza's stricken face and their grandfather's. 'Where are we going?'

'To Uryl.'

King Crovir grabbed Eleaza roughly by the arm and beckoned to Kaleb. He stood still, his eyes widening as he stared at them.

'I said come, child!' snapped King Crovir.

Kaleb startled, face blanching. King Crovir stormed across the passage and snatched his arm, forcefully dragging them both into the hall.

'No!' yelled Eleaza. She dug her heels into the floor and

fought his grip, blood thrumming in her ears and heart thudding wildly in her chest. 'I do not want to go to Uryl! You cannot make me!' She looked around. '*Father!*'

Kronos stood by the gilded chair, shock filling his face, his limbs seemingly frozen to the ground. Attracted by her shouts, servants appeared from every corner of the palace. They stumbled and backed into the shadows when they saw the king, their faces white with fear.

Her grandfather shook her, his fingers digging into her flesh. 'Stop that!'

'Let her go!' screamed Kaleb.

He punched and kicked at the king, tears swimming in his eyes. Their grandfather cast him violently to the ground before turning and slapping Eleaza across the face.

She gasped, head snapping sideways, pain and horror rendering her speechless. A ringing noise drowned her hearing. Kaleb's muffled shout reached her dimly, as did some of the servants' cries. Then a hand clutched the end of the scarf sitting around her shoulders. She turned, relief flashing through her, gaze searching wildly for her father's face.

Instead, she found Emet. He stood trembling, fingers digging into the fabric his grandmother had woven.

'No.' Her voice rose, panic lacing her words. 'Emet, *go!*'

He shook his head and gazed up at the king. 'You cannot take the princess. The Red Queen charged me with her care.'

Though his voice quivered with fear, a trace of defiance underscored his voice.

King Crovir stared at him. Fury and distaste twisted his features when he registered Emet's hold on the scarf. His hand snaked out and closed around the boy's throat.

Emet choked, his eyes widening, feet swinging helplessly beneath him as he was lifted off the ground.

'*Stop!*' shrieked Eleaza. '*Let him be!*'

She doubled her efforts to escape her grandfather's cruel grip, hitting and kicking him with all the strength in her small body.

King Crovir ignored her and studied Emet's reddening face, as one would gaze upon an insect.

'You forget your place, slave,' he said in a voice devoid of emotion.

Kronos took an unsteady step toward them. 'Father, no. Stop—'

Then she heard it. A snap. Like a branch breaking.

Emet stilled in King Crovir's grip, his body suddenly limp, his features going slack, his eyes staring. Empty. Unseeing. Dead.

Eleaza's breath froze in her throat. Her legs sagged beneath her and she collapsed to the floor, arm still in her grandfather's vicious hold, her brother's horrified screams and the servants' shocked cries echoing in her ears.

Emet's body thudded softly to the ground as King Crovir let go. The latter grimaced and wiped his hand on his tunic before yanking her to her feet.

She lolled in his grasp, her gaze locked on Emet's face, unable and unwilling to comprehend what had just passed.

'You will accompany us to Uryl as well,' King Crovir told her father.

Her grandfather walked over to where Kaleb lay shuddering, face white with terror. He hauled her brother to his feet and dragged them both toward the exit, tugging on their arms when they stumbled and fell, the servants scattering helplessly in their path.

All the while, Eleaza stared over her shoulder at the dead boy on the ground, his fingers still clutching the scarf that had slipped from her shoulders.

CHAPTER THIRTY-ONE

Helena stared at Mila unseeingly, her face as white as a sheet. All around them, her siblings and cousins glanced at each other, their pain and horror plain to see.

'That is—' started Tobias.

'What I suspected all along,' interrupted Baruch in a harsh voice.

Hosanna's hand closed over his clenched fist on the table.

They were in Larraak, where Navia had convened a secret gathering. It had taken some of them a day to get there from their respective cities, the storm that swept across the plains from the mountains to the east slowing their progress. Only Kronos and the kings' wives, bar Helena, were missing. It was Mila who had insisted upon it.

'I only want mother to come for the time being,' she told Navia and Jared when they were still in the desert. 'It will be less suspicious than having all the wives in your city.' She frowned then. 'I will go to Issin to talk to Kronos personally. But only after I speak with the others.'

Navia hesitated before nodding. Then she closed her eyes

and concentrated. In the moments that followed, Mila knew she was sending out a direct message to the others' minds. It was rare and taxing for her to communicate in this fashion with Immortals but it was the fastest way to get everyone to Larraak.

Aäron had accompanied them and stood leaning against a wall to her left, arms folded across his chest, posture relaxed and face composed.

Mila was not fooled. She could tell he was tense from the way a muscle occasionally twitched in his cheek.

'And you saw this? All of it?' whispered Helena, glancing from Mila to Navia.

Navia nodded. Mila clenched her jaw and slowly dipped her chin.

Helena rose and walked over to wrap her arms around her. Mila blinked before relaxing in her hold, a wave of relief flooding through her and causing her breath to catch in her throat. The burden she had carried since Romerus's death seemed to lighten fractionally. She felt the wetness of tears against her temple and gripped her mother's arm tightly.

Rafael rose and paced across the room, fingers spearing through his hair.

'But why?' he said in a tortured voice. 'Why would Crovir do such a thing?' He paused. 'Was it— was it because of Hazaara?'

Helena slowly straightened. 'No, Rafael. Children, you must not blame yourselves. What you did for Hazaara all those months ago was the righteous thing to do.' She paused. 'Even if Mila had not defied him and stoked his rage, Crovir would likely still have killed Romerus some day.' She closed her eyes briefly. 'For the longest time, I had sensed his growing bitterness toward our father. But never in a thousand years did

I think he would act upon his base desire.' She swallowed convulsively. 'He is truly a monster.'

Mila startled, recalling Romerus's final words before Crovir stabbed him.

'At least Mila was there to witness it, however horrifying it must have been,' Helena continued. 'Otherwise we would be none the wiser as to the true identity of his killer. No doubt Crovir would have found another innocent soul to blame instead of admitting that Romerus died at the hands of his own son. His firstborn.'

'Will King Bastian believe us if we talk to him?' said Aäron in the hush that followed.

Helena looked at him and hesitated. 'This I cannot answer.' She sighed. 'Although they equally share ownership of the Empire, the love Bastian has for Crovir knows no bounds and often renders him weak. I have seen it firsthand, over hundreds of years of being in their company. He worships the ground his older brother walks on and has always had a hard time giving credence to any misdeed Crovir is accused of.'

Baruch frowned. 'Father is loyal to a fault but we *must* apprise him of this. He has to listen to reason.'

Malachi stirred and looked between Mila and Aäron. 'And what of the rest of what you have told us, cousin? About this… human alliance and this army that would see Uryl fall?'

Ysa narrowed her eyes. 'I am also keen to hear more about that.'

Mila's gaze shifted to Aäron. He studied her for a moment before nodding.

And so she spoke, of what they had already told Navia and Jared in the desert, of the promise made over one hundred years past by a former governor of Parsah, of the secret cities and the recently-elected human king, of the vast army amassing in clandestine locations throughout the Empire and the men and women still joining their ranks, of Kadavan and the prisoners and governors they freed.

'You took Kadavan?' Tobias said hoarsely, his face draining of color.

Ysa grimaced. 'Of all the things we have just heard, *that* is what concerns you the most?'

Baruch frowned. 'It is a big *that.*'

Rafael studied Mila, doubt lacing his voice when he spoke. 'So what are you saying, cousin?'

She looked down at her hands where they lay on the table, a storm of thoughts and emotions twisting through her. Then she raised her head and met their gazes one by one, ending last with Aäron. The expression in his blue eyes stilled the tempest inside her heart and mind.

She took a deep breath and spoke the words she had uttered that night in the prison fortress. 'The Empire must fall.'

Tobias blinked and drew back in shock.

'What?' said Baruch in a low voice.

'For the good of all, we must end our dominion over this world.' Mila's voice softened. 'It was never ours to rule. Neither was it our destiny to enslave the human race.'

'What do you mean?' whispered Hosanna where she sat next to Baruch.

'Romerus said so, on the night he died.' Mila swallowed. 'That he never wanted the Empire, never asked his sons to conquer all those cities and nations. He said—' her voice caught in her throat, '—he said he had made a promise, to the One who bestowed upon him the gifts that made Crovir and Bastian Immortal.'

'A promise?' Phebe repeated.

'What—what promise?' mumbled Beatrix from pale lips.

'That he would allow them free will,' Mila replied. 'That he would not interfere with their actions. As if the paths chosen by Crovir and Bastian all this time were a—trial of sorts.'

'A trial for what?' said Baruch.

Mila shook her head. 'This I do not know.' She studied them again, her gaze flittering over their various expressions, seeing doubt and unease and fear. 'All that we have done since the time of our births has been for one purpose only. To grow this empire. An empire drenched in blood and erected on the bones and skulls of thousands of innocent souls.'

A snort escaped Tobias. 'I never thought I would see the day the strongest and most successful among us at expanding that very empire grew a conscience.'

'Tobias,' Ysa said miserably.

'He is right,' said Baruch. A muscle jumped in his jawline as he stared at Mila. 'Do you understand what you are asking us to do, cousin? To go to war with our own fathers? Do you know the anarchy that will follow?'

Mila observed her eldest brother and cousin, the two most powerful Immortals after her. The generals of the Empire's army.

'We have been blind. All these years, we have been living in a dream. No, a *nightmare* created by our fathers.' She paused, her gaze shifting to Aäron's piercing blue eyes once more. 'Ask yourself this. What is it that you want? Deep down inside, ignoring the fact that you are princes and princesses of the Empire, ignoring your immortality and other unearthly gifts, what do you truly wish for, for yourself and your children? What destiny would you choose to carve if you had free will?'

THEY APPROACHED THE CITY FROM THE NORTHWEST AS DAWN

swept across the land, aiming for one of the smaller gates to avoid the commotion that would no doubt greet her arrival.

'Are you sure you would not rather wait out here somewhere while I bring Kronos to you?' said Jared as the walls of Issin came in sight.

'No,' replied Mila. She narrowed her eyes at the distant ramparts. 'If I am to do this, I will do so at our palace. Besides, I must talk to the men stationed in our barracks.'

'Mila is right,' said Helena above the drum of their horses' hooves.

Their mother had decided to accompany her and Jared to Issin, while the others returned to their cities to reflect on her words and make their decision.

'You know where I will be waiting,' Mila had told her siblings and cousins when they departed Larraak the night before.

They had nodded, their expressions grim, before whirling their horses around and heading for the gates of the city.

'They are a sight to behold,' Aäron had murmured from where he sat atop his own steed.

Mila had studied him, sadness spearing through her. From that point until their meeting with Darius and the other leaders of the alliance, he would travel north and west to join the various factions of their growing army and coordinate their plans.

'Be safe,' she said quietly.

Aäron smiled, unspoken words filling the silence between them, before turning his horse staround.

She had watched him leave, her gaze latched on his wide back until he faded from view, conscious of her mother and Malachi's curious stares, and Jared's shrewd one. Only Navia had observed her with a degree of empathy. As they headed into the palace, Mila had wondered if her cousin's compassion had anything to do with her own forbidden feelings for Jared.

She had slept fitfully in the short time until their departure for Issin, her dreams filled with images from the events of the last Half Moon. It was when she unconsciously stretched her arm out and could not feel Aäron's warmth that she had awoken and realized she had gotten used to him being by her side. She had lain in the dark and stared at the ceiling for a long time, a deep yearning filling her.

They left Larraak under a clear, starry sky, Abu dozing on the saddle before her as they raced across the dark land. He awoke when they approached Issin, a contented squeak leaving his chest at the sight of his home. He flapped his wings and rose into the fading night.

Mila let him leave, confident he would be waiting for her somewhere ahead. She lowered her gaze and studied the city growing on the horizon grimly.

Let us hope that he listens to reason.

All thoughts of Kronos and the confrontation to come fled her mind when they reached the gates. Though the soldiers shouted at the sight of her and Mila sensed their hostility, she could tell they were distracted.

She ignored Jared and Helena as they commanded the flustered men to stand down and guided Buros over to a captain who stood watching them, his face pale. 'What is it? What is wrong?'

The man stared at her as if he were seeing a ghost. 'Princess —my queen—'

Unease flashed through Mila. A call sounded in the early morning light. Abu's shrill cry. It had come from the direction of the palace.

Apprehension turned to alarm. Mila steered the stallion

around and galloped toward the center of Issin, the soldiers in her path scattering as she charged through them. She recognized Abu's tone. It spoke of death.

She found them on the terrace overlooking the city, outside the main hall, the hawk whirling agitatedly in the sky above.

Mila's steps faltered as she rushed toward the crowd of silent servants, acid burning the back of her throat when she registered the old woman sitting in their midst and the small body in her arms. Helena's gasp reached her dimly from behind.

Mila took no heed of the servants' shocked murmurs as she walked slowly through them to where Emet's grandmother sat, clothes still wet from the previous day's storm, her lined face expressionless as she gazed blindly over Issin.

Emet lay in her slack hold, his limbs locked in the stiffness of death, face blue and neck at an awkward angle. In his right hand was a beautiful scarf, now sodden with rain.

Blood roared in Mila's ears as she dropped to her knees beside the old woman. Emet's grandmother unfroze, head turning slowly until she met Mila's stricken gaze, her own eyes lifeless and dry.

Shadows fell across them as Helena and Jared joined their side.

'What happened?' said Mila's mother hoarsely.

Emet's grandmother glanced at Helena and Jared before staring at Mila once more. In her gaze, Mila read the terrible answer to the question her mother had just posed.

'He took them,' said the old woman. 'He killed my Emet and took the children.'

'Kronos?' said Jared, disbelief underlying his harsh tone.

'No,' Mila whispered before the old woman could muster a reply. 'Crovir.'

Emet's grandmother nodded. Helena cried out and crumpled to the ground. Jared swore. Mila stared at the dead boy, her body going rigid, ice filling her veins.

'He tried to stop him,' said Emet's grandmother. A humorless chuckle left her lips. 'This foolish child thought he could keep the princess safe. While her own father stood by and did nothing, he walked up to King Crovir and challenged him.'

Her laughter turned to low sobs and she hugged her dead grandson tightly to her chest.

'Where is Kronos?' Jared asked one of the servants.

'He—he went to Uryl, at the command of the king, my prince,' came the mumbled reply.

Mila lifted a hand and gently caressed Emet's cold cheek. Marks branded his neck, a dark chain of fingerprints. She knew without being told how he had met his death.

His innocent smiling face came to her mind from that day so many Moons ago, when she first met him in Uryl. Tears filled her eyes and blurred her vision.

'Did the king hurt my children too?' she asked softly.

Silence answered her. Her fingers stilled on the dead boy's skin before slowly curling.

Mila moved, her violent motion causing the servants to draw back, her fist striking the ground with the full power of her rage. She threw her head back and screamed. In the sky above, Abu's stricken shriek echoed the agony in her voice.

The floor cracked, spiderweb fissures spreading and widening across the terrace. Panicked shouts sounded from the servants and the soldiers who had followed from the city as a terrible force swept across the palace, forcing them back several steps.

The storm washed through Mila, raw, unrestrained, fury

like she had never before known turning her mind red. Then arms surrounded her, her mother and her brother fighting the tempest to enclose her body in their hold until the world stopped trembling and the air ceased to vibrate with the wrathful energy burning inside her.

CHAPTER THIRTY-TWO

Bastian studied the giant man who rested on one knee at the bottom of the dais in the throne room of Uryl. He reeked of sweat and filth, his missing teeth creating an unpleasant gaping void in his mouth when he spoke, his broken nose a swollen, deformed lump in the midst of his face.

Crovir sat stiffly in the ceremonial chair beside Bastian, face dark with anger.

'Are you certain?'

The troop commander from Kadavan swallowed and nodded.

'Yes, my king. Even as I speak, more cities answer the call of the governors who were once prisoners of Kadavan and the army of the enemy grows. But the Red Queen never revealed to us the exact location of the throne where the false human king sits. All I know is that the governor of Dur Untash is somehow involved and that some of the men were from Parsah.'

Though the soldier had recounted what had happened in Kadavan six nights past before he fled to bring them news of the prison break, Bastian could still not quite believe that his niece had had the audacity to pull off such a coup. It left a bitter taste in his mouth, one that echoed the lingering doubt he still felt following his conversation with Baruch on the day of Romerus's funeral.

Crovir rose to his feet.

'Thank you. You will be rewarded for your loyalty.'

The troop commander stood and bowed before turning and exiting the throne room. He passed Kronos on the way out and dipped his chin respectfully.

'Leave us,' Crovir ordered the men guarding the doors and the servants hovering in the shadows.

They scurried away, their footsteps fading in the distance. Silence fell inside the throne room.

'Now you see?' hissed Crovir. 'You see what she is capable of?!'

He glared at Kronos. The latter avoided his father's gaze, his face pale.

'We must gather our forces and exterminate this threat. Send a message to Tobias and Baruch. I want them here tonight and our army mobilized by morning!'

Kronos nodded. He glanced uneasily at Bastian and strode out of the throne room, his back rigid.

'What are you thinking, brother?'

Bastian startled and turned to find Crovir studying him closely. A sliver of ice danced through his consciousness at the expression in his older sibling's eyes.

It reminded him of their early years together, when they had set about conquering distant cities in foreign lands, the Empire a far-fetched dream they spoke of when they were full of drink and seated around a fire under the stars. Though their physical strength and stamina more than matched on the battlefield, Crovir had always possessed the more twisted personality of the two of them and had never shown pity for their enemies, be it man, woman, or child.

It was with relief that Bastian had relinquished control of their army to him and their children, to better concentrate on managing their vast and complex kingdom. When his eldest daughter Hosanna showed an uncanny aptitude for dealing with the governors of the cities they ruled, he had assigned her the task of being the Empire's main representative and liaison, along with the duty of collecting its tithes.

And so he insulated himself from the harsh realities of the conflicts that always simmered on the edges of their domain for a hundred years, turning a blind eye to his brother's cruel military campaigns and a deaf ear to some of the horrific tales he heard, preferring instead to lose himself in numbers and administrative ventures.

For his love for Crovir surpassed nearly everything in his life, even his love for his own children. There was an unbreakable bond between them, one they shared not only by virtue of their blood relation, but also because of something else, something intangible. It was the simmering energy of the gifts they were granted when they were but mere mortal children and lay dying of the sickness that had darkened all corners of the world. An unearthly life force that was in constant resonance between them, pulling them together, whether they wanted it or not. A connection that sapped at his once iron will in exchange for keeping the peace between brothers.

Crovir arched an eyebrow.

'Well?'

'I am thinking that you are right.'

Shock reverberated through Bastian when he realized that the words he had just uttered were a lie, the first he had ever told his brother in their hundreds of years of existence. It took steady resolve to keep his face neutral and meet Crovir's gaze unflinchingly.

The latter watched him for a moment longer.

'Good.'

Later that day, as he stood staring out over Uryl on the terrace outside his private quarters, still perplexed by the falsehood he had uttered earlier in the throne room and troubled by the treacherous thoughts filling his mind, a messenger delivered a parchment stamped with Baruch's seal.

Bastian dismissed the man and unrolled the scroll, lines furrowing his brow. He stilled when he saw the words within. He read the message again and gazed blindly into space for a long time. Then he burned the parchment and watched it turn to ash before he left his chambers.

BARUCH PACED THE GROUND BRISKLY, HIS BOOTS CARVING TRAILS in the dirt.

'He will come,' said Hosanna. 'Have faith.'

He glanced at her with a frown.

'Seriously, stop,' groaned Tobias. 'Just watching you reminds me of that time we were on that voyage on the South Sea.'

'You mean the one where you were sick?' said Ysa. 'Truly sick?'

'By Gods, you spewed everywhere that day,' muttered Rafael.

Phebe grimaced.

'Please, do not remind me. I was the first in his firing range.'

'Shut up,' grumbled Tobias.

Despite their lighthearted banter, Baruch sensed the same

tension that thrummed through his veins in their stiff postures and troubled eyes.

They heard it then, the sound of rapidly approaching hoof beats. As one, they turned and stared west, down the gradient of the hill where they stood waiting, past Romerus's citadel in the distance and to the vast city beyond.

But it was not from Uryl that the horses approached.

Puzzlement flashed through Baruch and he raised a hand instinctively to the blade at his waist as his gaze swung north. He stared at the two figures storming across the plains toward the hill.

'Mother?' Tobias murmured in surprise a moment later.

Rafael frowned.

'Jared?'

They glanced at each other, faces reflecting Baruch's own bewilderment.

Jared reached them first and pulled up sharply. He leapt from his horse before the creature came to a halt, grabbed the bridle of his mother's steed when she slowed beside him, and helped her down.

'How did you know we were here?' said Hosanna as they approached.

'Navia,' Jared replied in a hard voice.

Rafael narrowed his eyes.

'What is wrong?'

It was Helena who replied, her voice as cold as her son's. 'Crovir went to Issin and forcefully took Eleaza and Kaleb from the palace. He killed a servant boy who tried to defend the children.'

Baruch rocked back on his heels. 'What?'

'Are you certain?' Tobias said harshly.

'Yes,' said Jared.

'Mila?' whispered Hosanna in the stunned hush, her expression stricken. 'And Kronos?'

Jared gritted his teeth. 'We took her to Larraak. Navia came to meet us halfway. She had a vision of what was happening and heard Mila screaming in her mind. She managed to calm her down, somehow. Beatrix is with them. As for Kronos, he left Issin with Crovir.'

Phebe covered her mouth with her hands, a soft whimper escaping her lips. Tears filled her eyes.

In the shocked stillness that followed, they heard another horse approach from the west. Bastian appeared below them a short while later.

He was alone.

He climbed the slope rapidly and dismounted in the shallow depression where they had left their steeds, before making his way toward them. Unease flashed across his face as he drew near.

His steps faltered. 'I was not expecting to see all of you here.' He frowned at Baruch. 'You said you wanted to talk?'

'Did you know?' said Baruch, his mouth full of ash.

Bastian stopped in his tracks, mystified. 'Know what?'

'That Crovir had taken Eleaza and Kaleb from Issin?' said Helena. She crossed the hilltop until she stood face to face with her step-brother. 'That he is planning to use them as collateral if Mila dares challenge him?'

'What—what are you talking about?' demanded the younger king.

Helena told him of all that had come to pass, of the true identity of the one who had killed Romerus, of Mila's flight from the Empire and her shocking discovery in the Zagros Mountains and the plains beyond.

Bastian listened wordlessly while she spoke, blood draining from his face, his expression aging in what seemed a matter of heartbeats, shoulders sagging and frame stooping as if an unbearable load weighed him down. It was when Helena mentioned Kadavan that he finally interrupted her.

'I know. I know about Kadavan and the army.'

Another wave of shock coursed through Baruch. 'How?'

Bastian gazed at him blindly. 'The troop commander who was in charge of the prison came to the palace this morning.'

Jared drew a breath in sharply. 'So he is aware? Crovir knows about the human army and what they intend?'

Bastian nodded.

'We have to warn them,' said Ysa.

Tobias turned to her, startled. 'You have made up your mind?'

Ysa walked up to him and caressed his face, her loving gaze unflinching. 'I made my decision that day, in Larraak.'

Baruch looked to Hosanna, his heart thundering in his chest, knowing that they stood on the precipice of something momentous, something that would forever change their world and the fate of millions of souls. She watched him for a moment before dipping her chin, her eyes bright and filled with determination.

'So it is agreed,' said Rafael, looking around their small group.

Bastian blinked, his expression finally clearing. 'What is?'

Baruch stared at his father, his pulse racing, blood roaring in his ears. 'We have to stop Crovir.'

'We will stand with Mila and the human army,' said Tobias.

Their words hung in the air, the meaning behind them irrefutable, reflecting the cold reality of their new conviction.

'You will turn against your own father?' Bastian said, his troubled gaze sweeping across Tobias, Ysa, and Jared before landing on Helena. 'And you your husband?'

'He killed Romerus,' said Helena quietly. 'And he blamed

our own daughter for the terrible crime he committed. Not only that, but he now seeks to control her actions by taking her children, his own flesh and blood, prisoner. Why can you not see it, brother? Why can you not see the evil that dwells inside him? The wickedness he wishes to tar us with, to drag us into the hellish nightmare born of his corrupted soul?'

Her voice shook, tears shimmering on her lashes as she gazed at the younger king.

'Because he is the other half of me,' Bastian whispered. 'He has always been. I cannot be without him.'

Helena watched him silently before raising gentle fingers to smooth out the lines on his brow.

'What will you do?' she breathed.

Bastian closed his eyes for a moment. The expression in their depths when he opened them once more was a knife driving into Baruch's chest.

'I do not know.'

Baruch clenched his jaw and felt Hosanna's hand slide into his, her shoulders shaking silently beside him.

They were all crying. For they knew. This was it. The beginning of the end. The dawn of the darkness that Hosanna had told Baruch Navia spoke of when they met in Nawaar, all those Moons ago. And they had chosen their side.

They would stand with the strongest and most righteous of all of them. The one who had started it all the day she made the fateful decision to spare a governor and a city. The one whose stark words in Larraak still resonated within them. The one who had convinced them to change the destiny that had been forged for them by a madman and dared them to take their fortune in their own hands.

Their cousin. Their sister. Their daughter. Their kin.

❄

CHAPTER THIRTY-THREE

Kronos watched the city burn below him, his face impassive. Shrieks and wails rose in the night, tortured voices echoing against the walls of the narrow canyon as skin blackened and flesh charred. Those who tried to escape the blaze fell rapidly upon the swords of the soldiers waiting beyond the wall, their scorched bodies finding relief in a swifter death.

It took a long time for the screaming to stop. It was only when the roar of the fire ravaging timber and thatch dwellings became the sole sound filling the ravine that Kronos finally wheeled his stallion around and trotted through his troops.

It is all her fault. Everything is. The blood of all these people is on her hands, not mine.

With hate for his wife a malignant blight slowly growing in his heart, Kronos ordered the soldiers south.

They met some fifty leagues north of the city of Nemrik, in a valley carved by the Tigra River, an army some three-thousand strong and growing.

Eight days had passed since Aäron departed Larraak, eight days during which he had met with the messengers who left Parsah over two Half Moons ago, on their mission to convene the leaders of the alliance and their troops. Eight days during which he could not see her face, could not touch her skin, could not kiss her lips.

In the short time that he had been separated from Mila, Aäron felt as if he had lost a part of himself. But though he ached to be with her, to fuse their bodies and souls together, he had little time to dwell on his yearning. There was a war to organize.

He stood talking with the governors and commanders of the various assembled factions, debating the plans he and Mila had started to put together in the hidden Parsah. It was as he was privately wondering at the fact that Darius had still not arrived with the troops from Dur Untash that the alarm sounded.

Aäron tensed at the distant sound of a horn coming from a hill to the east. It was a warning, one his men had been trained to issue upon seeing a potential enemy. Ignoring the murmur of nervous voices, he hurried from the makeshift table holding maps of the Empire and found his horse.

Kayan and a group of twenty soldiers joined him as he raced across the dark land toward the source of the signal.

'Do you think it is the Empire?' asked the captain as their mounts ate away the distance separating them from the elevation ahead.

'I hope not,' Aäron replied grimly. 'Otherwise this war starts tonight.'

It did not take them long to climb the slopes and find the

sentinels stationed in a shallow depression overlooking the plains that stretched toward the hazy, far-off peaks of the Zagros Range.

'What is it?' said Aäron as he lowered himself down beside one of the soldiers.

The man pointed. 'Over there, to the south. There are people coming.' He swallowed. 'A lot of them.'

Aäron narrowed his eyes in the direction he indicated. It was an overcast night, with clouds stretching across the heavens as far as the eye could see, blanketing out the moon and stars.

Then he saw it. Movement on the lowlands. A shifting in the darkness. Shadows where there should be none. His mouth went dry.

They were only three leagues away.

'Return to camp and raise the alarm,' he told Kayan briskly. 'We must—'

That was when they heard it. The sound of another horn. One they knew all too well.

Kayan drew a sharp breath. 'That is—'

Apprehension filled Aäron as he stared at the mass of people approaching across the plains. 'The distress call of Parsah.'

He headed down the hill and onto the lowlands with some ten men while the others returned to the camp. Then, as the moon finally pierced through the grey mantle covering the land, the first among them came into view.

'Megash?' Aäron whispered hoarsely.

He dug his thighs into his steed's flanks and galloped toward his brother, his heart thundering in his chest.

They met a moment later. A sleeping Gilgamesh sat in the saddle in front of Megash, head lolling against his father's chest.

'We found you,' the younger prince muttered in a tired voice, his shoulders sagging in relief.

Aäron stared past him to Nisuna and the baby in the sling around her chest, then to the thousands beyond, most on horses, some on carts, a few even on foot.

His gaze found his brother's face once more. 'What happened?'

MILA URGED BUROS ON, A COLD WIND WHIPPING AT HER HAIR and numbing her face. The stallion responded to her command, breath leaving his muzzle in fast pants as he accelerated, muscles moving powerfully below her.

'Slow down before you kill yourself!' Ysa shouted behind her.

Mila paid her no heed, her gaze focused on the hills outlined against the reddening sky ahead.

Day had broken by the time they reached the location of the meeting point she and Aäron had agreed upon with the commanders in Parsah and Dur Untash. They pulled up sharply on a ridge above the valley, their horses rearing up and stamping their hooves at the abrupt halt. Next to them rode one of the sentinels who had been posted to the south to watch for their approach.

Abu squawked and fluttered onto Mila's shoulder as she stared down the escarpment, his feathers stroking her left cheek briefly before he folded his wings and gripped her armor with his claws.

'This army looks larger than the one you spoke of, cousin,' said Hosanna.

Mila frowned. She was right. There were at least five thousand souls below them.

They made their way down the cliffside and soon reached the edge of the vast camp stretching along the banks of the Tigra. Silence fell around them as they trotted through rows of tents, the crowd stopping and staring, some faces hostile, most fearful. The banner of the red eagle flapped atop dozens of poles, the crimson bird stark against its pale background.

Mila realized it was the first time she would ride into battle under a pennant other than that of the Empire.

'There are injured people here,' murmured Phebe.

Mila remained silent, her troubled gaze sweeping the sea of bodies until it landed on the center of the camp and the figures who stood waiting under the shade of a canopy. She had eyes for only one of them.

As Aäron's features swam into sight, his lips curving in the faint smile she had become accustomed to, Mila allowed herself to feel again for the first time in days.

The horror and agony that had possessed her in Issin swept over her once more, causing her breath to catch in her throat. Though still raw and fresh in her mind, the pain had eased slightly in the company of her siblings and cousins.

They reached the canopy and dismounted. Then, unheeding of the eyes watching them, Mila crossed the ground to Aäron and wrapped her arms around his chest. He froze for an instant before enfolding her tightly in his hold.

Gasps sounded from all around. Mila ignored the shocked murmurs that followed and felt a modicum of peace sweep through her as she listened to the strong heartbeat underneath her ear.

'Not exactly the best way to kill those rumors, you two,' muttered someone close by.

She stepped back and looked past Aäron to find Megash gazing at them wryly. Governor Tanis stood beside him, eyes round, mouth opening and closing soundlessly.

'What are you doing here?' Mila frowned at Megash. 'You are several days early, are you not?'

Before he could reply, low voices rose behind her.

'Are those two, you know—?' Ysa muttered.

'What, fornicating?' said Hosanna bluntly. 'It looks like that might be the case, yes.'

'Hosanna!' Beatrix admonished.

'Seriously, your mouth is as filthy as that of your husband,' murmured Phebe.

'I could not agree more,' said Beatrix acerbically.

'What is going on?' Malachi asked.

'Keep up, brother!' snapped Hosanna.

Aäron took hold of Mila's chin and gently tilted her head. 'What is wrong?'

Mila registered his weary expression and the fresh creases on his brow. There was something else. Something deep in his eyes that caused unease to coil through her.

'Crovir took Eleaza and Kaleb to Uryl.' Her tone turned bitter. 'They are now prisoners in the citadel, although my— *father* would argue otherwise.'

Aäron stiffened and let go of her, his face darkening.

Mila indicated the camp. 'What happened here?'

A baby's wail rose from somewhere close by in the hush that followed.

'Dur Untash and the Parsah on the plains, the one the Empire knew of, are no more,' Aäron replied in a dull voice.

'What?' said Hosanna, her voice echoing the shock coursing through Mila.

'It is true,' said Megash with a dip of his chin. His gaze found Mila. 'It seems someone betrayed us.'

'So the men we sent to warn them were too late?' whispered Ysa, her face pale.

Confusion washed across the faces of the governors and commanders gathered under the canopy.

'What do you mean?' said Aäron, his eyes searching Mila's face for answers.

'The troop commander from Kadavan defected,' she said stiffly. 'He reached Uryl the day after Crovir took my children from Issin and told the kings what happened at the prison and what he knew of our plans.'

'We sent messengers to alert the governors of Dur Untash and Parsah,' said Hosanna. Lines furrowed her brow. 'Those men are no doubt dead.'

Troubled murmurs rose around them.

'We suspected the traitor was you, at first,' grumbled Tanis, staring at Mila with a somewhat guilty look.

Phebe frowned. 'Who destroyed Dur Untash and Parsah?'

Aäron closed his eyes briefly and took a shallow breath. Dread filled Mila at his expression. A flash of intuition followed.

'Kronos?' she said hoarsely before he could speak.

Aäron swallowed and nodded.

'Darius survived the fires at Dur Untash, although he is badly burnt,' Megash continued, anger and sadness lacing his voice.

'Fires?' repeated Phebe.

'Yes. After soldiers surrounded the canyon in the deep of night, they tossed barrels of oil from the heights above, straight down into the city. All they had to do after that was fire flame-lit arrows from outside the walls. Those who did not suffocate from the smoke or burn in the flames were killed when they tried to escape.'

Mila's gaze switched between Megash and Aäron. 'The troops? Governor Edras?'

'Only a hundred men survived of the thousand odd who

were based there. Most suffocated when smoke filled the caves or perished in the flames when they went to help the people in the valley.' Aäron paused. 'Governor Edras is among the dead.'

'And Parsah?' said Hosanna.

A tortured expression washed across Aäron's face. 'We had no soldiers based at the Parsah on the plains. There were only citizens there, some three thousand of them. Men and women who would have been ready to join our ranks if and when we asked. Most of them are dead. Kronos stormed the city with troops from Uryl and slaughtered nearly every living soul within its walls. Once our sentinels detected the smoke coming from that direction, Megash and soldiers from our palace went to the aid of those who survived the massacre.'

A horrified gasp escaped Beatrix. Hosanna uttered a colorful curse.

Mila raised a hand and gently touched his cheek, her heart breaking all over again at the agony in his blue eyes, anger and torment twisting her gut.

'I am sorry,' she whispered.

He clasped her fingers tightly. 'Why? It was not your fault.' He inhaled shakily. 'Megash and my father decided to mobilize the army in the hidden valley there and then, in case the soldiers of the Empire discovered its location. They arrived last night, with the survivors from Dur Untash and the fallen Parsah.'

Mila glanced around. 'And the king?'

Megash shook his head. Exasperation underscored his voice. 'He stayed behind with some two hundred soldiers to guard the city and its people. He would not leave the place of his birth.'

'So they know we are coming?' said Tanis with a scowl. 'The kings in Uryl?'

Mila nodded.

Megash stared at Hosanna and the others before frowning at Mila. 'There are only six of you here. Does this mean you did not manage to convince the other Immortals to join our ranks?'

A grim smile flashed across Mila's lips in the expectant silence. Megash's eyes widened.

'Bar Kronos, we will all stand with you,' said Ysa in a hard voice.

'We have been recruiting soldiers from the cities under our command and the garrisons we felt might be sympathetic to the rebellion,' said Hosanna. 'The others are bringing them here.'

'You are going to need plenty of manpower if you want to defeat the army of the Empire,' Phebe added dryly. 'These are men who have been trained by us throughout their years of battle. The skills they have learned are the ones we acquired over hundreds of years of conflict.'

As startled voices rose from the crowd, surprise mingling with elation, Aäron studied Mila intently. 'King Bastian?'

Mila shook her head slowly.

'My father did not say he would take the side of Crovir,' murmured Hosanna. 'But he did say he would not go against him.'

Mila gazed at Aäron, sorrow piercing her once more. 'My mother returned to Uryl, to protect Eleaza and Kaleb as best she can. She will die before she lets my father lay another finger on them.'

'The other queens have taken our children to a safe place in the South Desert, out of the reach of Crovir,' said Ysa bitterly.

'What now?' muttered Tanis.

'The plan has changed,' said Hosanna. 'Even as we speak, the army of the Empire is on the move. We need to attack now.'

The governors and commanders glanced at each other warily.

'But the rest of our troops are yet to arrive,' said Megash. 'There are more men and women joining us from the cities to the west and—'

'We cannot wait,' said Mila. 'Send messengers to meet them. Tell them we are moving south, as of today. If our suspicions are correct, then Tobias, Baruch, and the others may very well cross paths with the army from Uryl on their way here.'

CHAPTER THIRTY-FOUR

'*To me!*' shouted Navia.

Scores of men responded to her command, stumbling and backing away across the battleground until they reached her side, blood weeping from their injuries, some dragging fallen companions with them.

Navia moved toward their enemy, soldiers of the Empire who once stood beside her and who now faced her on the field of war, faces filled with deadly intent under the late afternoon sun.

They had come across the army yesterday at dawn, a few leagues from Qataara, on the eighth day after they made that fateful decision on the hill close to Romerus's citadel. By then, they had some three thousand odd men at their side, soldiers from the various garrisons and cities she and her siblings and cousins had traveled to during the past Half Moon, men who had elected to join the side of the human alliance planning to storm Uryl and depose King Crovir.

Her swords arced through the air as she danced between her opponents, blades finding flesh and bone easily while the soldiers froze, immobilized by the power of her mind, shields and weapons dropping from limp fingers. The men behind her rallied forth once more, cries leaving their throats as they charged toward the ones who were once their comrades in arms, their exhaustion overpowered by their will to survive.

'IS SHE NOT GLORIOUS?' SAID JARED.

He deflected a blow to his head with his shield and stabbed two soldiers, his gaze darting to where Navia fought some distance away with an entourage of soldiers, sunlight glinting on her bloodstained weapons, her face a study of grim concentration.

Baruch swooped beneath a circle of spears and twisted on his heels, his swords humming as he slashed at the men around him.

'Really?! You think now is the right time to be indulging your life-long infatuation with my sister?'

'You just do not appreciate her,' Jared retorted sullenly, striking down two more men.

Unease filtered through him as he studied the battlefield. Though they had gathered considerable troops in the past Half Moon, their numbers were overshadowed by the regiments of the Empire, currently some five-thousand strong and growing as more battalions arrived from the south. Although he suspected Kronos was somewhere among them, he had yet to see him.

The whistle of arrows came from the sky once more. Jared narrowed his eyes.

They never learn, do they?

He pierced a captain in the gut with his sword and raised a hand toward the two hundred or so deadly projectiles sailing through the air toward him and the soldiers who fought at his side, men from the garrisons at Omran and Duruin faithful to their campaign.

The arrows stopped some twenty feet above their heads before dropping harmlessly to the ground as they had on countless occasions before, the clatter lost in the cries and the clash of swords resonating across the plains.

'Do not falter!' he shouted to the soldiers beside him.

They nodded, expressions hardening with resolve despite this being the thirty-fifth hour of the battle.

Jared lifted his blade in the air before pointing it forward. At his signal, the soldiers protecting the archers at his back dropped behind their shields. Then his men rose and fired their bows toward their enemy.

RAFAEL EVADED TWO SWORDS, BLOCKED A THIRD WITH HIS STAFF, and jabbed the spear-headed ends into the chests of the soldiers around him. He finished them off with blows to the head as they doubled over, aiming for the fragile bones over their temples.

Another four soldiers surrounded him.

He smiled grimly. 'Well, that is not very fair now, is it?'

He twisted a ring in the middle of his staff, releasing the twin blades from inside.

'Looks like you are finally getting serious!' yelled Tobias as he watched Rafael take down the enemy encircling him.

'I normally heal these bastards. It is a bit hard to have to kill them now!' he shouted back. 'And should you not be worrying about yourself?'

Air left Tobias's lips in a gasp as he dove to the ground, avoiding the swords and spears heading toward his back and head. He rolled, leapt to his feet, twisted at the waist, and brought his right leg up and around, his heel smashing powerfully into the jaws of the soldiers behind him, sending them crashing to the dirt.

Rafael scowled. 'Now you are just showing off!'

Tobias grinned, then looked over to Jared.

'Brother, do you recall that time at the Nahal River?' he called out, elbowing a soldier in the face before slashing another two across the neck.

Jared blocked the spear aimed at his chest and looked around with a frown as he kneed his attacker in the gut. 'What, you mean—?'

'Yes,' said Tobias. 'There is a dry stream bed running across the plains a few hundred feet south from where we are standing.'

JARED SCANNED THE BATTLEGROUND, PULSE RACING.

'We will need to move our men back!' he said with a nod. He turned and shouted over to his right. 'Navia!'

She spun on her heels in a low crouch, swords carving through three enemy soldiers before she gazed his way.

'We have to get our soldiers away from here! Tell them to retreat!'

He felt her power touch his consciousness, ghostly fingers seeking out his thoughts. A shiver danced down his spine at the intimate contact. Her eyes widened for a moment as she registered his plan. Then she dipped her chin briskly.

In the moments that followed, Jared heard her voice in his head as she communicated the urgent command to their men the way she knew best.

As the soldiers drew back, he charged forward, Tobias and

Rafael at his side. Two hundred feet later, he stopped and crouched down on one knee. Then, with his brother and cousin protecting him from attack, he laid his hands on the ground and closed his eyes.

Dirt danced around his fingertips as he sent faint tendrils of elemental force through the earth, seeking out weak points and cracks in the rocks beneath the shallow channel where water once coursed.

He took a shallow breath before unleashing his powers.

THE GROUND SPLIT AHEAD OF JARED. NAVIA WIDENED HER stance to maintain her balance and watched with bated breath as the fissure snaked south before splitting to branch east and west, heart thundering with excitement at this indomitable show of force.

Alarmed cries rose from the enemy as violent tremors shook the earth, cries that turned to panicked shouts when a rift appeared beneath their feet, where the streambed once lay. The break expanded, forming a crevasse some half a league in length and fifty feet wide. Hundreds of soldiers were swallowed by the chasm, their screams tearing the air as they fell to their deaths, their consciousness winking out from Navia's mind.

Stunned silence spread across the battleground when the reverberations died down moments later.

KRONOS SCOWLED FROM HIS POSITION ON THE HILLS TO THE northeast, rage burning through him as he watched the earth consume his troops, his stallion prancing agitatedly beneath him. He signaled to the troop commanders at his sides. Then, blade glinting in the sunlight, he rose in his saddle and stormed down the slope toward their enemy.

Behind him came the rest of the Empire's army, their angry roars splitting the very heavens.

BARUCH WATCHED THE SEA OF BODIES DARKENING THE HILLS AND plains to their left. 'Son of a—'

'Fall into formation!' Tobias shouted.

The soldiers hesitated before responding to his command, years of training coming to the fore despite their evident fear. They moved across the battleground and positioned themselves behind their shields, locking the metal buckles together, spears protruding through the gaps at the top. Organized rows soon enclosed their troops on four sides.

'Archers, in position now!' yelled Jared.

Behind the lines of soldiers with shields, hundreds of archers stretched the strings of their bows and aimed their arrows at the sky.

Navia gritted her teeth when she felt the murderous intent of the thousands of men galloping across the flatlands, the hordes thinning as they spread out to encircle them. While the ground trembled and the battle cries of their enemies tore the air asunder, she reached deep inside her chest, to the source of her powers, and prepared to unleash the ungodly force dwelling inside her heart.

Then she felt it. Faint voices that grew rapidly inside her mind, gathering in momentum until their roars eclipsed that of the enemy thundering toward them. Rising above it, full of such power and determination it sent a shiver down Navia's spine, was a hauntingly familiar consciousness.

'Mila,' she breathed.

She looked north, her siblings and cousins following suit as they too perceived the noise.

Charging across the plains toward the army of the Empire, an awe-inspiring sight to behold, came thousands of soldiers, golden banners depicting a red eagle streaming above them.

And there, leading the men and women, the heads of the human alliance and her Immortal kin at her side, black stallion moving powerfully beneath her while her armor-clad hawk circled in the sky, came the Red Queen.

CHAPTER THIRTY-FIVE

CROVIR SWIPED THE TRAY OFF THE TABLE, SENDING THE CARAFE and tumblers crashing to the floor. The liquid within stained the marble as red as the rage filling his heart.

'You mean to say that even now, there are more humans joining the ranks of those traitors?' he hissed.

Kronos nodded from where he sat, a servant carefully wrapping a bandage around the wound in his arm while another cleaned the gash on his head.

'I barely made it here from Duruin,' he said with a grunt.

Crovir gritted his teeth. Over fifty days had passed since Kronos and the Empire's army first clashed with the human alliance now advancing steadily toward Uryl. Fifty days during which their enemy vanquished every city and outpost from Qataara to Omran, forcing the Empire's soldiers to gradually retreat south.

But it is not just the human alliance that is our foe in this war, he thought bitterly. *That all our children bar Kronos have elected to stand against us is truly unforgivable. She has thoroughly corrupted them.*

A crimson mist filled his vision at the thought of his lastborn child. Mila, the one he always suspected could one day topple him. The only living witness to the terrible act he committed nearly two months past.

He scowled. *She will not defeat me that easily.*

He turned to Kronos. 'Send for them.'

Kronos stared, his eyes slowly widening. 'You mean—?'

'Yes.' A thrill of satisfaction coursed through Crovir. 'They will not see this coming.'

BASTIAN STOOD OUTSIDE CROVIR'S CHAMBERS, HANDS FISTED AT his sides as he listened to his brother plot with his nephew. The agony and doubt that had filled his every waking moment since the last time he saw his own children and his half-sister on the hill outside Romerus's citadel finally crystallized into an inescapable truth.

He had to stop this war.

He twisted on his heels and headed deep into the palace, his resolve growing with every step.

MILA TIPPED THE JUG OVER HER HEAD AND CLOSED HER EYES AS the cascading liquid cooled her skin and washed away some of the grime and blood from the past day. She was splashing more water on her neck and arms when someone entered the tent.

Aäron stopped near the opening and studied her with a grin. Abu spread his wings where he perched on a chest and flew onto his shoulder as he walked toward her, the hawk letting out a contented squeak when Aäron tickled his chest.

'You are looking mighty fine, Red Queen,' he drawled. 'That hair color suits you.'

Mila touched her recently-dyed locks self-consciously. They were a vibrant red. It was Hosanna who had suggested the change.

'Though you are scary enough as it is on the battlefield, I suspect this will make you stand out even more and truly strike fear in the hearts of our enemy.'

Having indulged her cousin on a whim on the eve of their latest battle, Mila now harbored mixed feelings about the change. But she could not deny that it had caused the Empire's soldiers to falter on many an occasion in the past days.

Any regret she entertained was replaced by concern as she examined the fresh wounds marking Aäron's skin. Despite his easy smile, he had suffered many injuries today.

It had been sixty-six days since they encountered the Empire's army outside Qataara, where they came to the aid of her brothers and cousins and the soldiers who had decided to stand at their side. Of all the outposts and cities they conquered as they progressed south, Girisu had proven the hardest to crush. Bribed by King Crovir's promises of untold riches, the men at the garrison and the amassed army outside it remained fiercely loyal to Crovir and Kronos to the bitter end. It was only that evening that the human-Immortal alliance finally took the fort, after their fiercest engagement yet.

With the Empire's army falling back toward Uryl, they had a night's reprieve in which to rest and heal, something they had rarely enjoyed over the past two months.

When he was not busy fighting or getting brief periods of sleep, Rafael spent his time taking care of their soldiers' wounds, Phebe working tirelessly at his side. The additional energy the Immortal couple spent looking after the injured men and women in their ranks had started to take its toll and the circles under their eyes darkened with each passing day. Only Mila, Tobias, and Baruch showed no sign of fatigue among the Immortals, their endurance bolstered by hundreds of years of leading the most aggressive conflicts the Empire had seen, although none of them had ever been in a war that had lasted this long.

Despite the fact that Rafael had tended to him on several occasions already, Aäron showed more wounds day by day, sleep deprivation and physical exhaustion rendering him more vulnerable on the battlefield. This only served to remind her of the stark difference between them. That he was a human with but one life, whereas she was an Immortal with all seventeen of her lives still intact, the only one among her kin who could make that claim.

This realization made her feel powerless in a way she had never before experienced and the fear that he would perish in this war grew steadily inside her, a darkness that threatened to swallow her very soul.

He closed the gap between them, an anxious look washing across his face at what he read on hers.

'What are you thinking?' he said, tilting her chin gently with a finger.

Mila hesitated before taking his hand and lifting it to her cheek.

'I am scared,' she admitted in a low voice.

Her fingers fluttered over a cut on his temple and another on his arm, anguish spearing through her at the thought that he had suffered pain.

Aäron cocked an eyebrow. 'What, these?' He indicated his wounds. 'They are nothing.'

Mila shook her head and bit her lip. 'No. I am scared of losing you. This war could drag on for another month still and you could—'

Aäron covered her mouth with his hand, a frown creasing his brow.

'Stop right there,' he said in a hard voice. 'I always knew such a day might come. I realized it when I became a soldier in Parsah, and even more so after I joined your army. Every single man and woman outside this tent is also conscious of this fact. If we fall, we will not rise again. We will succumb to eternal rest, unlike you Immortals.' His lips curved in a faint smile. 'But for us, it is a sacrifice worth making.'

Mila closed her eyes briefly before staring into the bright blue gaze above her once more.

'What of me?' she whispered. 'The thought of spending hundreds of years without you is intolerable. I might as well—'

He kissed her then, his mouth landing on hers with a fierceness that matched his expression, fingers closing around her head and locking her in place while he ravaged her lips.

'Never say that again!' he gasped a moment later, their heated pants mingling as they struggled to catch their breath. 'Never say that you would follow me in death! What of Eleaza and Kaleb? What of the rest of your kin?'

Mila inhaled shakily, remorse bringing a bitter taste to the back of her throat.

'You must live,' said Aäron, his tone turning heartbreakingly gentle. 'Promise me this. That you *will* live. That you will never look back. That you will carry on treading the path that was always yours to follow. A path where your strength and compassion will relieve other human cities and nations of any misery and tyranny that afflict them. A path where you champion the weak and the just and all those who will stand next to you.' He paused and softly wiped away the tears trembling on her eyelashes. 'I grew up despising you and your kind,' he continued in a voice that quivered. 'But yet, here I am. Standing at your side, willing to lay down my life for this noble cause. And for you, my queen.'

Mila closed her arms around his waist and rested her cheek against his chest, listening to his strong heartbeat, imprinting the sound in her mind so she could recall it later, in the hundreds of empty years to come, until her very last moment upon this world.

They reached Uryl at dusk the next day, the scattered troops they encountered on the way dispatched with ease. But instead of the last stand they expected to have to make outside the capital, they found the city deserted, its gates open and its army absent, the signs of a fierce battle in evidence. The thrones of the palace stood empty and pyres of the dead burned on the plains.

It was as she stood in the shadows of the kings' statues in the main plaza with Aäron, Megash, and her Immortal kin, unease filling her while the human alliance celebrated jubilantly around them, that the alarm came.

Mila's anxiety at not finding her mother and her children in the city intensified as she stared toward the gates leading to the moat, her hand on the handle of her sword.

A commotion accompanied the fading sound of the horn. Then, the crowd parting before him, silence spreading out in a slow circle where he passed, sitting tall and proud on his stallion, came King Bastian.

He pulled up a short distance from where they stood and dismounted, his gaze never leaving her as he approached. He was dressed in full battle armor, a sight Mila last recalled seeing over a hundred years ago.

'I have been waiting for you,' he said coolly.

'Helena? The children?' Mila said between numb lips.

'I got them out of the city and took them to Eridug ten days ago,' said Bastian. 'Most of the citizens from Uryl are there now, along with some six hundred soldiers who wish to join your alliance. Helena will take Eleaza and Kaleb to meet the other queens in the South Desert tonight.'

A wave of relief washed over Mila at this news. Aäron squeezed her shoulder lightly.

'Does your presence here mean you are willing to stand with us, father?' said Hosanna, her face pale. She looked around the plaza and at the evidence of a conflict they had not instigated. 'Was it you who took Uryl?'

Bastian dipped his chin. 'Yes. I had to end this madness.' He stared at Mila again, his expression hardening. 'When the time comes, you must let me take care of Crovir. Can you promise me this?'

Mila returned his gaze unflinchingly amid the surprised murmurs rising around them. 'I cannot. For the sake of Romerus. For the sake of my children. For the sake of the boy he killed in Issin and the thousands of lives he has taken. If I get to him first, I *will* stop him.'

Bastian watched her for a silent moment, a muscle jumping in his jawline.

'You are indeed the child of my brother!' he snapped. A frustrated sigh left his lips. 'I expected no other answer. We will settle this later. Come, we must gather everyone and hurry.'

Tobias frowned. 'Why? And where to?'

Apprehension filled Mila at the look in Bastian's eyes.

'The reason you did not find Crovir here today is because he is gathering a second army from the North, one he has kept a secret from everyone except Kronos it seems,' he said bitterly. 'It is an army he has amassed over many years, barbarians and mercenaries from the farthest reaches of the Caucasia Mountains and the frozen lands beyond. The very worst kind of warriors, those who would spill the blood of their own kin in exchange for riches. There are more than five thousand of them, not counting the army of the Empire, and they will crush anything and anyone in their path on their way here.' He paused, an anguished grimace twisting his features for a moment. 'It is folly I could no longer ignore, hence why I am standing in front of you right now.'

Horrified gasps sounded from the commanders and captains within earshot. Aäron's knuckles whitened at his sides as Bastian's words were conveyed through the crowd.

'We must warn the troops in the other cities and outposts,' said Baruch.

Mila looked at him and the rest of her kin before meeting the eyes of the leaders of the human alliance, her gaze landing on Aäron last. As panicked uproar spread around them, she saw the same icy resolve dawn on all their faces.

She turned to Bastian. 'When will they get here?'

'Three days, four at most.'

CHAPTER THIRTY-SIX

Bastian's prediction proved to be wrong by several days. By the time they reached Eridug at dawn, the fires of the barbarian army and the Empire's soldiers were already visible on the horizon to the north.

More than half the women and nearly all the children at the fortress had already disappeared into the desert, on their way to the relative safety of the coastline of the South Sea. The rest refused to leave, determined to stay at their husbands' sides to the very end. Many joined their ranks, arming themselves with whatever weapons they could find at the garrison. Along with every able-bodied man and youth from the capital, they stood atop the ramparts of the defensive wall, soldiers once loyal to the Empire beside those of the alliance, their fear overshadowed by their will to survive as they faced enemy troops nearly double their size.

Having arranged their men in a thick defensive square around the fortress, the Immortals and the human leaders took the full brunt of the initial attacks. Over a thousand men perished on that first day. Everyone knew this would be the decisive battle of the war.

On the morning of the second day, Hosanna fell, struck in the neck by an arrow. Rafael healed her, and Phebe and Ysa protected her body until she awoke from death. In that time, Baruch killed nearly a hundred men in his wrath. That evening, Malachi suffered a death, victim of an axe injury that cleaved him from navel to neck. As he lay bleeding and unmoving, Navia unleashed a psychic blast that extinguished the consciousness of nearly two hundred enemy soldiers.

When Navia was struck in the heart by the errant spear of a Caucasus mercenary on the dawn of the third day, Jared went berserk, his elemental powers creating a sandstorm that choked and buried hundreds. Later, he too perished, overcome by nearly ten dozen men.

And so all the Immortals met their death at least once as day turned into night, even King Bastian. All except Mila, whose body vibrated with an ungodly energy that made it impossible for anyone to harm her.

On the fourth day, the Empire's army breached the east flank of their defenses and reached the fortress. As she fought to reestablish the fallen front with Aäron, Megash, and Governor Tanis, the screams of women and children rose at their backs.

'Do not look away from the enemy before you!' Mila shouted at the distressed soldiers around her. 'You will hold this line so that no more of them may pass!'

The men steeled themselves at her command and faced the Empire's army while Eridug burned behind them. By the time the sun set, their defenses had all but fallen and they were forced to retreat from the outpost.

❄

'ARE YOU CERTAIN THIS WILL WORK?' SAID HOSANNA GRIMLY, HER breath leaving her lips in shallow pants.

Mila frowned. 'This is likely to be our last charge.' She glanced at the battle-weary soldiers gathered on the elevation behind them. 'It is the only strategy Aäron and I could think of that may give us an advantage in the current situation.'

'It is a clever one,' said Baruch.

'But unpredictable,' murmured Rafael.

'We have never tried anything like this before,' added Ysa.

Tobias shrugged and wiped sweat from his face. 'We do not exactly have a choice. And there is a first time for everything.'

Jared winced and pressed a hand against his chest before gripping his broadsword. 'I agree.'

Beatrix cast a worried look his way.

They were standing on a low hill to the northwest of Eridug. Stretching out before them was a battlefield covered in the corpses of those who had fallen these past days and nights, desert sand crimson from spilled blood and gore.

The sky reflected the color of death as the sun raced toward the horizon from the dark side of the world, the reddening heavens ahead rendered even more ominous by the vast flocks of carrion birds circling above them. The creatures' shrieks and screeches bounced off the sand dunes as they alighted on severed limbs and heads.

Beyond the remains of the dead stood the enemy's army, their vast troops outnumbering those of the alliance by a significant fraction. Behind the southern frontline of the silent hostile mass, flames continued to rage through the last outpost of the Empire, the black smoke spiraling from the burning buildings more evident as night turned to day. Shrill screams occasionally tore the air. The thick, metal gates guarding the garrison lay buckled and twisted from the constant battering they had received.

Even though Jared had recovered from his death and had his injuries healed by Rafael, there was still some residual stiffness where a dozen swords had entered his heart only two days before. And it was not exactly as if he had had time to rest and recover since.

He looked at Navia where she stood in full battle armor to his right. For all that he had repaired the hole in her chest shield, he could still see traces where the spear had torn through the metal.

He knew she had experienced several deaths in the years before she became a regiment commander, but he had never seen her perish in front of his eyes. Witnessing her fall for the first time had filled him with a fury like none he had experienced before, and he swore he would do his utmost to never have to suffer such a sight again.

As if she sensed his thoughts, Navia glanced over at him before gazing at the soldiers of the alliance behind them. The expression he glimpsed in the depths of her green eyes in that brief moment sent an ache through his heart that had little to do with his recent wounds.

He knew then with the utmost certainty that she harbored the same forbidden feelings for him as he did for her.

'ARE YOU READY, COUSIN?' SAID MILA ON HER RIGHT.

Navia's gaze shifted to the Red Queen, the bittersweet emotions raging through her heart abating in the face of the indomitable, pale gray eyes staring back at her.

'Yes,' she replied in a confident voice.

As the primary tool of the first wave of their attack, she stood in the middle of the line of Immortals leading the final assault.

'Let us go then, sister,' said Baruch to her left.

He flashed her a fierce smile. Navia gazed lovingly at her older brother and nodded. Then she gripped the bloodstained broadsword in her hands and raced down the incline, a savage sound tearing from her throat as she reached inside herself to the source of her powers.

Her siblings, cousins, and the army of the alliance followed after her, their own battle cries tearing the air asunder as they charged toward the troops rushing across the plains to meet them. When a third of the Empire's soldiers had crossed the field, Navia let her abilities loose and focused on the minds of the enemy's sweeping numbers.

Thousands froze in their tracks behind the initial tide, bodies immobilized for the briefest of moments by the terrible energy gripping their heads.

It was all the time the alliance needed.

As the enemy troops faltered, Jared clenched his jaw and released his elemental powers. Sand rose between the soldiers of the Empire in the forefront of the surge and those temporarily crippled behind them, thick, fountaining walls of spinning grit some ten feet high that lifted many off their feet and sent them tumbling to the ground.

With Navia continuing to advance, paralyzing further sections of the enemy troops with her mind, he raised more walls, separating their startled enemy.

Mila smiled savagely.

If their numbers are double ours and their assaults overwhelm us, then the best way to fight back is to divide them.

It was Aäron who had spoken those words the previous evening, during a brief reprieve in the war. Mila had stared at him, surprised once more by his tactical reasoning.

In the past, whenever she had led the Empire's troops into battle, their numbers and fighting skills had always outweighed and outclassed those of their enemy, and they had crushed entire cities by the sheer might of their advance.

This war was different. A lot of the men they faced were warriors the Immortals themselves had trained. Not only were they often more skilled than the soldiers of the alliance, they were also more numerous.

'What do you propose we do?' Bastian had said.

Aäron had dragged the pointed end of his sword in the sand and sketched out an outline of their surroundings. 'The sand dunes to the north and south of the main battleground could provide cover for a surprise approach. If we position our forces on this hill by dawn,' he indicated a line to the northwest of Eridug, 'the enemy will not see how many of us are missing from their location on the plains. We can move half of our troops around under cover of darkness and place them here and here.'

He indicated the sand dunes on the drawing and frowned. 'We need a way to carve up their army into more manageable divisions. I think we stand a chance of winning this war if we overpower them in small groups.'

Hosanna's brow furrowed. 'How though? We cannot exactly build walls to separate them.'

Mila stiffened as the idea suddenly bloomed in her mind.

'Yes, we can,' she breathed, turning to Jared. 'Sand. You can use the sand to divide them.' Her gaze shifted to Navia. 'But we have to make sure they do not come at us all at once. So we need a way to stop their charge, if only for brief moments.'

Navia's eyes widened. 'You want me to restrain them with my powers?'

Mila nodded. Aäron looked around the circle of surprised faces before gazing at her.

He grinned. 'That could work.' His smile faded. 'It does, however, mean you will have to hold the frontline with less men for the rest of this night.'

Tobias glanced at the other Immortals. 'We can do that.'

Baruch nodded, a faint smile on his lips. 'Indeed we can, cousin.'

Mila had studied the drawing in the sand with narrowed eyes. 'We could do with something else. Something that will grant us the element of surprise even more.'

As she tore into the first of the enemy soldiers with her blades, Mila heard the distant roars rising from the north and south. Through a break in the whirling sand walls surrounding them, she caught a glimpse of Aäron charging down the sand dunes to her left on Buros, his own steed having perished two days past. Behind him came the hundreds of men who had lain hidden in the sand most of the night with some of the leaders of the alliance.

On her right, riding at the forefront of the southern wave of their troops, came Bastian, Megash, and the other governors.

In the sky above, Abu whirled, his armor glinting in the rays of the rising sun, his shriek telling her that their strategy was working.

Then his body disappeared in a brilliant light as the men and women she had left on the elevation behind raised their shields, the polished metal catching the golden light of the Heavenly orb as it emerged above the opposite horizon, turning its radiance into a deadly weapon that blinded the enemy's troops below them while sparing those of the alliance.

The arrows came next, Jared and Aäron's archers rising behind the soldiers with the shields and raining their deadly projectiles on the sightless army on the plains.

KRONOS SHIELDED HIS EYES AND SWORE AS HE WATCHED THE SKY darken with hundreds of whistling arrows through his parted fingers. He raised his shield and blocked several of the projectiles while dozens of men fell around him.

An arrow struck his right thigh, another his stallion's neck. He ripped them out of their bleeding flesh with a vengeful cry and turned toward the enemy troops swooping down the sand dunes to the north. Fury filled his heart when he spotted a familiar figure riding a black stallion. He dug his thighs into his horse's flanks and raced toward the man who had taken away the woman he once loved more than life itself.

MILA WIDENED HER STANCE TO KEEP HER BALANCE WHILE THE ground shifted beneath her. Ripples danced across the plains as Jared moved the very earth, creating rises and dips where there were none, and fissures that widened to swallow the Empire's men.

Meanwhile, the Seer ran through their enemy, forcing hundreds to their knees with her own unholy force while her blades carved through flesh and bone, her cold face filled with a light that seemed to burn from within, blood staining her hair, skin, and armor crimson. All around her, the alliance's soldiers closed in for the kill.

Abu's call suddenly came from above. Mila's heart stuttered in her chest at the apprehension she detected in his cry. She followed his body with her eyes as he dove toward the land to the north. Then, between a gap in the walls of sand that still stood, she glimpsed the white stallion and saw Kronos close the distance that separated him from Aäron.

She moved, her feet carrying her across the ground before her mind completed the command, fear twisting her stomach.

CHAPTER THIRTY-SEVEN

THE BROADSWORD HUMMED PAST HIS EAR AND SLICED A SLIVER of hair from his temple. Aäron dropped beneath Kronos's next swing, air leaving his throat in a grunt.

They had abandoned their horses and fought on the desert sand while their men clashed violently around them. Kronos let out an incoherent roar and stabbed at him once more.

Aäron blocked the blade before it could pierce his skin, muscles burning as he strained to push the Immortal's sword down. Their blades clashed again and again, Kronos's anger visibly rising as he failed to cut him.

He had just deflected another blow when pain suddenly bloomed on his right flank, wrenching a gasp from his lips. Aäron glanced from the dagger that had slipped under his armor to the grinning man who held it. It was the troop commander from Kadavan.

Abu swooped down from the sky, an angry shriek leaving his chest as he clawed and pecked at the soldier's head and face.

Aäron jumped back just as Kronos knocked the hawk out

of the air, his broadsword carving through the bird's armor and breaking his left wing before sending him crashing into the ground some dozen feet away.

Despite the knife in his flank tearing across his flesh, Aäron raised his sword and blocked strikes from human and Immortal soldier alike.

Then he saw her. She raced across the plains toward them, her blades striking the men in her path in lightning-fast moves, red hair streaming behind her, rage and panic painted across her beautiful features.

He gripped the dagger buried in his waist, ripped it out, and slashed the Kadavan troop commander across the neck.

Fire bloomed in his back in the next moment, robbing him of his breath. It seared straight through his body and out his chest, paralyzing him.

Mila watched Aäron turn and slash the Kadavan troop commander's throat with the dagger that had been lodged in his flank.

Then, as the giant soldier gargled and choked around the red flood fountaining from his neck, Kronos's broadsword entered Aäron's back in a violent thrust. Aäron gasped, eyes widening and body stiffening as the blade tore through flesh and bone and exited the left side of his chest.

Mila stumbled, shock causing her to falter for a heartbeat.

A scream left her lips with her next breath. *'Nooooooo!'*

Navia looked around as the agonizing cry tore through

her mind and echoed in her ears. Her eyes widened as she beheld the scene several hundred feet to her left.

AÄRON SLOWLY COLLAPSED TO HIS KNEES, HIS BLADE FALLING AT his side. He barely felt any pain when Kronos yanked the broadsword out of his back.

The Immortal's shadow engulfed him and the faint hum of the blade came again as he swung it down to cleave Aäron's head from his body.

It never touched his skin.

METAL CLASHED AS MILA BLOCKED KRONOS'S SWORD WITH A trident dagger a foot from Aäron's neck. Her own broadsword found her former mate's flesh in the next moment, carving through bone and gristle, slicing through his right forearm just above the wrist.

Kronos screamed, his sword thudding onto the sand, still gripped in a hand that was no longer attached to his body. He stumbled backward, fingers clutching at the scarlet jets spurting from his severed flesh.

Mila followed, dropping her broadsword and reaching for the second trident dagger in the sheath on her right thigh. She crossed the twin blades across his neck and slashed his throat.

Kronos's eyes widened above her, disbelief overshadowing his fear and rage. Then he fell to the desert, his blood staining the sand beneath him.

Mila turned without a backward glance and rushed to the side of the man who lay dying a few feet away.

'Watch out!' someone shouted nearby.

She dimly recognized Governor Tanis's voice as she dropped to her knees beside Aäron. His eyes were closed and his face pale. Blood gushed from his wounds.

'For the love of the gods, Red Queen, get a hold of yourself!' roared Tanis, blocking two soldiers' blades before they could reach her.

Mila ignored him and lifted Aäron's head onto her lap, her tears spilling over and landing on his face, the agony searing through her body a wound that would never heal.

Tanis gasped as the soldiers converging on them suddenly froze in their tracks. In her mind, Mila felt the Seer's power and knew her cousin would stop anyone who got too close to her in this timeless moment of loss.

Aäron's lashes fluttered as her tears landed on his lids. He opened his eyes a heartbeat later, dilated pupils constricting as he focused on her face.

'Do not cry,' he said in a low voice.

His face blurred as more tears filled Mila's vision. She wiped them away angrily, not wanting to miss a single instant of this precious time she had left with him.

Blood spilled past Aäron's lips as he took a rasping breath. They curved in a gentle smile and his gaze roamed her face, as eager as she to carve this moment in his mind.

'Find me in our next lives,' he whispered. He raised bloodied fingers to her cheek and stroked her skin for the last time. 'I will give you my heart a thousand times over.'

Mila clutched his hand, engraving his features in her memory and absorbing his fading heat into her body as he went limp in her hold, his blue eyes closing for the last time, his face relaxing as death claimed him.

'And I will give you mine a thousand times more,' she murmured brokenly.

She brought her lips to his, stealing his last breath, sealing it deep inside her.

Mila held him for a while longer as the war raged around them, until Megash reached her side. The younger prince collapsed to the ground with a tortured sob, fingers moving frantically across the gaping wound in his dead brother's chest.

She kissed Aäron's eyes and placed his head in Megash's lap. 'Protect him.'

'What?' Megash mumbled, tears streaming down his face.

Mila rose and walked over to her wounded hawk. She gathered the squeaking bird gently in her hands and left him by Megash before collecting her sword and trident daggers from where they lay in the sand by Kronos's body.

As she turned to face the battlefield, the ground split at her feet.

Then a terrible blast erupted from her body, throwing men to the ground a hundred feet around them. She advanced across the plains, the power of her steps cracking the earth and making it tremble, her rage causing the very air to shimmer and sending sand spiraling in angry, twisting funnels, her eyes seeking the masses before her for the one she truly wanted.

It ends now.

Navia gasped as the dreadful force washed over her. She reached out and steadied the minds of her kin and as many of the alliance as she could with her own, protecting them from the paralyzing effect of Mila's wrath. Never before had she witnessed such violent energy from the Red Queen. She leaned against the physical pressure buffeting them, struggling to maintain her balance.

To her right, Jared anchored himself to the ground with

one hand and held on to the other Immortals with his elemental powers. Soon, the only ones left standing in the middle of the battlefield were them.

As Jared's walls of sand came crashing down, Navia finally saw Crovir up ahead, on the eastern edge of the plains. The Immortal king had been driven to his knees by the weight of his daughter's fury.

MILA STARTED TO RUN, FISSURES SPREADING ACROSS THE ground in her path, her gaze focused unblinkingly on the monster who had given her life, fire filling her veins and heart.

Crovir fought the sandstorm lashing at him and slowly crawled to his feet, his broadsword held in a white-knuckled grip. His face paled when he saw her and he turned to run. He was too late. He twisted at the last moment to block her strike.

An inhuman roar left Mila's lips as she leapt in the air and brought her broadsword down, cleaving his blade in two when she landed in front of him. As her father stared numbly at his shattered weapon, she spun and slashed through his armor, the edge of her sword carving a red trail across his body from his left shoulder to his right hip.

Crovir cried out and stumbled back, hand fumbling for the dagger at his waist. Mila swung her blade around again.

It clashed against another, sparks erupting in the air where metal met metal, the sound ringing in her ears and echoing across the battlefield.

She turned her head and met Bastian's gaze.

'Stop!' he shouted.

'Get out of my way!' snarled Mila.

She slid her sword down his in a flash of sparks,

sidestepped around him, and brought her blade up to slash Crovir's neck.

Bastian blocked her attack again, his movement lightning fast despite the pressure of her rage, his agony painted across his face.

'Stop, I am begging you,' he said brokenly. 'He is my other half. Let me be the one who ends this.'

'What?!' gasped Crovir, ashen-faced. 'You would—you would *kill* me, brother?'

Mila shook her head, blood roaring in her ears, heart burning with incandescent fury. 'I cannot. I *will* not.'

She met Bastian's tortured gaze. The Immortal king suddenly gasped and stiffened.

In her mind and from across the battlefield, Mila heard Navia's terrible scream. Her own pulse stuttered, shock overcoming her rage for an instant.

Crovir grimaced behind Bastian, hands locked around the broken sword he had used to stab his brother in the back.

Bastian gazed blindly at Mila for a timeless moment. A defeated expression washed across his face. He closed his eyes briefly before turning and taking Crovir in his arms, the shattered blade still embedded in his flesh.

Crovir cried out and struggled in Bastian's hold.

The younger king gripped his brother firmly and looked at Mila over his shoulder. 'Do it now.' His gaze shifted to his children and those of Crovir where they raced across the battlefield toward them, love and sadness reflected in his eyes. 'They will not let you kill us again. You must remove our hearts while we still breathe, so we can never rise from death.'

Mila blinked. 'What?'

'*Let me go!*' screamed Crovir. Terror twisted his features as he fought his brother's embrace. He gave Mila a frantic look.

'Do not do this, daughter! I will forgive you your sins! We can start over again! It will be as if nothing happened—'

Rage surged through Mila at his lies.

'*Now, Red Queen!*' roared Bastian, tightening his hold.

'*No! Mila, stop!*' screamed Navia from across the plains. '*Do not do as he asks of you, please! There has to be another way! There has—*'

Mila closed her eyes for a moment and felt Navia's powers wash over her in a desperate attempt to stop her. Then, tears spilling down her cheeks, her own unearthly energy overcoming that of her cousin, she drove her sword into Bastian's back, through his heart and into that of her father.

She ignored the other Immortals' cries of horror as she yanked her blade out of the kings' bodies. She dropped to their side when they fell to the ground and carved their beating hearts out of their chests, the organs heavy in her hands before she cast them to the sand.

Then she released the sword and looked up at the sky, a howl of rage and pain erupting from the depths of her soul and rendering the air, her kin falling to their knees around her, their anger and sorrow sweeping over her.

And all around them came a faint smell of spices carried on a warm breeze that coursed across the battleground.

CHAPTER THIRTY-EIGHT

From the time of Romerus's murder to the end of the war at Eridug, a hundred days passed in all.

Of Kronos they found no sign, though his bloodied hand remained where Mila had left it.

As for the ones who had died in the battles that had raged across the Empire, be they friend or foe, their remains burned on giant pyres that turned the skies above the land dark with smoke from Qataara all the way to the South Sea.

And in the plaza of the kings, in Uryl, the remains of Aäron, general of the human alliance and prince of Parsah, were given a royal funeral.

The queens returned from the desert with the children. Although Mila's heart rejoiced at holding Eleaza and Kaleb in her arms once more, she had to tell them the truth about what had happened to their father. Kaleb was the angriest of the two and it was a long time before he came to forgive her.

In the days that followed the passing of the Immortal kings, the Empire was officially disbanded and Megash was crowned the new ruler of the human nation that occupied the lands between and around the two great rivers.

Shortly after his coronation, the Immortals and the long-lived queens prepared to leave Uryl with the bodies of Crovir and Bastian.

'Will we see you again?' said Megash at the gates of the capital when they departed that evening, a solemn Gilgamesh and Nisuna at his side, the baby quiet for once as she stared wide-eyed from her mother's arms.

Tobias glanced at his siblings and cousins, his gaze lingering on Mila's empty face for the briefest of moments. The anger he felt toward her had started to abate and he knew Bastian's children felt the same way, especially after Navia had described what had happened in the moments before Mila killed the Immortal kings. For the Seer was the only one who had heard the words spoken by her father and the terrible request he had made of Mila.

Still, Tobias shuddered when he recalled what she had done. He did not know whether he would have had the courage to do the same.

He had told his kin so the day after Crovir and Bastian's deaths. 'However much you disapprove of her actions, Mila knew what needed to be done. And Bastian realized she was the only one fearless enough to do it.' He had turned to Baruch. 'You heard what your father said on the hill near the citadel. That he could not live without Crovir. That they were two halves, unable to survive without the other. So he chose to die with his brother.'

A muscle had jumped in Baruch's cheek. Hosanna had laid a hand on his shoulder, tears swimming in her eyes.

'What do we do now?' Ysa had murmured.

It was Navia who had replied. 'We bury them. In the deserts

to the west, where none may find their resting place. This is why I requested their remains not be cremated.'

Tobias had stared at her. 'Why do you—?'

'Because I have seen it,' Navia had said, her green gaze hard. 'I have seen what must be done.' She had glanced at the other Immortals. 'And it requires all of us to do it.'

Tobias gazed at Megash presently in the flickering light of the flaming torches framing the gates and laid a hand on his shoulder. 'No, I do not think you will see us again, my friend.'

The newly crowned king released a sigh.

'There is no need to look that relieved,' muttered Baruch.

Guilt flashed across Megash's face. 'I am sorry. It is just that chaos tends to follow in your steps.'

Nisuna slapped her husband on the back, a scowl darkening her features. Tanis chortled behind her.

Tobias smiled. 'We shall attempt not to interfere in the matters of humans from now on.'

'Ha! That I cannot wait to see!' said Tanis.

Baruch sighed. 'You doubt us still, governor of Cayon?'

'Do not worry,' Hosanna muttered acerbically, 'we will outlive him over a hundred times.'

Tanis glowered. 'Well, I cannot help being human.'

'Nor can we help being Immortal,' said Tobias.

He offered his hand to Tanis. The governor hesitated, then shook it, all the while muttering under his breath.

Mila walked over to Gilgamesh and crouched before the boy. 'Be as good a king as your father will be and lead your people well, young prince.'

Gilgamesh swallowed and dipped his chin, giving her a grave look. He reached out and petted the hawk on her shoulder. Broken wing long healed by Rafael, Abu stirred and butted his head against the boy's hand.

Then, the Immortals turned and disappeared into the night.

'HERE?' SAID JARED. 'ARE YOU SURE?'

Navia nodded. Jared stared warily at the mountain before them.

Over a month had passed since they left Uryl with the bodies of the dead kings and crossed the South Desert. Surprisingly, the corpses had remained as fresh as the day the Immortals fell at Eridug, although their hearts had started to change color slightly. In order to protect them from decay, Rafael had created a strange mixture of oils and herbs and preserved the remains inside two large clay pots.

It was the Seer who guided them to the massifs that bordered the Red Sea, some forty leagues east of the city of Nuburu on the Nahal River. After leaving their children with the queens at an oasis in the desert, they proceeded east toward the towering range filling the horizon.

'There is a pair of natural caves that we can use for our purposes,' said Navia, indicating the peak above them. 'They are some thousand feet above us though.'

And so, while Jared used his elemental powers to create an ascending tunnel from the base of the mountain, his siblings and cousins carved two gigantic tombs from a large block of granite Mila found on the other side of the mountain.

It took a Half Moon for them to complete what would be the final resting place of Crovir and Bastian's bodies. During that time, when they were not working and sleeping, they sat around fires and reminisced about their childhoods, focusing on the happy occasions that had marked them. It was a bonding experience they very much needed to heal the scars left over from the war.

After Jared breached the first cave and enlarged it, smoothing the walls and ceiling out to make a perfect, domed-shaped chamber, they carried the tombs up the tunnel and placed them in the center of the floor, arranging the stone coffins so the heads faced the west and the feet the east, the brothers forever gazing in the direction of the rising sun. Under Navia's mysterious directions, Jared also created a complex closing mechanism in each casket.

They dug an opening in the ground near the southwest wall of the chamber and fashioned steps that spiraled down to the smaller cave below. There, Jared smoothed out the walls as per Navia's instructions and fashioned two giant pillars in the middle of the chamber, directly beneath the dead kings' tombs. Within each column, he sculpted an alcove and in them they laid the clay pots containing the hearts.

'Now what?' muttered Hosanna as they stood gazing at the final remains of the Immortal kings.

'We tell their stories,' said Navia. She indicated the walls around them and the pile of bare parchment lying inside a stone box she had carved. 'The story of Romerus, the one descended from the first man and woman who walked this Earth, and his Immortal sons, Crovir and Bastian.'

Jared's eyes widened. The others shared surprised glances.

'What do you mean, the first man and woman who walked this Earth?' said Mila.

Navia's expression turned sad as she studied her cousin. Then she took a deep breath and started to speak.

She told them of the dreams and visions she had been having since the kings' deaths, of a history defined by the heavenly origins of mankind and the mysterious cures Romerus had received in the desert all those hundreds of years past. She told them of a future that would be wreathed in darkness for hundreds of years still to come, of devious deeds and twisted plots both man and Immortal made, of conflicts that would be a scourge upon this world for countless generations.

'You mean, even after all we have suffered, our children's children will go to war with one another?' Hosanna whispered.

'Yes,' said Navia. 'For there are many among them who will revere Bastian and Crovir, and who will always blame the younger king for the death of the older one.'

They listened, faces pale with anguish, struggling to grasp her uncompromising predictions as she continued to talk of the war that would tear the descendants of Bastian and Crovir apart, and the plague that would finally bring it to a close. Only Mila seemed somewhat unsurprised by the Seer's words, her eyes cool, as if she expected no less of men and Immortals alike.

Finally, when all hope seemed to be lost and the agony of what was to be their legacy weighed down heavily upon them, Navia smiled tremulously and told them about the marked ones who would come after them, the descendants who would inherit their powers and more. They who would be mankind and the Immortals' hope for a way out of the shadows ahead.

Jared's heart slammed against his ribs in the stunned silence that greeted her final words. 'You mean, our souls will be reborn?'

Navia dipped her chin. 'In a sense, yes. A piece of the souls of those descended of a union between a son and a daughter of Romerus will be reborn again.' She crossed the floor and pressed a hand against Jared's chest. 'Those who will come after us will not remember who they were in this life. Although our children and their children will manifest our abilities to some extent, a part of us will only come to exist once more inside the hearts of the ones who will be the true beneficiaries of our gifts.'

Jared swallowed convulsively.

❄

THEY SPENT ANOTHER HALF MOON CAPTURING THE STORIES OF Romerus and the dead kings in script form on the stone walls of the second cave, creating a beautiful, circular tapestry that told the tale of the Empire's rise and ultimate fall.

On the scrolls the Seer had carefully prepared, they inscribed their own narratives, the stories of twelve Immortal princes and princesses and their unique skills, Mila penning Kronos's story as well as her own. These they left inside the smaller stone box, which they placed between their fathers' tombs.

On their last day in the desert, Navia removed two chunks of gold from her saddle and asked Jared to fashion a seal for each tomb in the design she sketched in the sand, the sun encircling the middle of a cross. Before he closed off the access to the smaller cave, Navia herself engraved the marks that the ones who would inherit their ungodly powers and pieces of their souls would bear from birth.

To Mila's consternation, she carved out a giant trident dagger in the space between the pillars that held the hearts of Crovir and Bastian.

'Why?' Mila murmured, grief filling her.

Navia took her hand and squeezed her fingers. 'Because just as you are the most powerful of all of us, so will your heir be the most formidable of our scions. And *this* is the mark she will bear.'

They left the mountains after Jared secured the coffins' lids and sealed off the tunnel, heading into the desert as twilight claimed the world. From the oasis, they traveled north and crossed the West Sea to the Land of the Hatti.

There they were to part ways, as Navia had told them they should, some to venture east while others veered north and west. Though separation would not prevent the future war between their descendants, it would delay it for as long as possible. On the last evening they spent together, they feasted and cried and drank late into the night while their children slept around them.

In the morning, as they embraced each other for the final time, Navia bestowed the seal to Crovir's tomb to Baruch and the seal to Bastian's tomb to Tobias.

Then, while Beatrix and Malachi watched on with melancholic expressions, Navia walked up to Jared and raised her hands lovingly to his face. With tears glistening in their eyes, they shared their first and last kiss.

EPILOGUE

Days soon turned to months and months to years. As the sun and the moon rose and set on hundreds more, the children of the original Immortal princes and princesses settled in cities once ruled by the defunct Immortal empire, their identities and origins a carefully kept secret from the humans around them. Their lineage rapidly grew and spread itself across the world, their children and their children's children bearing their own offspring and casting them to the four winds.

Many became nobles in mortal societies and the Immortal ones that soon flourished in the shadows, their wealth and power growing during their long-lived existences.

It was later that rumors of beings who could survive death started to emerge, giving birth to the wildest of fables. As once-forgotten tales of Immortals spread across humanity and were retold over and over again to generations that followed, their existence became enshrined in myths that would continue to fascinate mankind for thousands of years to come, and give rise to strange alchemy that promised to deliver a cure for death itself.

Among the epics that evolved was one that was not so much fable as it was truth. A tale of a woman who came to be revered and feared in equal measure, a warrior who fought with two trident blades, her quest to protect and guide humanity taking her to all corners of the world. A goddess whose legend was engraved into some of mankind's most sacred religious texts.

AROUND THE TIME THAT WHISPERS STARTED OF A WAR BREWING between those who called themselves members of the Bastian race and those who claimed to belong to Crovir's lineage, on a hill in a cold land populated by hundreds of lakes, an old woman climbed the snow-covered slopes to a tree that had long since shed its leaves.

In the large residence that straddled the land below, a young woman stood by the window and gazed at the gibbous moon that bathed the world in an eerie light.

'Should we not go with her?' she murmured, staring at the hillside.

Her great-grandmother came to stand beside her.

'No, child,' said Eleaza. 'This time is for my mother and her alone.'

Tears glimmered in the eyes of the young woman. Behind them, the extended family that had gathered to say their goodbyes wept quietly.

Eleaza smiled and glanced at Kaleb where he sat at a table, his face dark with grief.

'Do not be sad,' she told her great-grandchild. 'She is not. For she shall soon be with the one she has been waiting to join for over a millennium now.' She turned to stare out of the window, her eyes just about making out the shape of her mother sitting under the tree high above them. 'I wish that you too could one day find a love as great as theirs.'

THE WARRIOR WATCHED THE STARS SHIMMER ABOVE HER, HER heart at peace and her soul content for the first time in a long time. Just as she did every day, she closed her eyes and brought the sound of his heartbeat to mind for the last time, along with the heat of his body and the feel of their final kiss.

Mila smiled. 'Wait for me, Aäron.'

CROWS DARKENED THE HEAVENS ABOVE THE HILL. THEY LANDED in the tree and crowded the snow-covered ground beneath it, blacker than black, blotting out all whiteness. Their shapes blurred as Eleaza's tears finally spilled over and stained her cheeks. She wiped them and watched all the way to the end, until the last bird leapt into the night and disappeared with the flock that faded fast in the direction of the moon.

IN ANOTHER LAND TO THE NORTH AND EAST, IN A CITY BUILT inside a vast cavern under ice-covered mountains, an Immortal with a missing hand gazed upon his hundreds of offspring, children born of human women he had mated with over centuries, and the children who came after them.

Fire filled his soul as he thought of all that he would accomplish through them to regain what was once lost, to retake a world that was rightfully his as an Immortal prince, to bring back dead kings and gods.

'I shall name you…Kronos,' he murmured to the assembled mass.

And they bowed before him, pledging their eternal alliance to his cause.

IN THE KINGDOM OF HEAVEN, THE ARCHANGEL WATCHED AS THE Immortal War began and darkness spread across the Earth. And he waited.

For the wheels of fate to turn.

For souls to be reborn.

For the destiny of mankind and those who could guide them to the path of redemption to unfold.

THE END

The Immortals' adventures reach their epic finale in Destiny.
Read an extract at the end of the book now!

FAMILY TREE II

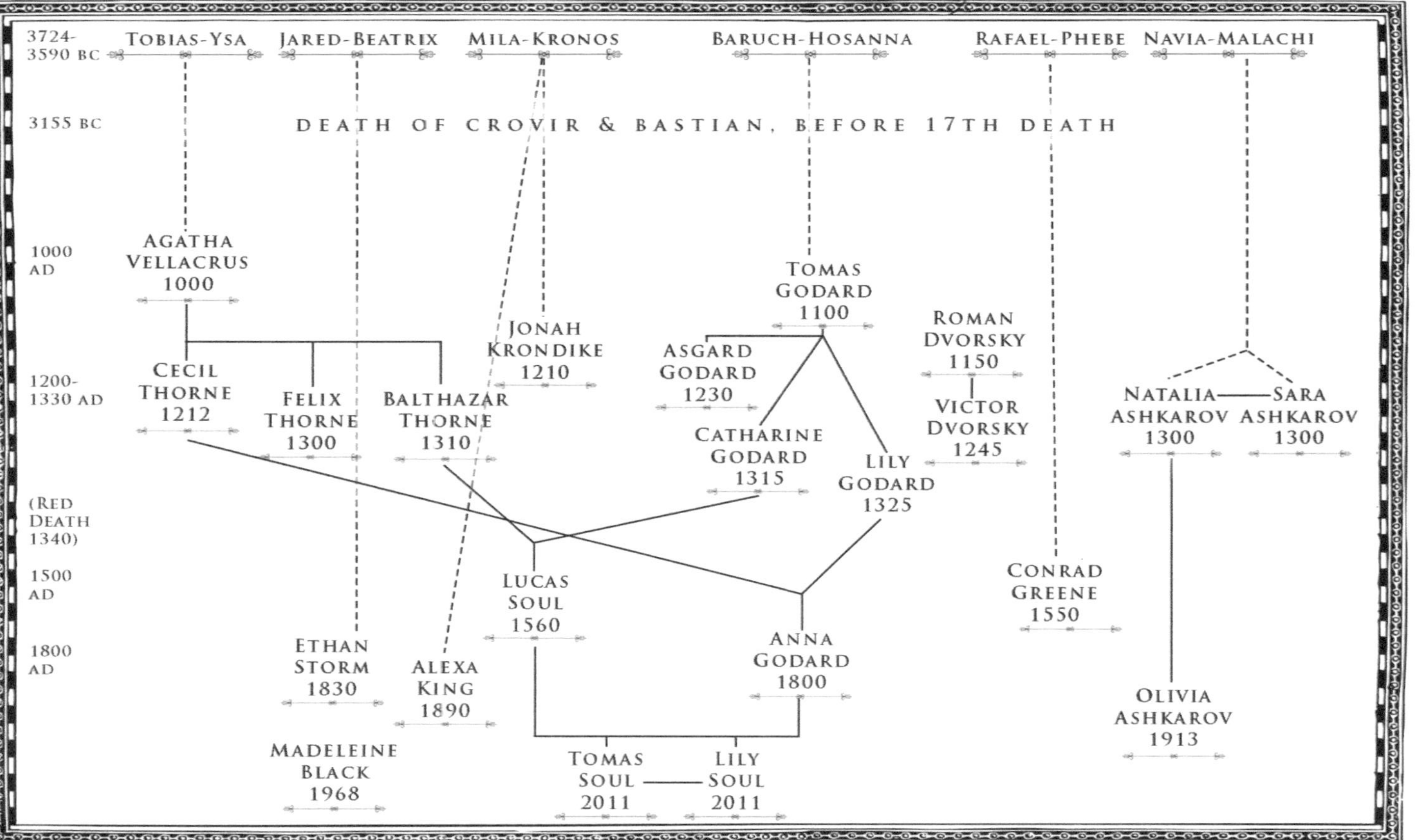
3724-3590 BC
TOBIAS-YSA
JARED-BEATRIX
MILA-KRONOS
BARUCH-HOSANNA
RAFAEL-PHEBE
NAVIA-MALACHI
3155 BC
DEATH OF CROVIR & BASTIAN, BEFORE 17TH DEATH
1000 AD
AGATHA VELLACRUS 1000
TOMAS GODARD 1100
1200-1330 AD
JONAH KRONDIKE 1210
ROMAN DVORSKY 1150
NATALIA ASHKAROV 1300
SARA ASHKAROV 1300
CECIL THORNE 1212
FELIX THORNE 1300
BALTHAZAR THORNE 1310
ASGARD GODARD 1230
VICTOR DVORSKY 1245
CATHARINE GODARD 1315
LILY GODARD 1325
(RED DEATH 1340)
1500 AD
LUCAS SOUL 1560
CONRAD GREENE 1550
1800 AD
ETHAN STORM 1830
ALEXA KING 1890
ANNA GODARD 1800
OLIVIA ASHKAROV 1913
MADELEINE BLACK 1968
TOMAS SOUL 2011
LILY SOUL 2011

THE REBORN SOULS

Mila - Alexa King
Aäron - Zachary Jackson
Tobias and Baruch - Lucas Soul
Jared - Ethan Storm
Navia - Olivia Ashkarov
Rafael - Conrad Greene

DESTINY EXTRACT

PROLOGUE

April 2013. KOFA Range, Yuma Proving Ground, Arizona.

The man looked beyond the scorched plain at his feet to the dark peaks to the east. The burnt wreckage of a helicopter and the twisted shells of dozens of army vehicles dotted the landscape around him, the only evidence left of the devastating psychokinetic blast Olivia Ashkarov had visited on the men of the secret R&D base where she had been kept prisoner.

The bodies of the humans who had died in the firestorm had been removed from the site in the last twenty-four hours, their deaths officially put down to an unfortunate training accident. As for the Immortals who had perished at their side, their remains had long since been scattered by the winds coursing through the mountains and desert, bones and flesh turned to ash by the flocks of crows that had descended from the crimson skies the day before.

The only trace left of Jonah Krondike was the warped silver

ring the man held in his hand. It was pure chance that had led him to it.

Although he had known that searching the buckled, black carcass of the helicopter would prove futile—that he would not miraculously find Krondike injured but alive inside—he had still done so. Agony and rage had flooded him at his failure to uncover any vestige of the man he had worshipped all of his life.

It was as he had slowly paced the area around the impact site, his carefully cultivated, dispassionate expression masking his fury, that he had stumbled upon the metal band. It had become wedged under a rock some twenty feet from the wreckage, its polished surface dulled by dirt and desert sand. The writing upon it was almost unrecognizable, the engravings distorted by the incendiary explosion that had engulfed the helicopter. Still, he had seen the ring enough times to know it belonged to Krondike.

He did not care about the humans and Immortals who had met their end during the intense battle that had taken place inside the Kofa Mountains and beneath the desert plains at the eastern edge of the Yuma Proving Ground. Nor was he unduly worried about losing the covert research facility and the US Army faction who had been working closely with Krondike for decades.

As for the death of William Gunnerson, the four-star general who had been in charge of the rogue group assisting them, he had ordered the man's assassination himself yesterday morning.

There was only one thing that preoccupied him right now. One thing that ate at him, that gripped him to the point of obsession, that consumed him like little else had in all the centuries of his existence.

Jonah Krondike's death.

He clenched his fist, the ring digging into his palm so hard it nearly cut his skin.

'Are you okay, sir?'

The man turned to the Hunter who had spoken.

'Yes, I am,' he lied with a neutral stare.

'We're being called back to base.' The Immortal indicated the mouth of a cave about a mile behind them.

'Go ahead,' the man murmured. 'I'll be right with you.'

He took a shallow breath, cast a final glance at the remains of the crumpled cage of metal where Jonah Krondike had met his end, and twisted on his heels. He headed for the Jeep where his escort waited, his mind filled with a single thought.

They will pay. I will make them pay for your death.

Get Destiny now!

ACKNOWLEDGMENTS

To all my friends who helped make this possible. You know who you are.

To you, my readers. Thank you for reading Origins. If you enjoyed my book, please consider leaving a review on Goodreads or on the store where you purchased it. Reviews help readers like you find my books and I truly appreciate your honest opinions about my stories.

Make sure to sign up to my store newsletter for special deals on my books and new release alerts. Or you can sign up to my author newsletter to get upcoming release notifications, sneak peeks, and giveaways.

FACTS AND FICTIONS

Now, for one of my favorite parts of writing my books. Here are the facts and fictions behind the story.

Mesopotamia

When I planned the novels of the *Seventeen* series, I knew the fifth book would be the origin story of the Immortals. While researching when and where to base the formidable empire they once ruled so as to meld it with the known factual history of the time, the 4th millennium BC and the birthplace of one of the most advanced, ancient human civilizations made logical sense.

Mesopotamia was famed for being one of the earliest known 'cradles' of civilizations, the other two being the Levant and the Nile River Delta. It included the lands between and around the Rivers Tigris and Euphrates (known by their old Persian names of Tigra and Ufratü in *Origins*), in what is now modern East Turkey, Syria, Iraq and Kuwait, and saw mankind's transition from the Stone Age to the Bronze Age, the beginnings of agriculture, the invention of writing, architecture and animal husbandry, and the origins of a class-based human society.

Of all the incredible kingdoms that took root in those fertile lands, from the Sumerian, Assyrian, Babylonian, Akkadian, and the later Persian and Parthian empires, one struck the deepest chord in me and formed the backbone of the human alliance that would rise against the Immortal kings in ORIGINS and become the first human empire to lay claim to the throne of the fictional Uryl.

That civilization was that of Sumer and the capital of the Immortal Empire, Uryl, is a play on the factual Uruk, a Sumerian city said to be the largest in the world at the time, and which was similarly situated on the banks of the Euphrates River. The other cities and garrisons of the mythical Immortal Empire are also based on factual Sumerian cities, as are those of its extended territories in Ancient Anatolia, the Aegean Sea, the Nile River Delta, the Indus Valley, the Yellow River, and the Levant.

GILGAMESH

For those of you with some knowledge of history and religion, Gilgamesh will not be an unfamiliar name. He was a Sumerian King thought by some to be a mythical demi-God and by others to be a true historical figure. His father was Lugaldanda, one of the Kings of Uruk, and his mother was Ninsun, a goddess descended of a sky god and a goddess of the Earth. Gilgamesh is the subject of a series of Sumerian poems entitled THE EPIC OF GILGAMESH, on which many fictional stories, games, and comics have been based.

While studying the Sumerian King list inscribed in a variety of archaeological artifacts recovered from Iraq, the oldest and most fascinating of all being the Weld-Blundell Prism in the Ashmolean Museum in Oxford, I fell in love with the story of Mesh-ki-ang-gasher, the founder of the First Dynasty of Uruk. Hence, I decided that Gilgamesh's father, and the first king of the human empire that would follow the fall of the Immortals in ORIGINS, would be Megash, and his mother would be Nisuna, a play on Ninsun. Although I never overtly addressed Megash and Nisuna's relationship in ORIGINS, I hope

I hinted heavily enough to show that theirs was a marriage based on love, mutual respect and a deep attraction, with a large modicum of sexual humor, which often exasperated Megash's fictional older brother Aäron.

As for Gilgamesh, he is but a boy in ORIGINS and I loved depicting him as an incredibly intelligent, solemn child whose relationship with Mila, the Immortal Warrior, would inspire him to accomplish the great deeds of his unparalleled future and establish him as a legend of his times.

TIME

As you may have deduced from reading ORIGINS, I carefully avoided using time references such as seconds, minutes, and hours in the story. It made for some convoluted writing while I tried to be as historically accurate as possible, by not using units that didn't exist then.

The Sumerians invented a sexagesimal system (a numeric system based on the number sixty) for counting time, angles, and distance. Why sixty? The common theory among historians is that people in those days used their thumb to count the three segments of the four fingers of one hand (making the total of segments twelve) and then multiplied it by the five fingers of the other hand (making that total sixty). Sixty and twelve became incredibly important numbers in the civilizations that followed, and the twelve lunar cycles and twelve constellations of the Zodiac all derive from the ancient Sumerian system of counting, as do the modern systems of calculating geographic coordinates.

The Sumerian Calendar was a lunisolar one, based not only on counting on the human hand but also on the phases of the moon and the sun.

A year was the time needed for the Earth to complete one orbit around the sun, and hence became known as a solar year.

It was equivalent to 360 days or the 360 degrees of the sun's ecliptic path through the celestial sphere.

A month was the time needed for the moon to orbit the Earth, and hence became known as a lunar month. It was equivalent to thirty days and was further divided into four phases; the new moon, the first quarter/half moon, the full moon, and the last quarter/half moon. Each phase was thus roughly equivalent to seven days.

The day was the duration of the Earth's full rotation upon its own axis. Day and night were each further divided into twelve periods each, ranging from sunrise to sunset and sunset to sunrise. Hence, the first hour of the day would be around the modern 6am, whilst the first hour of the night would be around the modern 6pm. Making the sixth hour of the day midday and the sixth hour of the night midnight.

In ORIGINS, I use years, months, full moon, new moon, half moon, days, and portions of days to denote time. The use of century and millennium did not come until the later Roman, Julian, and Gregorian Calendars. Fun fact: century is derived from centuria, the basic 100-man-strong fighting unit of the Roman Legion.

DISTANCE

Just as counting time started out based on the human hand, so did the concept of distance, with the addition of barley and wheat in the mix. Yes – the grains. A grain formed the most basic unit of distance measurement in ancient Sumer and was equivalent to some 2.7mm. One finger was equivalent to six grains and a foot equivalent to twenty fingers.

Since I did not want to be throwing grains and fingers all over this book, I opted to use feet and leagues instead, one league being equivalent to some three miles or the distance a man could walk in one hour.

Inventions

Most of the inventions of the first advanced human civilizations, particularly those of the Sumerians, I attributed to the Immortals.

From the potter's wheel to the chariot, from agricultural techniques such as mono-cropping and ploughing to methods of irrigation using shadoofs, canals and dykes, from animal domestication of mouflons (wild sheep), aurochs (wild cattle), and onagers (wild donkeys) to farming, from metallurgy and pottery to architecture and the building of Ziggurats, from writing to mathematics, from beer brewing to ice houses, from legal and administrative processes to advanced weapons and military formations and training – all were passed down from the Immortals to the Sumerians in *Origins* and form the primary reason why they ruled for so long and had such a long-lasting impact on the human civilizations that came after.

Immortals would continue to influence the technologies and inventions of the following centuries and millennia, as well as mold the history of mankind through various wars and political intrigues.

Military Structure and Weapons

The Stele of the Vultures is the oldest known historical document known to man. Assembled from a series of fragments discovered in the ancient Sumerian city of Girsu and now residing in the Department of Near Eastern Antiquities in the Louvre Museum in Paris, the stone tablet narrates a war between the Sumerian city-states of Lagash and Umma, and the victory of Eannatum, the King of Lagash at the time. It has been dated to around 2450 BC and shows the use of helmets, pikes, shields, battle axes and chariots at the time, as well as the phalanx military formation, where soldiers arranged themselves in a rectangular mass behind interlocked shields with spears and pikes protruding in front and above. This is the battle formation used repeatedly by the Immortal-Human Alliance during the war to defend and advance against the army of the Immortal kings.

With the Bronze Age just beginning at the time of ancient Sumer, swords and daggers were made of copper alloyed with arsenic, tin and bronze, and often overlaid with silver, gold, and gems. Other weapons and protective guards used at the time were similarly made.

As for the Immortals and their soldiers' battle outfits, these consisted of metal breastplates overlying chainmail dresses and tunics, leather elbow guards and shin greaves reinforced with polished bronze plates, metal helmets, and leather sandals and short boots. Along with broadswords, they used daggers, battle axes, bows and arrows, and spears. Note that broadswords are not factually accurate to the time, being inventions of 16th and 17th century Europe. Sumerians used sickle swords instead, which were slimmer, shorter and curved.

I thought broadswords were more kickass. Who wants to fight with a cheese stick when they could have a power sword?

MEDICINE

Though disease was very much still blamed on the influence of spirits, gods, ghosts and demons at the time, Sumerians were among the first human civilizations to have professional medical practitioners, although one was known as a sorcerer (*ashipu*) and the other as a physician (*asu*). The sorcerer was responsible for identifying which god, demon or organ system was at fault for causing an ailment and then referred the patient on to the physician, who would use herbal pills, potions, and creams to try and cure the illness. Asus used washing, bandaging, and plasters as well as the first known surgical techniques in their practices.

As for the joy plant mentioned in ORIGINS, it was indeed the opium plant, which exudes latex from its seed that contains morphine and is used to make the modern day heroin and other synthetic opioids. The oldest known reference to the opium plant comes from the Sumerians around 3400 BC and they referred to it as the 'joy plant'. It was mostly used in the form of vapors, suppositories and poultices for pain relief and during surgical procedures, and was also combined with hemlock to put people quickly and painlessly to death.

And that's it for the science and technology lesson folks. Visit my website at www.adstarrling.com to check out more Extras!

BOOKS BY A.D. STARRLING

SEVENTEEN NOVELS

Hunted

Warrior

Empire

Legacy

Origins

Destiny

SEVENTEEN SHORT STORIES

First Death

Dancing Blades

The Meeting

The Warrior Monk

The Hunger

The Bank Job

LEGION

Blood and Bones

Fire and Earth

Awakening

Forsaken

Hallowed Ground

Heir

Legion

ABOUT A.D. STARRLING

Visit Shop AD Starrling and buy all of AD's ebooks, paperbacks, hardbacks, audiobooks, and exclusive special edition print books direct.

Want to know about AD Starrling's upcoming releases? Sign up to her author newsletter for new release alerts, sneak peeks, giveaways, and more.

Follow AD Starrling on Amazon.

Join AD's reader group on Facebook
The Seventeen Club.

Check out this link to find out more about A.D. Starrling
Linktr.ee/AD_Starrling.